Inside Stories
for Writers and Readers

Inside Stories
for Writers and Readers

Trish Nicholson

collca

Collca

An imprint of Collca Limited
24 Comforts Farm Avenue
Oxted, Surrey, RH8 9PB, England
www.collca.com

Inside Stories and *From Apes to Apps* first published as ebooks in 2013 by Collca

This edition published in 2013 in Great Britain by Collca
Inside Stories and *From Apes to Apps* © copyright Trish Nicholson 2013
Inside Stories cover photograph © copyright Trish Nicholson 2013
From Apes to Apps cover photograph © copyright Glenda Powers – Fotolia.com

ISBN: 978-1-908795-01-4

The moral right of the author is asserted.

Covers and text design by Mike Hyman, Collca

Contents

Inside Stories for Writers and Readers

How to Use This Book

As a supportive, inspiring friend you can visit any time for a quick cuppa and a word of encouragement, or stay with for an entire evening. But *Inside Stories* also contains the resources to stimulate discussion in groups and workshops as well as for personal inspiration. This is *your* writing and reading companion to enjoy however, whenever, with whoever you choose.

If you disagree with some of the critiques, think of better endings or openings for the stories, are stimulated to read or write something new, then it has done its job.

You can simply read the whole book, or dip into it: a detailed Table of Contents enables you to access any topic, article or story. Each themed chapter has two of my stories to demonstrate some of the points covered in discussion, with analysis and critiques given after each story (to avoid spoilers).

Reading this book might not make you rich and famous, but it will inspire you to better writing and more perceptive reading.

If you are reading the print edition, my essay exploring how stories came to be so critical in our lives – *From Apes to Apps: How Humans Evolved as Storytellers and Why it Matters* – is bound in with *Inside Stories*. The digital version includes an extract.

Introduction

"Stand still, traveller and read."

In a letter to a friend, Mark Twain claimed not to like reading novels or stories. When challenged that he wrote them himself, he replied, *"Quite true: but the fact that an Indian likes to scalp people is no evidence that he likes to be scalped."* It seems he was being characteristically contrary because a comment elsewhere to his daughter penetrates the heart of storytelling: *"It is so unsatisfactory to read a noble passage and have no one you love at hand to share the happiness with you. It is unsatisfactory to read to oneself anyhow – for the uttered voice so heightens the expression."*

Stories and their telling are a shared encounter. A story is not complete until the listener or reader has experienced it and achieved his or her own understanding. Oral storytelling may no longer be a regular occurrence for most of us, nor reading aloud by the fireside, but audience and storyteller are coming together in new ways. All writers are readers, it is part of our obsession with words, and the number of readers who have started to write is increasing. Everyone, it seems, is writing these days. It's getting harder to tell readers from writers – maybe there is no significant difference other than a tilt in one direction or the other. We are all born storytellers: our brains function around narrative; it is inescapably the way we perceive and understand life and the world around us.

Certainly, the relationship between readers and writers has changed radically with digital communication. Readers want to know their favourite authors; follow them on social media; learn the 'inside story'; post reviews, and become more involved. Writers set up websites; write blog posts, and open Face-book and Twitter accounts to interact with their readers. Some authors use digital media to write interactive stories, where readers can choose alternative plot paths and outcomes. We love talking about the stories we read, and I have never met a writer who didn't enjoy talking about their craft or gain something from sharing the ideas and stories of other writers.

Thinking through these changes, I thought it was time to celebrate stories in a way that brought readers and writers together – an inclusive book – this volume is the result, aimed to inspire both writers and readers to a deeper appreciation of that 'chemical reaction' between two 'voices' when a story resonates with a reader. And there is a whole chapter on 'voice.'

Many of the insights in *Inside Stories* are applicable to any length of fiction, but the focus is on short stories. There are several reasons why I chose to do this.

On a practical level, the brevity of short stories allows us to see their wholeness, to understand more clearly how the various components of a story such as theme, structure, character, are woven into a seamless tale – they can be read and reread in minutes. The fifteen stories included here are my own because only these can I analyse fully, tell you what inspired them, how they were written – or rewritten – and share what critiques have said about them.

Literary short stories offer a particular and unique writing and reading experience: they are not simply stories that are short. Although infinitely varied – defying any agreed definition – the compactness, depth and language required to tell a complete story in as few as 500 words, or even as many as 5,000, has created a recognizable form that many would claim is the most difficult in fiction writing. Every single word in a good short story has significance – in sound, rhythm and image as well as meaning. An experience of a life condensed yet deeply penetrated, a short story can provide rich insights not only into our own lives as readers, but into the craft of writing.

Despite the challenging nature of the form – or perhaps because of it – many successful novelists began their career by writing short stories. Others, like Alice Munro, made the short story their career. Teachers of creative writing encourage students to learn their craft through writing and reading short stories as well as longer prose. The form has a great deal to teach us.

Finally, in a fast-moving world where images and texts stream endlessly passed us, our attention spans shorten accordingly. We expect *everything* to be offered in 'super concentrated' form, not only the laundry powder. It is nearly twenty-five years since Saul Bellow issued the warning: *"The modern reader…is perilously overloaded."* And the volume and range of published material has swelled enormously since then.

Short stories should be ideal reading in such an environment, but popular though they are with readers, publishers are wary of them and critics and reviewers pay them scant attention. They deserve better, so the form has a major character part in *Inside Stories*.

But this is not a 'how-to' book. Rules for writing can be useful guides, but even standard strictures on punctuation and grammar have been creatively and successfully flouted on occasion. For me, there are only two unbreakable rules: keep reading, and keep writing. So this is a book of 'show and share' rather than 'tell and teach', and I have included 'also-rans' as well as winning or shortlisted stories because we can learn from reviewing our problems as well as our successes, and sometimes, our reasons for writing have nothing to do with competitions or publication.

Because we need structure to avoid muddle and to make ideas accessible, I divided *Inside Stories* into chapters that emphasize certain topics, but the problem is that the magic of a good story is in its wholeness. Character, voice, form and theme have to mesh in our minds and on the page as a holistic experience for a reader. Though we are obliged to talk in parts, the inclusion of complete stories reminds us of this wholeness, and I mention connections in the text to integrate the various points.

Each chapter is a bit like a workshop: exploration, followed by articles to dig deeper into particular aspects, and then a couple of stories are analysed to illustrate the chapter's topic. The illumination and encouragement from attending a reading or writing group can last for weeks, but the benefit of having such insights in a book is that you can go back to 'listen' to something you only half heard the first time, and pause when you want to ponder, make a pot of coffee or pour yourself a beer.

Much of the inspiration for this book was sparked by the joys, frustrations, whinges, moans and exaltations of writing and reading friends on four continents – this is my 'thank you' for their company over that rugged landscape.

~~~

1: Inspiration

"The artist is not a special person; every person is a special kind of artist." Michael Michalko.

If I was writing this book in the era of my Celtic ancestors, it would begin: "First, catch your cow and skin it." Short of vellum on which to write, Saint Columbus once transcribed ancient myths onto the hide of his favourite heifer. It is all so much easier now. Not simply the availability of pen, paper and keyboard, but because our understanding of how the mind works has improved and we now know that creativity is not confined to the few favoured by the Gods.

Inspiration and creativity are often treated as one and the same but I find it useful to consider them separately. Creativity is a capacity in our brain to imagine an original idea, or new combination of existing ideas. We are all born creative. Its focus and how it is used may vary; our upbringing and education may enhance or dull it, but it is there, an essential part of being human.

And it is not limited to art, music, literature and poetry. The nine Muses in Greek mythology each had separate spheres of influence which included science and astronomy. Plumbers, engineers, teachers, pastry cooks, astrophysicists, truck drivers, parents, doctors and accountants can all function more or less creatively.

The only limitation is that creativity involves taking risks – letting go of self censorship and the fear of others' judgments – to tap an inner source of imaginative and unstructured thought. Obviously, some tasks provide more scope for such experimentation than others. But for writers and readers, our own inhibitions are the only restraining force. And like all our other mental faculties, the more we use our creativity the better it will serve us.

As writers, we have nothing to lose. It doesn't cost us a cow, nor do we have to chip our words laboriously into stone. We can correct, delete, edit with ease; no one is looking over our shoulder except our miserly inner critic. Imagination is one of the few things in the world that is still absolutely free. All we need is to ignite the spark. As readers, we can delve more deeply into what we read, find new levels of stories to savour and new ways to share our enlightenment with others.

I think of inspiration as the light switching on: the awakening, the revelation of an idea arising from our creativity and invariably beamed at some specific enterprise. It may be entirely internal – a moment of understanding, a flash of awareness, or even a creeping realization of something we had not appreciated before. Or we may express it in writing – a new story idea; the solution to a problem in an existing one; the perfect active verb we searched for all week, or a driving urge to write a review even though we have never written one before.

But the Muse does not make door-to-door deliveries. There are only pick-up points. We have to go out to meet her. To activate creativity and release inspiration we need to stimulate it. We all have the power (inherent originality), but first we have to shift out of those gears that restrain our thoughts, and free-wheel to places of illumination.

For writers, this is different to simply 'getting started', putting something on the blank page in the morning; all kinds of activities and word games can help with that, some are included in the first article, *My Writers' Toy Box*. What I seek as inspiration is the deep idea or quirky 'take' that will form the unique heartbeat of a story. For this, we need engagement with real life – past or present – even though we may eventually project the story into the future or into an imaginary world.

It is no coincidence that the mother of the Muses was Mnemosyne – Goddess of Memory. The pick-up points are in our own experience and surroundings, including our understanding of other people's lives. From these we wrest originality: the previously unknown and unseen. How do we find it?

Our heads are like wheelie bins, full of what other people have already seen and heard and put in there. So our perception (the brain's interpretation of what our senses show us), latches onto these familiar images – they are quick and efficient...and stale. And yet, each of us is a one-time-only blend of inherited and acquired traits. Think about that for a moment. There is not another one of you in the entire universe (even if you have an identical twin).

Your thoughts can be equally singular if you nurture them well enough to know and express them as only you can, whether they concern a person, a book, a feeling, or discovering that single word that says it all.

Sometimes an idea will suddenly appear and we have no clue where it came from. This occasionally happens to me when driving; not an ideal situation for risk-taking, but a complete story can unfold during the course of a 17 km journey from town. Getting out, meeting people, participating in events, all stimulate creativity if we open our minds and carry a notebook.

I don't want to be a spoilsport but there is no magic in Moleskin. If you have a penchant for exotic notebooks, buy them if it gives you pleasure and the budget will run to it, but they will not generate better ideas. One reason is that their specialness inhibits us from sullying their pages with anything less than the epigram of the century, yet it is all those unguarded 'any old thing' thoughts that can take wing, and they can be scribbled into a mini ring-bound pad (four for a pound) without a qualm.

Most of my stories originated from characters, someone I knew, a stranger I observed and, on one occasion, a deceased person's possessions on a junk stall – I'll tell you about that in the next chapter. Dedicated readers and writers become people-watchers, eavesdroppers. Queues provide excellent opportunities because we are close enough to hear and smell people as well as surreptitiously scrutinize them. 'Waiting' offers a precious moment of free time to indulge our senses. That man standing behind you, irritatingly pecking at his iPhone, may be a writer jotting a note about you.

I found one of my favourite characters in a long line at the London Road post office in Brighton. Pension day, pressed together by urgency, we shuffled forward a toecap at a time. The only gaps were either side of an odorous old lady muffled in a woolly hat and an 'Oxfam-model' leather coat trailing along the floor. She smelled of apples when they've turned brown and spongy in the middle. (If you can't wait to meet Maisie, you don't have to. She stars at the end of the last chapter in *A Man of His Word*. You can go there now and come back later if you wish. I'll still be here).

Like many writers, I am equally familiar with the frustration of sighing over the third pot of tea for lack of an idea. But once I work through self-doubt and start to think constructively, two processes have always been helpful: divergence, and synthesis – maybe there are no new plots, but there are always unique combinations, outcomes and journeys in revealing them.

To use divergence, take a situation from your life, a newspaper, film, a favourite television series, or someone else's past, and radically alter some key elements. It's a form of the 'what if' question. If the caring person was stressed by circumstances to expose another part of their nature they were unaware of – to be violent or cruel for example – how would the story resolve? If a 'walk-on' character was given a source of power to change the action, what sort of tale would result? If the setting was in another country, a different time, or on a space station, what new challenges would the protagonist face?

The possibilities are endless, and this form of thinking can make a stimulating activity in a writers' group if you all read the same story, work out your individual divergences and compare the results.

Synthesis – the combining of separate components to work together in forming a unique whole – is what we do in constructing a story anyway, but if you take two or three disparate elements that do not normally act together, they can spark inspiration for a story: a child wandering into a casino; a file of confidential documents found in a toilet cubicle, or a rock band stranded by snow in the Pyrenees, forced to seek shelter in a convent.

Divergence and synthesis work well for inspired reading. Imagining how the story might look if written from a different point of view, or focusing on what is not said and thinking about why, can deepen understanding of what the writer is trying to convey. Novelist Vladimir Nabokov urged serious readers to re-read. His definition of a 'good reader' was someone with imagination, memory, an artistic sense and a dictionary.

And deliberately reading two totally different genres on a similar theme is a brain-teasing way of appreciating the power of storytelling and where that power comes from. Or you can read the book then see the film; compare the screen characters with your own images of them, consider the two different ways in which the story was told and work out why you prefer one rather than the other. Identifying what engages and excites you in a story can lead you to new authors as your personal tastes develop; why limit yourself to what everyone else is reading? Many factors create a 'best seller' – quality of reading and depth of meaning are not always among them. Sometimes they are merely shooting stars.

The following three articles expand various ways of provoking inspiration: while at your desk; with visual cues gathered from elsewhere, and by using the most unlikely situations – in this case, doing the household laundry. Finally, we read some stories; I share what inspired them and what competition judges and professional critiques have said about them.

~~~

Articles:

My Writer's Toy Box

If I wake in the morning with perfectly formed sentences scratching at the inside of my skull to get out, I leap at the laptop and bash away at the keys like I'm playing ragtime on the piano. But on the other 360 days I need my toy box.

My favourite toys are: three books; a wooden egg; a tiny woven basket with a lid; a picture of Gaudi's workshop and a portrait of Beethoven. In case the value of these to a writer is not immediately obvious, let me explain.

Serendipity:

Books, you might think, are tools rather than toys, and I do use them as tools especially when editing my work, but when I want to create – get the right side write-brain in gear – I play. Opening them at random, I close my eyes, put my finger on the page and look to see what I've picked. I might do that three times, write down what I find and let it slide between the grey cells for a while. If I prefer the word above or below where my finger landed, fine, cheating is allowed – no rules.

When I played this game yesterday with one of my favourite books, I discovered the Titanic was provisioned with 800lbs of tea and 8000 cigars; *balderdash* is a Norse word; the Scoville Scale measures the hotness of chillies, and I must ensure this article avoids *floccinaucinihilipilification* (being assessed as worthless). I could have found Roman numerals, Cockney rhyming slang or the names of wedding anniversaries.

What was I playing with? – *Schott's Original Miscellany* (Blooms-bury). In addition to mental stimulation, it is a rare source of that specific detail – what Sol Stein calls 'particularity' – that can give a piece of writing resonance and authenticity. But beware: it can be addictive.

Words and Sparks:

I've used various paperback editions of *Thesaurus* since my school days, but at a car-boot sale recently I found a hardback tome so bruised and faded I had to read the flyleaf to find the title: *Roget's International Thesaurus*. Instead of just the 27 words for 'death' in my Collin's paperback edition, the *International* has four whole columns of words, phrases and associations: 'life' has only two. It's enough to make any writer turn to murder.

The quotes at the bottom of each page are fun too: *'Though an angel should write, still 'tis* devils *must print'*. (T. Moore). Or, *'If you wish to be a good writer, write'*. (Epictetus), which is what this treasure chest of words encourages me to do – and all for $2.

My third book-toy is *Brewer's Dictionary of Phrase and Fable*. There you will see that the saying, 'to get out of bed on the wrong side', is a superstition dating from the use of chamber pots and the importance of remembering on which side of the bed you left it when it was too full to move.

Well no, actually I just made that up, officially it is about bad luck associated with putting the left foot down first (and the left shoe on first), but you see what I mean about stimulus to imagination?

Hatching the Story:

My wooden egg, a mere two inches long and intricately carved with a pierced design, is filled with incense. Perfectly hand sized, the warmth releases a sensuous aroma. But this is not inspiration for writing erotic romance; a delight to hold though it is, the play value is something quite different. It was another junk-stall treasure – so begrimed all the little holes were bunged with dirt. It wasn't until I cleaned it up at home that I noticed it unscrewed in the middle. Inside, I found not only stale remnants of joss stick, but a tiny shiny key.

What did it open? Who put it there? Why the need to hide it? How did the egg come to be on the junk stall? It's a mind-set toy: these are the sort of questions I need in my mind when I'm struggling to write, when I want to look deep inside my characters' heads and hearts and into my own secrets, because I know that is where the key to story will be.

And Gaudi's design picture? He has always inspired me; in my childhood because I was too inhibited to draw and he seemed to have enough freedom of imagination for both of us. Looking at the shapes and colours in his buildings made me feel artistic even if I couldn't express it. Later, I realized his originality was perfectly matched with a profound understanding of structure.

The picture on my wall shows an assortment of cords and chains of varying thickness and length, suspended at overlapping intervals from overhead beams. It's a copy of an old grainy print and looks like a mess of cobwebs hanging from Miss Havisham's ceiling. But turn the picture upside down and you have the signature spires and catenary arches of classic Gaudi. For him it was an experiential design tool: for me it is a source of courage to turn my stories on their heads if they are not working – reverse the ending; switch to another point of view; begin in the middle.

Staying Focused:

The purpose of my other two favourite toys is more prosaic. The little basket is woven with consummate skill into a sphere, including the tight-fitting lid. Inside, I place slips of paper on which I have noted issues that persistently interrupt my creative thinking – the phone call I must make later, items for the shopping list, the extortionate plumber's bill. I press down the lid and there they stay until my writing session is finished: they won't be forgotten but they're out of my head and out of sight.

As for Beethoven, I find inspiration in his music and often play it while writing if only to feel his passion. The portrait I have on my desk is a reproduction of J. K. Stieler's 1819 original '*Beethoven holding the manuscript of the* Missa solemnis'. What does this do for me? His eyes look up from heavy brows into some vision beyond the viewer, his mouth set in concentration. He is completely absorbed. I gaze at him and there is not a semi-quaver of sympathy. The message is unequivocal: get on with it!

~~~

Use Your Eyes – to improve your writing

For those of us blessed with sight, vision is the most important sense through which we recognize the world around us. Before we are old enough to understand words, we see images that awaken in us the wonder and curiosity of our future creativity.

It is important for writers to realize this. If you can 'see' your characters, scenes and settings, you are half way to showing them to your readers, so they can 'see' them, too. This applies equally to non-fiction and fiction.

Some people have a particularly acute visual sense, thinking in images, patterns and spatial relationships, but even if you are not one of these, it is easy to strengthen and develop your visual perception. Photographs are a fun and effective way of doing this and have long been an essential tool in my own writing.

It is an old joke that the typical tourist 'clicks it now and sees it later'. Obviously, we risk missing the full ambience of a place if all we do is rush around taking pictures, but there is value in taking photographs to study later, even long after the event. And it allows you to stare at people in a way you would not dare to do otherwise.

Whether you are using your own photographs or other people's, here are some suggestions for using them to strengthen your writing:

Character: From holiday snaps or portraits, you can discern the contours of people's faces, their expressions, body language and responses to the proximity of others. Studying images of someone similar in age and status to your character can help you get to know them intimately – the way your readers need to engage with them.

Scene: Photographs of public and private places where people work, play, or simply travel through, enable you to appreciate how scenes work, why action changes, and how actors affect each other. Still photographs freeze each movement, making them more visible. Once you use this knowledge, your characters' dialogues and actions will have more depth and context.

Setting: Use landscapes and interiors to experience the setting of your story while you write, whether a dystopian desolation of rocks, ruins and desert; the mystery of forest or foggy streets; the visual clamour of a cityscape, or the intimacy of a park bench, a bar booth or a double bed. What details do you see? What do you feel? Let the reader see and feel through your eyes.

Start using a photographer's eye and you will soon realize how much has been passing you by without you noticing.

~~~

How to be Inspired by Laundry

Clothes tell stories and reveal secrets. On the washing line, they show important traits in your characters.

Let your mind linger on the laundry and you might feel a story idea wash over you. If you're lucky enough to have a washing machine you might watch them go round – who tangles with whom – springing open a fresh plot angle.

By hand, the tedium can be relieved by imagining each item's story. Think about the wine stains, split seams, bleeding colours, unexpected trophies in the pockets, what do they tell you about the person, *'the universe, life and everything'*?

But actually, it was other people's laundry I was thinking of.

I should caution you that the study of clotheslines as 'field research' is not without its hazards – it's best not to loiter too long in any one location and it's a criminal offence to remove and pocket even the smallest item – neither is it an exact science.

In Venice once, I used a line of washing as a landmark, confident that the distinctively coloured T-shirts in the middle distance would lead me back to the right *viottola*. Unfortunately, they must soon have dried, been collected and replaced by a new lot because I couldn't find them again and ended up hopelessly lost. But what is on the line can give you insights into the household – the likely ages and numbers of children and adults, their pastimes, tastes and budget – and fresh ways of describing characters.

How does your character hang the washing? Are some items discreetly hidden from view, tucked in between others, or brazenly exhibited for all to see? How is it pegged out? Higgledy-piggledy, hunched and creased as they were dragged from the machine, any old edge gripped onto the line, or neatly ... obsessively?

Instead of telling us:

'Cary was so affected by her new situation she became irrational and obsessive. At times she feared for her sanity,'

You could show us how she hangs her laundry:

'Tea towels first, then pillow cases, table clothes, going up in size to single sheets before the doubles – taking things down and moving them to another place on the line to keep the sizing accurate – it could take all morning, keeping at bay the thoughts that...'

And it's not only women who do washing. Is the man hanging out laundry in the next street a true partner in running the household, or a single father? How, or even if, he deals with dirty linen can tell you a lot about how he is coping. Indeed, his neighbours' assumptions about what they see on his washing-line could subtly mislead your readers until your devastating punch-line.

You probably have taps inside your house, and a washing machine, or at least a launderette down the street. Millions of people are less fortunate; they have to lug all their soiled clothes to communal tanks, or river banks. If this is your situation, or the setting for your story, the possibilities are equally promising.

Usually, a few friends or relatives gather to do this chore companionably; a chance for 'women's business', for scolding, encouraging and passing on wisdom about men, babies – the dialogue that might drive the next twist in your plot.

I don't want to scrub all the fun out of this idea by pounding it to death – but you get the general Dreft...er...drift?

~~~

Stories:

Sunlight on Stone

'But man does not create, he discovers.' Antoni Gaudí

Standing naked at the window, the dark hair of his belly coiled flat with moisture, Alec stropped his damp shoulders with a coarse towel and watched the column of smoke rising from a chimney behind the hill. An air current flattened the top – it looked like a cobra ready to strike.

He'd noticed the new place when he arrived last night – two cottages knocked into one, and a massive extension – big money, poor design.

No one had mentioned it at the funeral; respect for his father had subdued the urge to exchange and embroider local gossip. The whole community turned out to mark the passing of one of its own; he recognized most of them, people he'd known since childhood, distanced now by time and space. His father had been part of their daily lives, delivering the spoken word along with the post, heedless of hail or storm. As if to add its own farewell, rain accompanied them at the graveside. He'd been drenched to the skin.

There'd been no time to pack before he left. In his old bedroom he rummaged for sweater and jeans, kicking aside rugby boots left on a previous visit. No rugby these days. He missed it; playing winger kept you fit though he wasn't so quick at dodging the opposition now. He'd take a long walk up to the *stac* tomorrow.

Last year Sarah had been with him. She'd teased him about the way he walked, "I'd recognize you miles away, Alec," she said, "Heels down, head forward, as if you're late for something." Which he usually was. She'd fallen for his voice she told him once. But he hadn't enough of the right words.

He pulled on a thick woolly, glancing at the sad collection of his school paintings still tacked to the wall, their edges split and curled, colours faded. All he'd ever wanted to do was paint. That and fishing had defined his young life.

His father's dog watched from the doorway with a muted whine – she was probably hungry, so was he.

Sharing with Jess the oatcakes and ripe cheese he found in the lean-to kitchen, he stepped into the main room, its cosy familiarity comforting. He'd make up a fire later. It was a few years since he'd been here for more than brief visits but he knew where his father kept things – matches and baccy in a biscuit tin on the mantelshelf, whisky in the dresser.

He sat at the table, arms resting on rough-grained wood, nursing the glass between his hands. The relief, mingled with draining sadness, was unexpected and tainted with guilt. He should have been here more often.

Jess padded back and forth across the room, snuffling the empty armchair, finally settling beside Alec, her head on his knee, eyes still restless. "Missing the old man?" He ruffled her soft mane. "Let's go see Hughie."

There wasn't a time when he hadn't known Hughie; he'd taught him to tie his first fishing fly and indulged his childish art with too much praise. Between them – Hughie and his father – they'd almost filled that yearning void left in a young boy by the loss of his mother.

Hughie would know what was going on with this new neighbour.

"It's an eyesore right enough. His name's Morton – property developer from down south. Plans to build chalets or some such." Hughie gripped the edge of the table and reached for the bottle on the old black dresser behind him. "When he bought what remains of the estate he reckoned your father's croft should be included."

"He's no claim. It's been out of the estate since Gramp's time – it's freehold."

"He's now conceded that, but I hear his legal hounds are sniffing for cracks in the title." Hughie warmed to his favourite topic.

"That's nonsense, surely."

"It is. Drew up the deeds myself..."

Hughie's concentration switched to pouring the Laphroaig before continuing, "But if you'll not be here, Alec, only bide your time. He'll make it worth your while, I'm sure of that."

Was Hughie suggesting he sell, or just testing him? Dad would have wanted him to sell. The malt's warm, smoky sting released the tension in his throat. A decision could wait; he didn't want to get embroiled in all this right now.

"I'll need to fix the roof before I leave, anyway. Dad let things run down a bit."

Back in the cottage – his own now – he poured himself a dram and sat opposite his father's armchair; it was more comfortable than the one he was in but he hadn't the heart to use it. Jess tracked from one to the other before finally settling between the two.

He smelled the old man's pipe. Fancied he heard him rattling pan lids in the kitchen intent on one of his famous concoctions – you could last all weekend on one of his Friday-night soups.

A stroke, they said, swift and merciful, but he'd hoped for time to...to what? Neither of them had the gift of words for such feelings. Their deeply wrought bond was a blind sort of love, absent of real understanding. Do the trunk and the branch know the way of their connectedness?

His father had been sceptical of his passion for art. "Daubin' will nae keep body and soul together, lad."

As a compromise, he ground through the technologies and mathematics demanded of an architecture student – at least the art school was in the same complex. But doodles in the margins of his notebooks grew more disciplined, structured, less frequent, finally ceased.

His dragging heels left grooves of discontent in his student memories, but he did more than pass. His father came all the way to Edinburgh for the graduation – so proud he wore a suit.

He proved his mettle at Scott, McDonald and Whaley, Architects. And there he met Sarah. She captured his unwary heart with ease; he'd never met anyone like her – lively, lovely, golden Sarah.

He struggled to match her glittering life, her flamboyant friends. He was riding a bullet train without a ticket. On the fast track to her own triumphs Sarah grew impatient.

"I don't understand...What is it I don't give you?" he asked.

"You never have understood, Alec. That's exactly the point."

The finality of her words echoing in the clamping shut of her suitcase.

He filled the Sarah-space with more work, chagrined by this lack of originality. But as his confusion and bitterness eased he was drawn to a project of his own; spending evenings in the library, scribbling notes and rough sketches.

A few months later, he scooped up a coveted design prize, turned his back on success and bought an air ticket to Spain. Retreat? Advance? He didn't know which.

His father was dismayed. "And then where? How far to chase an illusion?"

Illusion perhaps, but body and soul moved further apart with each new commission he undertook.

The senior partner was unimpressed. "Gaudi? A bit...esoteric isn't it?"

It wasn't Gaudi's architecture but his artistry that compelled him. His sketches weren't trying to copy or even interpret the master's style; he was looking for the spring of Gaudi's artistic energy to somehow release his own. A forlorn hope maybe but it was all he had.

During his first few days in Barcelona he lost his way. The Gothic alleys – filled with a dank odour of cold stone and stagnant air – all looked the same.

He persevered. Followed the itinerary he'd worked out for himself. In the undulating façade of La Pedrera he recognized the subtle mastery behind apparent freedom of form. Decorative detail, especially in Park Gruëll, revealed similar contradictions: delicate line with bold colour; deceptive simplicity, and everywhere many layered symbolism. Though he paid homage to the incomparable imagination of the man, his restless tramping brought him no closer to his goal.

Under the awning of a cafe in Plaça Reial, he drained his second cup of coffee and pulled his battered sketchbook from his pocket. One evening in the library he'd written, 'the passion of unformed talent' – what he hoped to find was youthful idealism. Here he saw only the grand expressions of the mature Gaudi – it wasn't genius he sought, it was some initiating spark, even just the dry tinder.

He flicked through his earlier sketches, reluctant to continue what now seemed futile exploration. Gaudi had drawn inspiration from his native Catalonia, maybe that's where he should go – or just return to Edinburgh.

A young waiter brandished a coffee pot, eyebrows raised. Alec nodded. Eyeing the open sketchbook as he poured, the waiter grinned. "Artiste, Señor? I also. Estudiante." Alec shook his head. The waiter shrugged and moved away.

Alec slid down the chair, stuck his feet out under the table and stared unseeing into the heat of the square, his coffee untouched.

The waiter's question had scratched another scab off Alec's doubts: yesterday, like a bad omen, someone had stolen his travel bag from his too-cheap room – it contained all his painting gear.

"Order lunch, Señor?"

Alec jerked upright and looked around; the place was filling up. "No, no thanks." He hated the hassle with menus; too often picking blindly something that turned out unpalatable. The crowds and traffic oppressed him – he should get out of the city.

Before leaving the cafe he searched his guidebook for a shop that sold art supplies.

On the windswept plains of Catalonia, among the honeycombed, honey-coloured hills around Reus, where Gaudi was born, Alec rented a small casa.

How the intense light here foreshortened distance intrigued and excited him. It drew out colours, vibrated them into vivid shapes, dissecting them with deep shadows. He walked along dried riverbeds and through prolific olive groves. Sketching their gnarled trunks he scribbled, 'ancient monoliths tilted with the weight of their own history'.

He looked up into the mountains – tried to capture their ochre mornings, their indigo evenings. In the hills he rambled through ruined castles; set his easel overlooking villages strung out across the plain like beads of a rosary, each clustered around its church tower.

In the family restaurant without table cloths where he ate his meals, la dueña kept a place for him until late. With her encouragement, he learned enough Catalan to gain some understanding of his surroundings. Despite contrasts to the landscape of his childhood, he was aware of a subtle affinity, a barely perceptible tension.

Vivid though it was, with its soft red earth and ever-changing sky, the image eluded him. Half-finished, abandoned artwork littered his room. His feverish efforts were still products of his head not his heart.

But he was painting again.

When news of his father's sudden death reached him, it seemed even by this his father mocked his ambition. That he should think this shocked him. He'd taken the first plane home.

Alec spent most of the week replacing broken slates on the roof. When he refitted a window and tightened loose door hinges in Hughie's cottage, he heard that Morton had already issued an eviction notice to a local family.

"Technically he has the right of it." Hughie shook his head. "But damn it, the man has no heart."

Having failed to find any flaw in Alec's title, Morton had written with an offer to purchase. Alec pushed it to the back of his mind. Events were dragging him away from his painting again; he wanted to get back to Reus.

Planning an early breakfast, Alec picked up the kettle and yanked off the lid. He turned the tap and sweet peaty water ran darker than usual before dribbling to nothing. Bloody debris caught over the inlet – it happened occasionally after heavy rain. He trudged through bracken to midway up the hill where a slight levelling-out marked the underground tank into which the land drained. As a boy he'd been there often with his father.

He removed the obstruction easily but the blockage was deliberate; he was sure of it. He'd ignored the letter – though the offer was attractive – now Morton was pressing his point.

It was tempting. If he sold he could afford to set up his own practice, choose his clients – he was good enough, he'd proved that. He checked around the cottage; a few more days and he'd have it weather tight and tidy.

The night Alec finished the work he slept badly. Struggling free of tangled bedding he dressed in whatever was lying around, left the cottage, and scrambled down the bank towards the beach, Jess tacking ahead engrossed in her own mission.

Morton was offering an excellent price – the bastard had increased it after interfering with the water supply: carrot and stick. He was obviously determined to have the cottage; might even go higher if pressed.

Alec stopped and gazed at the familiar landscape of his youth: rocky spurs either side of the bay fractured and worn by fruitless efforts to hug the restless sea to its shore; stunted bushes, backs bent towards the prevailing winds, and gleaming water so white yet so full of colours.

He walked across the *machair* – recalling its tickly scratchiness under small bare feet – to where skeins of kelp marked the tide's retreat, and filled his lungs with sea-smell.

The air here was so different to the dusty plains of Catalonia, light and colours, too. His thoughts seemed to strain between the two: their pride and spiritual strength; their rich heritage thwarted by the political ambitions of others. The soils of both bore the blood of loyal sons – the price of freedom neither had won.

The crunch of his boots on loose stones sounded too loud in his ears; it cancelled out the soft tittle-tattle of shingle stirred by a rising tide – a more fitting chorus to the plaintive call of grey plovers scuttering along the water's edge. He stooped to pick up a pebble, traced the quartz veins with a fingertip, felt it silky-wet on his palm – a stained-glass pebble brought to light by the ocean that shaped it.

It reminded him of Gaudi's intricate mosaics – tiny pieces of broken ceramic and glass recycled and reassembled into new symbols – stories within stories.

A breeze riffled his hair. Gone was the gusting wind and rain that had orchestrated his father's memorial service. A thin cerulean wash of morning sky seemed to offer eternity.

He would fill that emptiness.

He whistled up Jess and strode back to the cottage, anger quickening his step. Clambering into his father's old land rover, flinging sweaters off the seat into the back where Jess already sat alert, he started the engine, wrenched it into gear, and bounced it along the stony track in the direction of Morton's house.

~~~

Story Analysis:

The initial inspiration for this story was the Neil Gunn Writing Competition in 2011, on the theme '*a wrong turning*' – a quote from Gunn's short story *Highland River*. I found the original lines: '*Our river took a wrong turning somewhere! But we haven't forgotten the source.*'

Entries did not have to be about Scotland, but I had enjoyed living in the Highlands for many years and could write from direct experience. I was aware, too, of conflict between the Highlands as a source of local pride, and the economic pressures that led to generations of outward migration. So I placed Alec along this fault line to reflect the inner struggle between his artistic ambitions and his father's expectations.

Following my own advice in '*Use Your Eyes*', I refreshed my knowledge of the Highlands with photographs, particularly of the west coast with the "*tickly scratchiness*" of the *machair* grassland I had known so well. It seemed important to let the reader share what Alec saw, heard and felt, not only to describe the setting, but to show its significance to Alec's internal quandary. The physical environment of his youth was part of who he was and how his early dreams were formed. His quest for inspiration in Catalonia led to another artist's source – his "*wrong turning*'.

For his painter's perception and some personality traits, I drew upon the character of a real artist I had known, although their situations were entirely different. By unscrewing this *'wooden egg'* of my own experience I recalled tensions in relationships which indirectly gave a sense of reality to dialogue and inner thoughts. Such inspiration from deep within us does not necessarily result in specific elements of a story, but it can create a mood, an understanding that enriches a character's 'voice' and influences choice of words and images. The process can be painful, but no one claims that writing is easy.

The choice of Catalonia provided a contrasting landscape with some historical similarities and the opportunity to have Gaudi – always a fascination to me – as Alec's guiding light, but both required detailed research. I relied heavily on photographs and descriptions of Barcelona and rural Catalonia to attempt the same kind of intimacy with the environment that I experienced in the Scottish Highlands.

In a sort of reverse inspiration, I visited Catalonia a couple of years after writing the story, staying in a *'too-cheap room'* in Barcelona which backed onto the Plaça Reial, and spending a day of pure magic in Reus on Gaudi's birthday. As an endorsement of the power of imagination and careful research in creating settings, I had no need to change anything in the original story after my trip.

I had read in one of Sol Stein's books that opening a story with a naked protagonist was always a good hook. It gave me the idea, but the decision to use it was based on its appropriateness: it made Alec seem more vulnerable to the threat of the *'cobra'*, and allowed a quick transition to the reason he was undressed and his search for clothes in the bedroom with its echoes of his childhood dreams.

A professional editor who critiqued an early draft said I had made it difficult for myself by choosing the Highlands – *'so often romanticized'* – as a location: *'because you've picked quite a well-worn location, your language needs to work extra hard to make the story feel original.'* (He was not aware that the story was being entered for a specific competition). He praised the story arc – the change from Alec's uncertainty at the outset to his clear resolution at the end – but wanted stronger conflicts in Alec's dilemma: between the temptation to sell-out and the desire to stay; between respect and resentment of his father, and with a nastier Morton. He wanted the character to be pressed harder in making more difficult choices.

I addressed all of these issues in the final draft, finishing just within the required word count, but the overarching comment was that the story was too big to be given justice in a confined space and I should consider re-working it into a novel – a project for my old age perhaps.

So how did Alec fair in the Neil Gunn competition? *Sunlight on Stone* was selected for the shortlist of twelve.

The following year, I entered it in the 2012 Winchester Writers' Conference short story competition where it was Highly Commended. The judges use a score card against set criteria rather than specific comments: they awarded full marks for the opening, characters, and title; good marks for language, entertainment, dialogue and ending, but they were not at all impressed with what they call the 'plot/theme', or the pace. I agree, it is not a racy, plot-driven story, but I leave you, the reader, to decide whether or not it should be.

~~~

The Pink Bobble Hat

A lovely young man picked me up – before I hit the ground, fortunately.

I was walking along Regent Street looking in the shop windows and didn't notice the loose paving stone; I felt myself falling, a strange powerlessness like being sucked into a giant vacuum cleaner.

It's a pink bobble hat I was searching for, but nobody had one. It's not surprising of course; they are rather ghastly. But my friend, Rosemary, knitted one for me last Christmas during an unprecedented lapse in taste. Well, I can't find the wretched thing and Rosemary is coming to visit, so I'm desperate to replace it.

Such an extraordinary thing for her to make: in the fifty years I've known her, she's always been impeccably dressed, even when we were gals at Cheltenham Ladies College. I was the blue-stocking; more interested in my Theophrastus than the prevailing fashions, although I do remember being given an exquisite evening stole for my twenty-first birthday. It was made of black silk with a narrow trim of fur. I wore it at our graduation ball.

They were exciting days, the 1950s. There was still some rationing but we were all so positive about the future. And Ernest Hemingway won the Nobel Prize – such a vigorous writer. I met him once, at a party in Malaga, but he was a sick man by then. I wonder what Rosemary reads these days – she lives in Worcester, out in the sticks – I haven't seen her for years.

The lifestyle of an embassy wife made it hard to hold onto old friends, but I wouldn't have missed it. All those years in the Far East were such a thrilling experience – once I learned how to manage the servants: embassy widows can't afford them, unfortunately.

Well, the guest room is ready, and Rosemary arrives tomorrow. We've always been fond of each other and I'm so looking forward to seeing her again. I hope she won't think I simply discarded that dreadful hat; it probably went to the animal welfare people ... Oh, now who is that at the door just when I've made the tea?

"Rosemary! How lovely..."

"Hello, Meryl, I brought milk."

"Thank you, dear. So thoughtful. Oh, and you're wearing one of your pink bobble hats."

"I love it. Keeps my hair tidy and such fun. Didn't you give me this for Christmas last year?"

Poor dear, she seems terribly muddled. I do hope the next few days aren't going to be too tiresome.

"It's so lovely to see you, Rosemary, but I was expecting you tomorrow you know. But really, it doesn't matter a bit. The tea is just this minute made so do sit down, dear, you must be tired after that dreadfully long journey."

"Oh, Meryl, you've forgotten. I'm in the flat upstairs now. Shall I pour, my dear?"

~~~

Story Analysis:

The attempt to write about memory loss arose from a story competition which had that as its theme. A challenge because its forms and causes are complex and the word count was only 250. At that time, I happened to be reading a collection of Ernest Hemingway's short stories, finding some of them dated, and wondering to what extent readers in the 1920s and 1930s, who shared his experience of the times, appreciated his writing in a different way to modern readers.

Initially there seemed no connection between that and memory loss; only later did I realize his generation was now elderly, if they suffered from dementia they might remember only those early days, recalling them with great clarity. I decided to focus my story on senile dementia.

It also sparked another idea: for my protagonist to have a surprising past that contrasted with her present life – a sort of divergence – and I wanted her to be intelligent, privileged and active, to accentuate a dramatic change into dementia. Having made her a classics scholar and married her off to a diplomat, I thought: she could have met Hemingway, why not? It would be a clear and treasured memory.

During several weeks, the story was built up in this way, not from my own experience or observation, but from other things I was reading and thinking about: I was going out to meet the muse at external pick-up points. The different ways inspiration occurs is a constant source of wonder, but it comes from engagement of one form or another, not from fretting over a blank page.

More difficult was working out how to show the loss of memory. To be convincing, it had to involve simple everyday actions that others would notice but the sufferer might not; something as mundane as laundry – a misplaced hat – that also involved mixing up past and present. After a couple of false starts, I knew this story needed to be longer. Abandoning the competition, I developed it to 500 words – my favourite flash length. (I have never written a fully satisfying story shorter than 500 words: something I had to learn and accept about myself as a writer).

I gained enormous pleasure from writing this story because I became especially attached to Meryl for her unconscious naivety in devotion to the good life, hearing so clearly her slightly 'blimpish' accent expressing a sense of wonder and fun. That voice and optimism came from a friend of my mother's who had a similar past to Meryl's, although she remained mentally alert throughout her life. I can't remember exactly how the idea of the *"rather ghastly"* pink bobble hat came to me, but with Meryl's personality, I wanted something outlandish to portray her loss of memory and at the same time reflect her natural gaiety – undiminished because she is not aware of her problem. And she does remember the hat; she simply forgets whose it is.

A lot of tweaking was needed to avoid the end being obvious too soon, while leaving ambiguous clues. And I used carefully researched detail – Hemingway's party, the 1920s silk stole with the fur trim – to divert the reader, although the clarity of past memories and vagueness about the present are also clues to Meryl's state of mind.

The story was entered in Flash500 competition for the third quarter of 2012, where it was shortlisted. I requested an official critique – which I always do because it is extremely good value – and the version given above is the story edited, after the competition, to take account of the comments.

I'll explain the editing in detail because, in flash fiction, it is the fine points that count. On the critique's positive aspects: the title was intriguing and inviting; the opening was engaging and, in particular, effectively introduced the narrator and her age without spelling it out; characterisation allowed the reader to get inside Meryl's head, and the ending was both unexpected and enjoyable.

On the negative side were two problems. The chattiness of Meryl's voice was lost at the beginning of the fourth paragraph when their schooldays were recalled in a too bald and 'telling' way. To let you see my edit, the original sentence was: *"We were at school together, Rosemary and I – Cheltenham Lady's College – nearly fifty years ago. She was always impeccably dressed even as a young gal. I was the blue-*

stocking;" Which I changed to: *"Such an extraordinary thing for her to make: in the fifty years I've known her, she's always been impeccably dressed, even when we were gals at Cheltenham Ladies College. I was the blue-stocking;"*

The second problem was the final piece of dialogue from Rosemary, which sounded 'unrealistic' with too much 'telling' in the author's voice. The original lines were: *"Oh, Meryl. I live in the flat upstairs now and pop down for tea every afternoon. It's Isobel who comes on Saturdays. Shall I pour my dear?"* I seem to have had a misplaced need to tell the reader Meryl was well cared for. I replaced it with: *"Oh, Meryl, you've forgotten. I'm in the flat upstairs now. Shall I pour, my dear?"*

Initially, analysing stories in this way may seem time-consuming and tedious, but the choice of a single word has significance in short stories, developing the habit of reading more slowly and creatively opens up a new level of enjoyment and understanding.

~~~

2: Characters

"We find out a short way by a long wandering." Roger Ascham.

I could tell you I am tall – five foot nine – but I doubt that would interest you unless I can show you it's had a big impact on my life story, which I don't think it has, (if I told you my shoe size, that might be a different matter). When I read that a protagonist is fat, and make the effort to remember the fact, I get cranky when I find by the end of the story that the man's weight was irrelevant – I've carried 20 stone around to no purpose.

Tall, short, fat, thin, dark or blonde: they don't tell us much, although they can be turned into significance: 'Charlie tries to slip a magazine off the top shelf in the newsagents but he can't quite reach. Looking around for the shop assistant, he turns pale when he recognizes her – the wife's cousin.' But here, Charlie's lack of height contributes more to plot than character – maybe he will end in strife for his choice of reading. On the other hand, if his motivation is that his shortness makes him feel sexually inadequate, that might lead to a different kind of story – I'll think about that one.

Apart from such twists, general physical appearance is my least favourite way of reading or writing about people in fiction because it conveys so little about them. Neither of the protagonists in the two stories at the end of this chapter has a physical description. I hoped to engage the reader as a partner in the storytelling by allowing them to construct their own portraits from other evidence – what the characters think, say and do – because their physical appearance is not critical to their stories.

For fun, I asked the members of my writing group to read the shorter of the two stories (*Now's the Day*) and jot down how they would recognize the narrator in a line-up. If you want to play, too, read it now before I tell you the results, it's less than 500 words.

No one in the group had noticed the lack of physical description for the narrator until I mentioned it, yet each had their own clear picture of what he looked like and they varied widely: fat, muscular but flabby, skinny survivor, bushy ginger hair, balding, unkempt and smelling of drink, slightly stooped, jowly. Funnily enough, no one had considered his height, but everyone agreed he was a rough but likeable chap. If you read the story, how does that compare with your image of him?

Height, colour and girth we can see in the street any day and happily apply our own prejudices. What we cannot see is inside people's heads – to their true temperaments, motives and intentions – and we need to. Not out of idle curiosity, or even to tell a good story, but because we have evolved as social beings. During our development as humans, our survival has depended on working out what the other person really thinks and is likely to do next. We co-operate but we also compete, even, or especially, with those closest to us – our families and friends. Working with limited knowledge of each other, our lives become complicated. Generations of lawyers have grown rich from our 'getting it wrong'.

Aware of the need for this understanding, our clever ancestors, between chipping at stones and spearing the next meal, used their emerging language skills to tell stories: to teach, entertain, enthral, and in so doing, to provide meaning and the means of surviving in the world around us. Stories can provide us with identity and a sense of connection to our inner selves as well as to others. One of the many things we do through reading stories is to 'rehearse' social relationships with a minimum of risk. For the old storytellers, these interpretations of people's intentions were calculated guesswork from experience. Even with modern advances in brain science, they still are. We can never know for sure the thoughts of another.

And yet we crave stories that get inside characters' minds, so where do writers find their best guesses? *"Observation is our source of characterizations, but understanding of deep character is found in another place. The root of all fine character writing is self-knowledge."* Despite differences of culture, background, age or gender, *"the truth is we are all far more alike than we are different. We are all human.*

We all share the same crucial human experiences. Each of us is suffering and enjoying, dreaming and hoping of getting through our days with something of value. As a writer, you can be certain that everyone coming down the street toward you, each in his own way, is having the same fundamental human thoughts and feelings that you are." (Robert McKee).

I don't doubt it is true, but I find it both a comfort and a worry. A comfort because it gives us a rich source if we are prepared to take risks, free ourselves from fear and self-censure as we talked about in the previous chapter. But it's a worry because the road to self-knowledge is long and winding and strewn with sharp stones that hurt. And even after tackling that journey, our knowledge can be only partial at best.

Perhaps that is why short stories are often described as 'a matter of life and death'. Not because their authors subject characters to more emotional turmoil and destruction per paragraph than anyone else – although they do seem to – but because of the urgency inherent in taking on the messiness of the whole human condition with so few words: a whole grove of olives is cold-pressed to produce the extra virgin oil that is an original short story.

With barely room to swing a critic, word-eaters like settings, plots and back-stories have to be controlled with a few deft strokes. Character becomes the main focus: *"Characters make your story."* (Sol Stein). But there's rarely space for more than two or three and they have to do the job of revealing each other *and* turning the plot because the writer, though privileged to 'know' it all, cannot simply tell us – as readers, we need to see it played out so we can participate, too.

No wonder it is the most challenging form in fiction. A short story writer lacks the novelist's indulgence to sprawl elegantly with his protagonist's remorse and recrimination over ten pages: she must beam it to us in ten words. And shallow, stereotyped characters can't do the job. As we shall see in the chapter on structure and plot, in the arc of a story, characters change in some way in response to challenges. Stereotypes lack the potential to draw on hidden attributes, reveal new strengths or weaknesses, or struggle with inner battles sufficient to carry a story.

Complex characters have conflicting needs, divided loyalties and muddled attitudes like the rest of us: the fragile, wispy-haired old lady in the nursing home, smiling as you pass, who accidentally drops her book onto the floor out of reach and shouts, "Oh fuck it!" way beyond the whisper she intended, on account of her deafness; the sanctimonious preacher who drills a hole through the wall of the meeting room so that when the Ladies' Committee is in session he can peek up their skirts, or the model of rectitude, law-abiding and honest citizen who abhors violence, hiding the crimes of her son.

How much a writer shows us about a particular character and what is in his or her mind, depends on the point of view adopted in telling the story, i.e. through whose eyes we 'see' the tale. The consequences of this choice may be less familiar to readers who are not also writers, so the first article that follows – *The View from Here* – explores this topic from a reader's point of view.

The other two articles dwell on a few practicalities about finding and showing characters. The latter piece is one I mentioned earlier, about inspiration for character from a small collection of belongings on a junk stall. It may seem a little odd: it was written almost like a story in an attempt to 'walk the talk', i.e. to 'show' rather than 'tell' about using objects to characterize.

One of the difficulties I experienced in structuring this book was exactly where to place each story and article, given that everything is connected and leaks into everything else. If you are in 'character mode' at the moment, you might like to nip forward to the end of chapter 5 and read also the article *Hands up for Character* (which is down there to contribute to identifying 'voice' through physical description).

~~~

Articles:

The View From Here

On holiday in Kiev some years ago, Ira, our guide, who never left our side and was probably an undercover KGB agent, took us to each splendid site – the gleaming domes of Saint Sophia's Cathedral come to mind – pointed to a specific spot on the ground beside her feet and commanded: "You take photo here."

Excellent though her selected view points were, I have a strange fondness for taking photographs that are not exactly the same as everyone else's; an artistic freedom imperiously discouraged by Ira, though what state secret I might have uncovered by deviating to left or right is hard to imagine. And it is probably fortunate that, at the time, I was unaware of a more original method for capturing scenes through my lens.

An artist friend told me the best way to appreciate a fresh per-spective on a familiar view is to stand with your back to it, place your feet wide apart and bend over to look at it from between your legs. Luckily, such physical contortions are not essential for considering different frames of reference when writing or reading, as opposed to painting or photography, although comparable mental agility may be required.

When writers choose to tell a tale using the perception – point of view – of one character rather than another, they face implications as to what can be said and how it should be expressed, but writers know this, talking about it in familiar tones as 'POV'. Instead, let's turn around to see it from the standpoint of a reader who is not a writer.

When we read a story written from a 'first person' point of view, we are invited to identify with that character and what he or she sees, does and thinks; the protagonist narrates events talking directly to us as if sitting across the table sharing personal experiences and insights. He might say: 'I watched for the bus all morning, pacing back and forth in the dust, wondering if she would bring the child.'

In that situation, we are aware only of what he sees and feels; we cannot, for example, know what other, absent characters are doing or what any of them are thinking – we have to look for clues and 'wonder' like the protagonist, and make up our own minds as to his reliability in this respect.

I enjoy reading first person stories most: the intimacy of hearing confidences, and the emotional exercise in making the kind of assessments one makes on meeting a new acquaintance and knowing them by increments. Both of the stories at the end of this chapter are written from a first person perspective.

When a 'second person' point of view is used, the narrator addresses you, the reader, as if telling you your own story: 'You walked into the room and stared with dismay at your partner, the woman you thought you knew well enough not to...' The intention is to draw you into emotional identity with the story. It can feel like being placed in front of a mirror that starts talking at you. Alternatively, we may be 'hearing' the narrator speaking to herself, seeking detachment to resolve an inner quandary.

It doesn't usually work for me. Reading this point of view, I feel a need to push back the speaker from intruding into my inner space, planting thoughts and experiences that are not mine. I feel I'm given no choice in the matter of identification and have little real 'work' to do as a reader. That is simply my personal reaction, you may find the novelty of it refreshing and, indeed, a story may resonate with your own. Possibly because of reader ambivalence, this point of view is rarely used.

More often, we read stories written in the 'third person', where a narrator, who may or may not be one of the characters in the story, relates to us what the characters are doing and saying: 'Graham pushed roughly through the crowd, shouting his order before reaching the bar counter. The woman beside him glared at the company as if daring anyone to object.'

The narrator watches and listens, telling us what is happening and, sometimes, what he or she thinks about it, but we have only the narrator's guesses as to what other characters are thinking and feeling because the story is told through the narrator's – the third person's – eyes, and they can't see inside people's heads any better than we can. Instead, we sense Graham's urgency from his actions, and the woman's feelings from the suggestive 'as if'.

Sometimes the narrator is not identifiable, remaining 'silent' except for telling us what is happening. When this technique is used to show the actions of one main character – often the case in a short story – it can feel like a first person account. As we read, we could almost replace the character's name with 'I' – in fact, it is being led to do this subconsciously, i.e. to empathize, that makes the story feel so 'close' even though we learn the character's thoughts indirectly through the 'invisible' narrator's comments or questions.

To show you the difference, I could rewrite the first example like this: 'John watched for the bus all morning, pacing back and forth in the dust. Would she bring the child?' Writers call this 'close third' and I used it in the story in chapter 1, *Sunlight on Stone*.

You've probably also read the variant form of third person, called 'omniscient' point of view because the author – who knows everything, of course – tells us what everyone is thinking as well as doing. From this viewpoint, the episode at the bar could be written: 'Graham pushed roughly through the crowd, shouting his order before reaching the bar counter. After what he'd just witnessed outside he felt his legs would give way without a stiff drink. The woman beside him glared at the company. She wished Graham wouldn't get so excited, but she was ready to fend off any protests.'

To avoid reader overload and confusion, writers are urged to give only one person's inner thoughts and feelings at a time, maybe letting characters 'take it in turns' in different paragraphs or chapters, not in alternate sentences as I have done above. But even then, I feel less involved when reading an omniscient point of view: there seems little for me to explore for myself, and I find it harder to forget the author – because only the author knows all of those things – and be drawn into 'living' the story. This may be because I am reading as a writer; we each bring different perspectives to our reading.

A lot depends on a writer's skills, but as readers, we tend to have preferences for certain ways of being told a story, of being shown how a character experiences life. If you haven't given much thought to this until now, points of view might help explain why you enjoy some stories more than others.

In a short story there is rarely room for the complications of hearing everyone's thoughts and feelings directly, and in the tight restrictions of a flash story, even showing a narrator's role sufficiently to understand why they tell us what they do, may take too many words. For these reasons, most short stories are written from one point of view, and often from first person, but I once took on the challenge of writing a 500-word flash story – *Transpositions* – through three different points of view. I include it at the end of chapter 4 on structure because it was the structure of the story that enabled it to work.

Ira is not watching: writers may select whatever view point they wish, and as readers, we can choose whichever we find most satisfying to read.

~~~

Writers' Face-lift – generating story ideas

One of the best generators of story ideas surrounds us almost all the time in flesh, print or electronic pulse, the first image we focus on after birth – the human face. Each is a window on character...and story.

A friend had difficulty starting a new writing project because every time she thought of characters, they turned into someone she knew. This isn't necessarily a problem, familiar people and experiences are a rich source of inspiration for fiction, as long as we rearrange details so that no one recognizes themselves. But my friend's situation was slightly different: she was feeling inhibited by the presence of these 'characters' with their existing traits and quirks – what she needed was strangers.

With accustomed faces we can become lazy. Not 'seeing' them anymore. Taking for granted past knowledge, we make assumptions about the thoughts and feelings behind them. In a stranger's face we are more likely to notice, for example, the set of the jaw and tilt of the head, skin tone and texture, and eyes – how they move, whether they seem to be saying the same thing as the mouth.

Our interpretations of these signs may be totally at odds with the person's real nature (and likely to be as much a reflection of our personality as theirs), but for the purposes of fiction, that doesn't matter: we are creating characters to story with.

Opportunities for 'people watching' abound: on buses and trains, in shops, waiting rooms and restaurants, but it can be a bit dodgy to stare for long periods at strangers while we imagine their inner lives and past experiences: some people don't like it. So when it was my turn to create an exercise for the writing group, I decided to take along some faces we could stare at with impunity.

These could have been cut from magazines and newspapers or downloaded from the web, but personal snapshots are more engaging. I made 4"x 6" prints of a selection of faces from my own albums that no one in the group would have seen before, with some duplicated to allow for diverse constructions from the same image.

These are the tasks I wrote on the top of a blank sheet for each participant:

- Select two photographs and give the people names.
- Decide on their relationship to each other (a casual meeting of strangers; family members; new friends; old-time neighbours; professional interaction etc.)
- Write a brief back-story for each person: who they are, what matters to them, what they seek in life.
- Decide on a setting/situation, and write a few lines of dialogue between them.
- What kind of story could this develop into?

How did the exercise go?

As it happened, selecting and naming two faces and relating them to each other in some way, was enough to generate a story idea. The back-stories and dialogues either developed it further or changed the concept in another creative direction. I summarize below two particularly interesting 'dialogues' that came out of the session.

1. The chosen faces were of a middle-aged woman smiling and a young woman who, by chance, bears a likeness to her. In the story that emerged, these two faces were of the same woman, Kerry, at different ages. As a 21 year old, Kerry wrote a letter to the self she thought she would be in forty years time. The mature Kerry finds the letter, 'dialogue' taking the form of her reading it and responding with her thoughts, revealing the discrepancy between her young expectations and the tragic reality that has fashioned her life since. Ultimately, Kerry taps the remembered strength of her youth to overcome unresolved issues from her past.

2. The joker in the pack, the porcelain face of a harlequin doll with an inscrutable expression, was teamed with a four year old girl showing the viewer where she had recently lost a baby tooth. The doll, Annabelle, is Patsy's confidante. Patsy has been locked in her room by a mother who was "not really cross, but didn't even look at me". The dialogue between Patsy and her doll reveals the child's emotional insecurity in a story of dysfunctional family relationships. Annabelle is Patsy's alter ego, saying the 'bad' things, while Patsy tries to convince Annabelle that her mother does love her. Daddy's return from work uncovers the reason why Patsy was locked in her room and the crisis that now faces them.

Other ways to use this exercise:

- I don't believe in the existence of 'writers' block' but our creativity can become stale and jaded on occasion, and there is always that sneak thief of time and inspiration – procrastination. If you keep a collection of pictures from magazines, this is a quick and visual exercise to reignite a spark when needed.

- It is also a handy warm-up activity to meet with the muse before starting a writing session.

- If you already have your characters, looking for pictures that resemble the image you have of them in your head, can help you enrich their description and actions – they become more 'real' to you, and therefore to the reader.

~~~

Writing Character

It was the walking stick that caught my gaze. Its rubber tip worn down to a custom tilt; its handle polished by decades of grip and lean. To see such a dependable old friend abandoned to a jumble sale is a sad sight: it can mean only one thing.

She was 92 when she died. What was her name? "That old lady who lived on top of the hill? Don't know, luv." Nobody knew her anymore: her generation had gone, new people arrived; she became part of the landscape they passed through.

"These two harlequins were hers, too. Real porcelain – the hands and faces – amazing. From out East somewhere, I reckon." They were found on top of an old black and white television set when the house was cleared. They still smile, shyly; dusty and faded where a window must have stood behind them. Houses on hilltops have a lot of sun – and a lot of view. Perhaps she looked at that view more often than the television, and smiled at the harlequins' generosity.

The stall holder rummaged through the bric-à-brac – seeing I was interested – and brought out a flower fashioned from purple, leaded glass. "I reckon she made that herself, a bit rough – pretty, though, eh?" Yes. I bought it all for a few dollars.

Not a lot to show for a life, but a treasure chest for a writer.

The walking stick had a roughly carved 'mouth' and two 'eyes' of shell fragments: with assurance of her own identity, a sense of humour and imagination, she made it unique. Those who didn't know her knew whose walking stick it was.

And from what distant land had she brought the harlequins, wrapped with infinite care – inside tissue paper, inside a box, inside her suitcase? Or were they cushioned in a sweater in her rucksack, even further ago. Were they the Yin and Yang of a young girl's hopes, the romance that begins with shy smiles and ends in side-by-side fidelity by a window with a view?

Or perhaps she travelled much later in life, after the twosome had become lonesome: the harlequins a bitter-sweet souvenir of a life and love once known.

And the leaded glass flower – a bit bendy where it shouldn't be – was it made of gritty determination with shaky hands and cataract-veiled eyes? With an irrepressible desire to make a thing of beauty that caught the light, a small, stained-glass epitaph? Or was it the expression of her youthful vision – unfading, still smiling ... shyly?

No one here knows her name, but I like to think of her as Beatrice, who preferred to be called Bea.

~~~

I hope you have understood, now, why there is no introduction to this piece; no mention of useful techniques, advice, reasons. Quite simply: it is all in the seeing.

~~~

All those objects really did belong to *"that old lady who lived on top of the hill"*; I saw and bought them from a junk stall in our local market. I haven't written Bea into a real story yet, but I will one day. Many objects can contribute to the depth of a character: items on a bedside table; contents of pockets (produced by a character or found by others); clothes and how they are worn; a book being read, and things on a desk, a mantelshelf, or bookcase.

And in the limited space available for a short story, objects can do three jobs simultaneously: indicate setting, show character, and have some significance in the plot. As readers, our engagement and satisfaction are increased by being allowed space to interpret the significance of objects rather than be told everything. Look around your own home – what would someone know of you from what they see?

~~~

Stories:

Getting Rid of Agatha

What a pity Jeremy isn't here to see this. He'd be furious.

"Hold it up, Arthur. That's the way." The auctioneer rests both hammy fists on the ledge of the pulpit and leans out, leering at the punters from a face resembling a Sunday roast – ruddy, plump and glistening.

"Right, ladies and genl'men. Lot Fifteen. 'Ere we 'ave a choice piece. Mahogany swivel mirror with drawer. Nice bit of yer Victoriana. Turn it around, Arthur. That's the way. I'll start at two hundred, it's worth twice that, what-am-I-bid-what-am-I-bid, come on now. Two hundred thank you, madam. Two forty at the front 'ere. Any advance on two forty? It's a steal. Two sixty … two eighty at the back, thank you –"

I remember the day we bought that, Mother and I. We found it in a little antique shop in Pimlico, a present for my twenty-first birthday – good heavens, almost forty years ago. We spent hours rootling among the stalls in Petticoat Lane Market. Mother made a hobby of nostalgia. She treasured anything old and handmade, musing upon the lives of those who made them, or owned them – a natural storyteller. I was her only audience but an avid one; Father thought it all a lot of silly nonsense and my brother – ten years older than I – parroted whatever my father said.

"Lot Fifteen. Going, going, gone! For three-hundred-eighty pounds – lady in red at the back there. It's all right, Madam, the clerk will come to you."

That sold for more than I expected. This seems a strange place for auction rooms – a disused church, stripped bare except for a few worm-eaten pews. Voices echo eerily around the walls. It smells dank, musty with fruity undertones, a bit like those charity shops with racks of disreputable clothing. And those small, high windows give a sinister light. It could be a courtroom: the auctioneer looks more suited to the dock than the pulpit, but he has an excellent reputation – one of the best in the business I was told.

"Lot Sixteen. A lovely rosewood Davenport, ladies and genl'men. Open a drawer on it, Arthur. That's the way. A little gem of a writing desk, this. I can't start at less than five-hundred pounds …"

That was Mother's. She wrote all her letters on it, poetry, too, but she always hid that, even from me. She would sit at the Davenport in the little back sitting room after breakfast to answer correspondence – the coldest room in the house but her refuge from my father's constant hectoring. She made excuses for him. "Your father is such a clever man," she used to say. I think it was one of her ways of coping.

It was for Mother's sake I stayed, although as the years sneaked by I realized that doors were rusting up behind me, doors I thought would never open again. We both knew this, but it was something neither of us wanted to bring into the light.

Mother would have woven a wonderfully poignant story around each cherished possession going under the hammer. I want to reach out and feel again that silky patina where her own hands so often rested, but it's no good being sentimental now, she's been gone for fifteen years.

"All done at one-thousand-five-hundred pounds? The bid's at the front 'ere. Going, going, gone!"

Lots of people here today. The usual sprinkling of dealers in suits, trying to look disinterested, each with their own barely discernible nod or twitch to place a bid. The woman with a paisley wrap over her trench coat, gabbling into her mobile phone and jabbing a peremptory finger at the auctioneer, might be a collector's agent. But the others look like people simply hoping for a bargain, or wanting somewhere to stay out of the rain. I can see better standing at the back and I'm too churned up to sit down anyway. Each item in this saleroom is a page in someone's biography; sad to witness past lives broken down to lots and sold off – including my own in some ways. But I'm excited about the future, too, and that has given me so much energy these last few weeks.

"Excuse me, Miss Wells?" One of the auctioneer's men in his long brown dust coat comes up quietly beside me.

"Yes, that's me."

"We found this 'ere tucked right at the back o' one o' them drawers – thought you'd want it, like." He hands me a dusty, crumpled piece of paper, yellow with age.

"Oh, that was kind, thank you very much."

It crackles as I unravel it, and a thrill runs through me: Mother's handwriting. One of her poems – after all these years:

'Never let it be too late, so soon the summer roses fade, their scented petals too will fall …' Too late for Mother but perhaps not for me. Already I am beginning to weave my own story.

"Lot Eighteen. The real piece of resistawnce, ladies and genl'men. Georgian breakfront bookcase – leaded diamond panes. Genuine, take my word for it. Stand aside, Arthur, let the dog see the rabbit. That's the way. Now –"

My brother was left all the books, the first editions and classics. I was allowed to read nothing else as a young girl. That was no hardship – marvellous, inspiring writers: Hugo, Tolstoy, Hardy, Conrad, and Edgar Allan Poe, too. We didn't have Jane Austen and the Brontës, Father wouldn't give any woman writer shelf space; I had to wait to discover them later at school. My life was lived through other people's stories, then.

"One-thousand-three-hundred on my right … and four-hundred … five-hundred … is that a bid, sir, or a fly on your nose? Thank you, sir, one-thousand-six-hundred –"

The bidding's going well for this, I hoped it would, it's the best piece. When Henry Walsh, the auctioneer's clerk, came to the house the day after the funeral, he sounded cautious. "There are some nice pieces here, but you can never tell what they'll fetch on the day. I'd suggest you put a reserve price on the larger items." I didn't, though.

I picked out the most valuable pieces: they'll have to make what they can.

"– going, gone! For two-thousand-eight-hundred pounds. Gent in tweeds at the back, Henry."

Wonderful. And I'll never have to polish the beastly thing again. Father was fussy about his antiques, and he could be so cutting, making nasty comments out of a sour face resembling a wrinkled old washcloth that's turned smelly. "You'd never keep a man, Agatha, even if you found one," he said to me once. He must have known how cruel that was after poor Ronald. But little chance I had of finding anyone else. After Mother died I was too busy running the house, and visitors were definitely not welcome.

They say writers can be difficult to live with; disappointed and bitter academics are the worst. Surprisingly, his temper improved during those final years when I had to nurse him. He bore his pain with great dignity. I really couldn't leave then, of course. My brother had long since left home. Set himself up in a bachelor flat with all his geological specimens. But Jeremy was little better than Father, when he came to the house they both tormented me. It was like a game to them. And all those disgusting curries Jeremy insisted I make for him. The house reeked for days afterwards.

" – bring it to the front, Arthur. That's the way. Only a print of course but a nice 'eavy oak frame. Who'll start with forty quid?"

Oh dear. Ronald gave me that as an engagement present – Constable's Dedham Vale – he took me there that glorious summer. We fell so much in love with the place we decided we'd live there after we married. But then there was the accident. I could bid for it back … No. No more past. I've stepped into the future. In fact I doubt if anyone would even recognize me now after – well, I believe it's called 'a complete make-over'. And if I'm going to succeed it's important to have the right clothes. It's a bit like window dressing I suppose although it makes me laugh to think of it like that.

I've always been slim – "gawky" Father called it. I suppose I was a bit of a string bean as a teenager. They describe it as "leggy" these days; it's more of a compliment. The garden kept me fit. Father wouldn't hire a gardener but that pleased me. I lived for those early mornings when daylight dissolves a milky dawn and cobwebs beaded with dew festoon the shrubs. Those peaceful hours teasing out weeds, pruning and trimming, even struggling with that cantankerous old lawn mower were my happiest: they kept me sane. And after Father was more or less bed-ridden, Jeremy would come and read to him for hours, that at least enabled me to get away more.

"Lot twenty-two, now. Lovely oak dining table, they don't make 'em like this anymore, ladies and genl'men. Shove them books off it, Arthur. That's the way – "

It's hard to believe I wasted so many of my best years at that table typing up Father's indecipherable scrawl about Greek heroes nobody cared a fig for, while he and Jeremy talked, father and son – as if I was merely the secretary. I wouldn't wish illness upon anyone, but once Father was too incapacitated to leave the house, and I had to research books for him in the library, a whole new world opened up to me, especially after that helpful assistant showed me how to use the computer.

I'd never been encouraged to train for anything, and it wasn't as if I was stupid – I won the school prize for chemistry and mathematics. But I discovered such interesting possibilities through the Internet; some involve travel. Lady's companions for example. They are hard to find these days and apparently they can negotiate good terms. But now, I won't have to be at anyone's beck and call ever again.

Jeremy inherited the house, and the money. "I shall move in next month, Agatha," he said, "You can get Father's old room ready for me; it'll have to be redecorated." I suppose they thought they had it all worked out – I wouldn't have enough to find a little place of my own so I'd have to stay and look after Jeremy into his dotage. Not again. No more of 'Agatha' either. I use my middle name now, the one Mother had wanted – Yvonne.

" … going, gone! For one-thousand pounds. Lady with the blue 'at in front. Right. That's it then. Shift those chairs out the road, Arthur. That's the way. Thank you, ladies and genl'men for your hattention."

Oh. I've missed the last few items, never mind, a profitable afternoon. The old devil left me only the house contents, 'chattels' that cadaverous solicitor called them and made me feel like one, too. But my new life starts today: first, the French cuisine and language course, and then the Mediterranean cruise. You can meet some wonderfully engaging people on these trips I believe. Who knows what might happen?

A pity I couldn't put that rare Persian carpet from Father's old room in the sale – it would have got a good price – but the nice couple who bought the house wanted it left there. Just as well, since it covered up those new nails in the floorboards ... Jeremy was so surprised when I made his favourite curry without having to be asked.

~~~

Story Analysis:

I included this story because it uses objects – furniture – not only to draw characters but to reveal Agatha's back-story as well as her present actions. The nature of the items – the Rosewood writing desk, the valuable Georgian bookcase, a large, oak dining table – show something of the characters and lifestyle of the entire family and, together with the fateful picture of Dedham Vale, reveal Agatha's past life and promise of the future through her relationship with them. They enable flashbacks to be brief, focused and natural.

There is no physical description of Agatha either, apart from being slim and fit enough for gardening, and the suggestion that the *"complete makeover"* probably transformed a tendency to frumpishness. As a reader, was the lack of physical description a problem for you? Do you have your own 'picture' of her in your mind? I envisaged someone of the appearance of Joyce Grenfell in a subdued form, about to metamorphose into her familiar energetic and animated persona.

Another purpose in the storyline was to see if I could write a tale where two threads ran simultaneously, so we have the auctioneer's patter interlaced with Agatha's recollections of her past, triggered by each lot of her household chattels coming under the hammer. The challenge was to make the auctioneer as 'audible' as possible, to inter-rupt Agatha's thoughts in a natural way, and that could only be done by using present tense which is often unpopular with judges and edit-ors, and may be awkwardly unfamiliar for readers. Sometimes you have to take risks to follow an idea. If it doesn't work, it's not a mis-take but a learning experience.

From many visits to auction rooms in the past, I discovered they are places to pick up bargains rather than to obtain true value for one's possessions, but that experience gave me the sound and rhythm for the auctioneer's 'voice', and the idea of increasing his 'audibility' by using the ubiquitous Arthur, and a signature phrase, "*That's the way*", which would become familiar to the reader so they would accept him chipping in at regular intervals. And I wanted him to add a touch of humour, using his physical description to signal that at the beginning.

I chose a 'first person' point of view so that Agatha's inner monologue could tell the story of each item, bringing the reader closer to her experience, and because I didn't need to show anyone else's thoughts, although the attitudes of Father and Jeremy had to be clear in their actions.

A small piece of my own life in this story is that the snippet of poetry is an excerpt from a poem by my own mother (Sylvia Taggart), who had died three years previously. But neither her life nor mine is in any way similar to that of Agatha or her mother.

The story above is a remodelling of the original version (titled *Going, Going, Gone*), in which 'Yvonne' auctions her inheritance of chattels, unknown to Jeremy, gaining revenge by leaving him with an empty house, and planning to use the proceeds for a cruise, with the possibility of finding a husband, or reverting to Plan A – a position as lady's companion, preferably overseas. But as two separate critiques pointed out, it was a weak plot.

After all the build-up, Agatha should do something more excit-ing at the end, but the comment was encouraging: "*I believed in her as a person, enough to be irritated that she isn't doing more with her freedom.*" The title, too, while appropriate, was "*not intriguing enough.*"

The second critique, from a judge, confirmed it was worth further work: *"This story deserves to work – with its artful intertwining of bitter-sweet memories and an auctioneer's lots. The theme of a wasted life being disposed of piecemeal, and the promise of redemption, is also potentially engaging."* 'Potentially', but it clearly didn't work. *"It ends a little too abruptly and ambiguously…The last line 'Jeremy will need to buy some furniture' is weak."*

Agatha needed far more than the proceeds of a furniture sale for a secure future, so I made my 'worm' turn more decisively: while I renamed the story *"Getting Rid of Agatha"*, she gets rid of the odious Jeremy at the same time. For this to work, I gave Jeremy a love of curry, and Agatha a relevant skill (chemistry). I felt she had sufficient motivation, considering the life she'd led and the imminent threat of its continuance with her brother. Apart from minor tinkering, the main changes were a new opening line and final paragraph: both going through several revisions.

What I learned from the experience was the need for balance: a story may be led by a character drawn in an original and effective way enacting a significant theme, but it still needs a convincing plot and satisfying end. Achieving this required critical feedback, and the time to reflect and edit. The best stories appear to inhabit the page effortlessly – the labour should not be visible. It may be a surprise to a reader to realize how much revision, editing and tinkering is required to give a story that ease; perhaps it is not asking too much for it to be read and reread with care.

~~~

Now's the Day

It's the bodies that bother me. The one behind the sofa has nae blood on him and I dinnae ken how he died. He's scrunched up on his elbows and knees like a praying mantis – his prayers were nae answered, that's for sure.

T'other one's in the back porch; a big man in a black fleece jacket lying flat on his stomach like a length o'carpet. A tyre lever's slipped from his hand and landed against the skirting board.

Did they break-in, then? I've nae memory o'that.

It's easy to see what did for the bearskin rug – it's stickin' out o' his back; a chisel for pity's sake.

I ken fine who they are. Trouble is I cannae figure why they're dead. I keep thinking, what if I'd bumped 'em off ma'self? If I were mad enough I could do it. Not tak the two o' them on, mind – not now. But one at a time – aye.

An icy finger's strokin' doon ma spine, 'cos it's nae one o' yon ordinary chisels with the yella plastic handle; it's one o'them proper turned wooden shafts – same as mine. But I have nae used 'em for years – have I?

It's doin' ma head in.

Got me in such a fankle I forgot ma medication. Took a double lot to make up for it.

Reckon I'm still shook up from the chase last night. Real dreich night it was, too. Rain lashin' doon so hard it pushed back the wind-screen wipers. Ian, the canny bugger, took us careening through back alleys. Dark shapes flashing past like an auld black and white film that's whuzzed off its spool.

A brick wall sped towards us; tyres screamed as the road tore off their rubber. "Christ, Man, yer drivin' like a loony," I said, "Where the hell are we, anyway?"

He slowed down passing the canal: a glint o' metal in murky water – a car bumper, maybe a body still inside, but we didnae stop.

Took me right back to those night patrols in Vietnam. Imagination in the darkness more terrible than reality.

We ended up in a bar with grime on the ceiling and sawdust on the floor.

I didnae get tae bed till nigh on dawn. Found the bodies when I got up.

It's nae good just lyin' low; they have ways of knowing. Aye, I've had ma fair share o'trouble on that score already.

I'll have tae go in. I ken there's no way out o'that.

Gives me the willies, though, that muckle place. Ye cannae go in quiet, like; the boots squeak on the linoleum. Folks look up as ye go by; not daring to speak above a whisper.

But I have tae know.

Surely, the lassie will let me renew it for another week.

~~~

Story Analysis:

In this case, both story and character are revealed entirely through an object – a library book – although we don't know that until the end. I chose a Scot because I have known many feisty Highlanders and enjoyed their dry humour. A friend had recently persuaded me to read his favourite author, Ian Rankin, not my usual genre but it hooked me, indirectly providing the story theme: the power of a story to take over one's life so completely as to "*forget ma medication*".

This also gave me the twist, and in laying clues and evasions, I tweaked a great deal in odd moments over several months to ensure that everything the narrator says and does could be happening in his house, or on the road, but equally could be 'lived' through the book he was reading. Though full of ambiguity, each detail has to be feasible once you know the ending because judges appreciate being surprised, but they don't like being tricked. Perhaps the sneakiest bit was having the protagonist talk directly to the author, but haven't you ever done that? The general 'feel' for the bodies and the chase came from reading Ian Rankin, but the chisel as a murder weapon is Alistair MacLean's – I read more widely to enhance my mood for the spirit of the piece.

It had to be written from the first person point of view, as if it were my own experience, and crowded with incident to make it all too close and fast for a reader to look around at what else might be happening. That was the easy part: a series of vivid scenes that did not have to fit into a wider plot, with mysteries I did not have to solve because the story's resolution lay in a different direction.

The *'medication'*, too, implies an unreliable narrator; you might give him the benefit of the doubt till you reach the dénouement. An ending can be too cryptic, though: nothing worse than reaching the punch-line and thinking, What? So I tried it out on a few friends. Not all of them 'got it' straight away, but the eventual dawning gave the others pleasure, so I decided not to change anything.

Without a physical description and with very little back-story, I relied on the protagonist's inner dialogue and actions to create a character with a distinctive Scottish 'voice'. Writing in dialect is a risk – it can put readers off – so I used only words and contractions that are widely known. I changed the original title, *The Victim*, to *Now's the Day*. You might recognize it: from Robert Burn's poem *Scots Wha Hae*, a battle-cry to Robert Bruce's march on Bannockburn to meet King Edward's English Army.

"Now's the day, and now's the hour: See the front o' battle lour, See approach proud Edward's power – Chains and Slaverie"

It seemed appropriate as my Highlander contemplates his own impending battle with the authorities in the library. (I had discovered the importance of titles; there are more thoughts on these in the next chapter).

For some reason since forgotten, *Now's the Day* was not officially critiqued, but it was shortlisted twice in Flash500 by different judges, and subsequently rejected for publication by a Scottish journal. This is its moment of glory.

~~~

3: Themes and Titles

"Storytelling is the creative demonstration of truth."
Robert McKee*

Have you ever read a story that is technically sound, makes interesting use of language, has believable characters and a plot that seems to work, but somehow it didn't quite 'gel', it felt flat, leaving you wondering why the author wrote it? I've written stories like that and struggled to work out what was missing. I now realize that in most cases it was lack of a clear underlying theme. Strong themes make strong stories we are told, but what do they mean by 'theme', and how to recognize it and show it in a story?

I've devoted a whole chapter to this because not only readers but many writers labour to distinguish between theme and plot. Not surprisingly, definitions vary because fiction is about life as we never quite manage to live it, and we are maddeningly complex beings with minds of our own. And an author is not the sole creator of a story. A writer offers a tale but the reader completes it. As readers we bring our own experience and attitudes to a text and may identify differing themes, or interpret meanings in our own specific way – I've seen members of a reading group throw pens at each other in passionate defence of their views.

The simplest description is that 'theme' is what the story is about, the central idea running through it – 'revenge', for example. But screenwriters might say that the theme only becomes clear with the dénouement, when you know the outcome – watching people emerge from a screening of Doctor Zhivago, huddled close to their partners, handkerchiefs dabbing eyes, you know, finally, it is not only about love, but loss.

To say the topic of a story is 'revenge' is only the start. We need to ask questions: What about it? How does it affect us? Is it ever a good thing? The deeper level of theme is what the author is saying *about* the topic through the 'who, where, why and how of the story'. What the conflicts are, how they are resolved, and what that shows us about revenge. In other words: the reason the story was conceived in the first place. Theme permeates not only the plot, pace and language – a dark tale contains threatening images and disturbing metaphors – but is expressed in the thoughts, dialogue and actions of characters.

I think of it as walking into a house where I might smell either coffee and baking, or the acrid odour of decay: it colours everything around me as I look for the welcoming plate of scones, or glance suspiciously behind the sofa and into the cellar for some impending horror.

Theme is like a pervading aroma that draws plot, structure, language, and characters' actions into a fully integrated focus and purpose – the story 'gels', becoming more powerful. What Robert McKee calls the 'controlling (or central) idea' of a story – the principal change that occurs in the story arc, and the reasons for it – I interpret as being this deeper meaning of theme. He emphasizes the importance of establishing the 'controlling idea' before writing so that characters, scenes, dialogue and everything else support, and are penetrated by, the theme.

Returning to 'revenge', the controlling idea might be that revenge is achieved at great personal cost to the avenger. For such a story to satisfy us as readers, the reasons for seeking revenge must seem justifiable, the character capable of the means of revenge: if by violence then he needs to be more of a Rambo than a nerd – the latter would most likely make a cyber attack. And we would have to believe that what the avenger loses through his act of revenge is truly important to him – the cause and effect must be logical.

In stating a cause and effect, a writer reveals an attitude, an approach to life and how it is, or should be, lived – the author is posing a truth as he or she sees it. (And to remind ourselves that we are talking about one part of a whole: that truth, and the way it is shown, is also related to the writer's 'voice' which we discuss in chapter 5).

In case this is starting to look too formulaic an approach to stories, remember that themes, subthemes and plots leave plenty of scope for originality and complexity, and so do characters. For one thing, they need balance: no person is all good, or all bad. The nerd may be a sensitive and passionate lover – perhaps jealousy was the reason he sought revenge. I might work on that story myself.

It takes time to think through the theme of a story. To curb my impatience, I have pinned to my study wall a quote from McKee: *"Yes, you can write a story without studying the theory – even a good one – but to write <u>consistently</u> good stories, you must learn the craft."* I would add to that: a little understanding of the writer's craft enlarges the consistent pleasure of reading.

One more aspect of a story coloured by its theme – and reflecting back to enhance the whole – is the title. When I started writing short stories the title was the last thing I considered; it didn't seem that important, merely an identity label – a bit like giving it a file name. My first few critiques soon put me right: my early titles were deemed *"uninspiring"*, *"appropriate but not intriguing enough"*, *"over used"*, *"irrelevant to the story"*.

Whether the reader is a man on the train, a publisher, or a competition judge, the first thing they see is the title: it can hook them into the story, or turn them away to answer their emails. Deciding on titles is still the bane of my writing life. They rarely appear without a lot of thought and effort, but I discovered a few helpful tips which I share with you in the first of the articles that follow.

My choice for the second article – a brief history of stories – may seem surprising but it is relevant to story theme. Although there are many lists of 'universal themes' in books and blogs about writing, I don't find them helpful because they are usually only topics – love, money, justice, revenge, ambition – not the deeper themes that lead us to a 'controlling idea' for the core of a story. Think for a moment about these two themes: 'love and hate eat at the same table'; 'no one has power over us until we submit to them'. What sort of stories might you read, or write, around them?

The popular topics are certainly universal, and probably have been since one of our early ancestors first said: "Hey! You took more than your fair share of mammoth." But the deep themes – how we interpret the causes and effects of human behaviour – and what we want to say about them; how explicit the moral or message should be, and who has the right to say it, have all changed over time. I find this perspective more enlightening in understanding the power story themes have in our lives.

~~~

Articles:

A Prose By Any Other Name

Just because your story title sits at the top of the page doesn't mean its sole function is to say: 'THIS WAY UP'.

It is the reader's first contact and first impressions leave lasting impact. It must intrigue, excite and promise all at the same time. A professional hooker focuses her enticement on what speciality she has to offer, fashioning her appearance and patter accordingly. Your story title must do the same.

Primarily, a title must relate directly to the theme and thus the content of the story in some way – that is the 'promise'. A funny story needs an amusing title. But it must also be original, eye-catching enough to excite, and contain an element – perhaps an unexpected combination of words – that intrigues. It is worth some effort, so I've listed a few ways to achieve the right mind-set for the task. Don't grasp the first title that comes into your head, trawl for ideas:

1. Annoy the staff in your local book shop and library by browsing all the book titles in your genre, checking them against the book blurb for an idea of content.

2. Access story competition sites on the internet to find winning or listed stories and check out their titles. A good site for this is www.flash500.com because they have a new contest every quarter with a 'long list' of about 40 titles. Only for winning

stories can you read the content, of course, for others, look for word combinations that attract your attention and think about why.

3. Construct a brief synopsis of your story and ask your writing group to brainstorm titles. Take all their suggestions home to work on later.

4. Write down the theme and 'controlling idea' or core message of your story. Can you reduce this is to two or three critical words? To one word?

5. Try out an image from the text that indicates the pervading atmosphere or mood of the story, or a snippet of dialogue loaded with meaning, especially a double meaning.

6. Construct a list of significant words from your story and play games with them: place an adverb or adjective with a noun that appears contradictory; reverse their order; combine two opposites; use two adverbs.

7. Think of some clichés that relate to the story and rewrite them in an original way e.g. 'Leave No Bone Unturned' for a crime story. Or 'A Turd in the Hand' for a funny tale about walking dogs in the park? Maybe not. But the important thing is not to censor too soon, note and consider all, even the craziest, suggestion.

8. Write your best title ideas on separate slips of paper, put them aside, and look at each one again later – pick out the top 6 possibilities for further thought.

9. Repeat steps 1 - 8 until you have the most exciting, intriguing, original title that promises your story theme.

~~~

A Very Partial History of the Short Story

"To be human one must have a story." Chinua Achebe

Stories propel the human project. In this, they represent both succour and jeopardy.

The compulsion for storytelling goes back to our ancestors foraging in the savannah. Scholars dispute the date when we first used symbolic thought and speech, and oral traditions leave no visible trace, but the extraordinary tool-making cultures of a million years ago would not have arisen without the power of narrative.

Once Upon a Time:

The boy, brought up by his elder brother, grows into a competent young man with energy and flare to increase the fortunes of their family enterprise. But his brother's wife becomes so infatuated she tries to seduce him. Panicked by the possible consequences of his unambiguous rebuff, she convinces her husband that he tried to rape her. In a jealous frenzy, he goes after his younger brother who, denying the accusation, escapes by leaving the country. When the husband realizes the truth, and further enraged by the loss of his brother, he kills his wife.

Is this from a popular magazine, a re-run of Dallas, or a plot line for a racy novel? None of these: it is a synopsis of the earliest known transcribed short story, written in Egypt about 3,000 BCE by that most prolific of authors, Anonymous. As an oral tale, the story is probably several thousand years older and yet the themes – lust, jealousy and betrayal – still resonate for us.

Creation from Conflict:

Our brains are wired to understand the world through story. Oral myths, tales and fables are repeated and embellished in every culture – to relate history, sustain belief, explain us to ourselves, or simply to lighten a dark evening – but however diverse, they share the core quality of all good stories: conflict and its resolution through transformation. Our theories of existence itself are based on conflict, whether the cosmic Big Bang, or Eve's desire for the apple – we all know the consequences of that, and for romance writers, the earth still moves.

As might be expected with this length of history, the stories have all been told before. There are no new plots. Even the 'classic' ghost story appears in ancient Rome. In the first century, Pliny the Younger wrote of a haunted house; the dead of night; clanking chains; the emaciated arm of a spectre pointing to a spot in the courtyard where...yes...buried remains were found entangled in fetters. No surprise it is such a struggle to be original.

Myths and other ancient narratives, however metaphorical or symbolic, are true in the deepest sense of understanding what it is to be human. They explain the unknowable, providing a means to live with uncertainty. Resolving conflict – be it psychological, interpersonal, or social – is the essential human story. For good or evil, ours is the capacity to imagine what might be, to seek it out, and to deal with the obstacles in whatever way our individual natures allow. Our tools – cell phones, cars, laptops – are different, but the needs and emotions that drive us remain a universal core of human nature and the foundation of our stories.

Before The Critics:

Ancient Celtic legends were originally in verse. A scholar's training was strenuous, taking at least twelve years. Their teachers believed sensory deprivation enhanced inspiration: students lay on the floor in darkness with stones on their stomachs to keep them awake. It might be worth trying this to overcome modern distractions of information overload; if no large stones are to hand, Chamber's *Dictionary of Quotations* is about the right weight.

Although early to adopt prose style, the Celts continued to compose in language rich in metaphor, riddle, and mythical knowledge. Emer, the highborn heroine declaring both her virginity and her love for Cuchulainn, describes herself as, '...*a goblet undrunk...a fire of hospitality, a path untrodden.*'

These stories were not mauled by critics or rejected by editors – they contained their own power. The word was sacred: although druids used an alphabetical code – the Ogham – inscribed on stone, Celtic 'writers' were forbidden to write anything down. The recitation of stories was part of their potency; they held 'truth' gleaned through inspiration from the 'other world'. Their themes were spiritual, their forms proscribed: only the trained and worthy could create and speak them.

Celtic storytelling concluded with a warning to those present, on pain of a curse, to repeat the story only in the right manner and in good faith in order to maintain the story's 'nourishment' – the force for good fortune released in the telling. A story was a blessing.

The Written Word:

Although oral storytelling is still a vibrant medium, the development of writing, and especially the invention of printing, allowed scholars to capture stories, fix them in ink like eels in aspic and lay claim to them. Easier methods of copying and distributing stories lead to more people reading them, but these were the elite: the language of literature and learning was Latin, which few had the education to understand. In England, only after Chaucer wrote his ribald *Canterbury Tales* in the vernacular, could lesser beings enjoy for themselves the ridicule of corrupt, canting clergy, and the honouring of their knights. Those who could read were still a minority, but Chaucer's themes questioned the social order. No longer controlled by the religious elite, stories lost their spiritual potency but began to accrue social power.

After Chaucer, the history of the English short story fades for a few centuries when it was overshadowed by other forms of literature – the Elizabethans preferred drama, eighteenth century Romantics fancied poetry and the Victorians would not be prised from their novels.

Elsewhere in Europe, especially France and Italy, the short story had long been well established. Chaucer, Shakespeare, Dryden and others harvested many of their plots from *The Decameron,* a book of saucy, humorous tales written in the 14th century by Giovanni Boccaccio, who had raided even earlier sources. Relevant since Genesis, *The Decameron* remains a well-spring of story ideas on the eternal struggle between the sexes.

And in France, Maupassant created a new model for the short story: original rather than derivative; tight focus on a single scene;

irresistible motive and, sometimes, a twist-in-the-tail ending. Admittedly, he was obsessed by the sex industry but his satire and facetiousness continue to hit their mark with consummate skill. Heir to the permissive society that delighted in Zola and Flaubert, Maupassant did not have to contend with the puritan ethics of his English and German colleagues whose stories, up to that time, had been constrained by the requirement to include moral lessons – the instructive element often overpowering the plot. The moral tenor of the times had tightened since Chaucer's day.

In Aesop's fables and Biblical parables, the moral premise – the teaching of appropriate behaviour and dire consequences of noncompliance – was explicit. In many cases, the theme was all there was to the story: characters were sketchy, action no more than required to make the point. In 18th and early 19th century England, although plots developed, moral instruction was still pervasive and explicit in stories as a means to educate the 'lower classes' – beginning to gain access to schooling in the three Rs.

Story writing in Germanic countries followed a more or less continuous thread from the Teutonic legends of Beowulf – gathering folk tales on the way – to the Doctor Faust stories of the 16th century and the Brothers Grimm (Jakob and Wilhelm) in the early 1800s. Their tales, too, were intended to be morally improving and educational; Wilhelm re-writing plots and even characters of traditional tales to comply with the protestant Puritanism of the times.

But this environment was about to change dramatically.

Then There Were Editors:

A big break for the short story in Europe, America, and Russia, came with the beginnings of mass education in the late 19th century and the emergence of popular magazines – in England, these ranged from the more literary *Gentleman's Magazine,* to the scurrilous 'penny dreadful' and inflationary 'shilling shocker'. At last, short stories – small but perfect prose orphans – had homes where they could receive thousands of visitors. And many are still worth visiting. The stories of Saki (aka Hector Hugh Munro) are a deep well of wit, insight, invective, and observations on the human condition that still chime: *'We all know that Prime Ministers are wedded to the truth, but like other married couples, they sometimes live apart.'*

Variety was the keynote – humour, horror, crime, romance, satire, grotesquery, or merely weird – the differing tastes of editors sparked the imaginations of popular authors such as Hawthorne, Scott, Stevenson, and Irving. But the greatest influence on the short story as an evolving genre sprang from writers who considered short fiction an independent literary form worthy of a lifetime's effort, notably Poe and Gogol, curiously enough, both born in the same year, 1809, though half a world apart.

And short fiction was lucrative for some. Editors paid Kipling hundreds of pounds for a single story – huge sums for that time. Chekhov was less fortunate: a struggling medical student with a bankrupt father, trying to support his siblings as well as himself, even his prolific output of humorous tales for the St Petersburg weekly journal, *Fragments,* barely made a dent in his debts.

In this fertile medium, magazines and literary journals spawned with abandon from the early 1900s, while short story anthologies and collections added new venues, drawing in writers worldwide. This dynamic interaction between editors and writers produced a golden age for the short story.

And Now?

We live in abbreviated times. For this channel-hopping generation addicted to texting and well adjusted to Twitter's 140-character yarns, the brevity and immediacy of the short story should appeal. One of the strengths of the short story in adapting to change is its boundless flexibility, described by H. E. Bates as having, *"...the indefinite and infinitely variable nature of a cloud..."*

Stories are no longer for the elite, and the reach of erstwhile village storytellers is international: stories belong to everyone. In whatever form, stories remain the essential and spontaneous expression of what is human.

The same plots and topics may dominate, but the range of deeper themes is greater. Life is more complex, faster paced. More of everything is available to an increasing number of people. The ambitions we aspire to, the aims we pursue and the antagonistic powers we confront to achieve them are richer and more varied in a global context. Bombarded 24/7 in a multiplicity of media by images of desirable goals and goods, we want more. Becoming inured to violence in world news, the horror in fiction escalates to satisfy our need for new, vicarious emotional excitement.

As a result, story themes are more complex and less explicit. Characters are always important, but the 'storying' – the intricacies of plots, causes and effects – becomes the dominant feature. The moral premise, the deep themes that underlay the thrills of the tale, may be harder to detect but are no less influential – probably more so because of their subtlety. And therein lurks the present danger.

Much as the advent of printing enabled the powerful to maintain their privilege by laying claim to stories, creating through them 'suitable realities' for the illiterate and disempowered, so the ascendency of corporate and political power in the virtual world can dominate the stories that define our lives. The deeper themes – the 'truths' of the spin doctors – are less explicit, ingeniously enmeshed in the disarming excitement of a well-paced story, but their impact on what we believe, how we think and who we are, remain as strong as ever. In resolving this conflict we must enhance the 'nourishment' of our own narratives by strengthening our truth as writers and sharpening our perception as readers.

[I develop these ideas further in the essay, *From Apes to Apps: How Humans Evolved as Storytellers and Why it Matters*, bound with this volume].

~~~

Stories:

Modus Operandi

Yes, he's my brother. The Press you said? Well, I suppose you'd better come in. You're the first one. No doubt there'll be others looking for things to dig up, entertain folk who don't have lives of their own.

No one ever asked before what I thought – or knew – but he looks so young, I don't know how much I want to tell after all this time.

I should say *was* my brother – Gary's been dead a good many years. You know he died in prison?

Took his own life. They didn't even tell me. Heard it on the radio. Refused parole – according to the newspapers he'd become very violent in prison. What else could be expected?

I suppose you're writing about those two local girls. The papers said they'd been buried within feet of each other on the river bank – exposed after the floods of course. You wouldn't think there'd be much evidence left after 40 years, but apparently one of them was wrapped in an old fishing jacket. I expect you know the police think it was my brother's.

What do I think? Well, you can't put a dead man on trial. He'd already served one life sentence for the death of his father.

It's Gary's childhood you want to ask about? Oh, I see.

Are you sure you won't have a cup of tea? People are always in such a hurry these days. It's all sound bites – is that what you call it? – click this and click that. I don't use computers nowadays but I expect you do.

All right. I'll get to the point.

Our father was a preacher. Loved the Old Testament. According to him we were all born in a state of sin and it had to be exorcised. He led an upright life himself; never drank or smoked, and wouldn't allow music in the house – chant of the Devil he called it.

Archaic ideas even in his time but he was as rigid as the gnarled old apple tree in the garden – a form of sickness I realized later.

A big man too – he had to duck under doorways. His hands were as wide as dinner plates. To see those long fleshy fingers you'd recognize the strength that was in them.

Is this what you want? The background?

Yes, I'll get round to that, but you have to understand the beginning, where it all came from. They didn't talk about this at the trial. I could have told them but no one asked me – I was of no account, just a twelve-year-old girl. Have you done any court reporting, young man? Well, whenever you do – remember that. People don't get to say what ought to be said.

While we grew up we didn't really know anybody around here – we were home schooled. You see, our mother died giving birth to me.

Strange, Father never took it out on me – it was always Gary.

Gary was only six and my father gave up preaching to look after us – a hard task for a man but he rejected outside help. We saw no one – no visitors or playmates. The house was outside the village then. Now it's become a town. He worked hard to provide us a sound education – I was a teacher before taking early retirement. Gary took after his father physically but not intellectually – he wasn't bright and that annoyed Father. There were beatings. That never helped anyone to learn and it didn't help Gary.

He never cried out though, and I think that angered my father more – as if he needed some response.

That was the start of it really. Gary would have got into mischief as little boys do, but by the time I was old enough to know what was happening he didn't need to do anything in particular to be punished. I remember how he crept into my room at night and I put ointment on the wheals and burns. The burns were the worst: they took a long time to heal.

Gary was a quiet boy – rarely spoke, even to me. He moved about the house like a shadow – you never knew where he was. Loved to be outside though – he looked after the garden from the moment he could hold a spade.

Yes, it was probably a stricter upbringing than most, certainly compared to today. It's not always a good thing. Gary was a sensitive boy. Make sure you get that down, because the newspaper reports were always about his violence in prison. There's more to people than what you see on the surface, you know.

Some people think their destinies are written in the stars. Do you believe in astrology? Well, you won't know what I'm talking about then, but Gary and my father were both born under the sign of Scorpio – passionate, loyal, and secretive. I was born on August 30th – Virgo. Virgoans are very practical people and they hate cruelty and injustice.

Young as I was, even I realized Gary needed love. When we found that kitten in the garden he spent hours playing with it – hiding in the shed. Father never found out: we'd become quite sly. I'll never forget the day I went down there with scraps for it and found Gary standing with his head bent, silent tears dripping off his face onto the kitten – it looked so small lying in his hand. It was dead. He hadn't meant to hurt it. After that, I said he could sleep in my bed so he wouldn't be alone. That's when I discovered how bad the nightmares were. And how, years later, I knew when he went out at night.

No, he'd never been in trouble with the police. They interviewed him after that first girl went missing. He wasn't a suspect: they did house to house interviews of everyone in the area, to eliminate them from their enquiries. I always follow the crime reports. Not fiction, only real cases, but they rarely find out what really happened – they don't ask the right questions. Anyway, Gary must have satisfied them because there was no further questioning. They hadn't found the body then, only her clothes, so they didn't know where or how she died. It was a tragic business. She'd got the last bus from town and was walking home.

Even at night we didn't talk, just lay there until we fell asleep, silent comfort to each other. I'd wake him if one of his nightmares started. If Father had known he would probably have killed us both, but he always shut himself in his room after supper. Only once did Gary start doing things to me I didn't like. He stopped when I told him, and never did it again. He was always gentle and quiet in my company. That's why it scared me so much – that terrible agitation a few months later – grinding his teeth, sweating, despite the cold. He'd come back later than usual from his fishing. I asked what was wrong, eventually he muttered, "It didn't happen right," – it made no sense, then, but it preyed on my mind.

I'm sorry, Gary's trial, yes. There was really no defence offered. Gary pleaded guilty to Father's murder. He refused to take the stand. The lawyer wanted to plead diminished responsibility but Gary wouldn't have that. The beatings were never mentioned. It wouldn't have helped – a psychologist would say it gave him a motive; you can find an expert witness to prove anything.

Then the second girl disappeared. Gary came home in a terrible state again that night. "Just tell me what you've done, Gary?" "She shouldn't have screamed," he said. I knew then. Dread clawed at my throat. There would be others: I had to stop him. But Father was more to blame than Gary, I knew that, too.

You doubt that he killed the girls as well? Certainly, the methods – the modus operandi – were different. They say the poor girls' necks were broken, but my father was stabbed through the heart with a fishing knife. It happened in this house – upstairs.

Surprising how easy it was. I used both hands but it only took one thrust – the Devil himself is vulnerable in sleep. Gary must have known but never said: he was always loyal. Maybe he realized it was for the best, too.

No, I never saw him again after the trial. He thought it better I didn't visit. It was his way of protecting me – I told you he was a sensitive boy. We were very close, you see.

Now I've got this far I could tell you how it was for me – as a young girl.

You've got all you need? Right then…No, no, I'll see you out – that old door won't open unless you have the knack.

~~~

Story Analysis:

Initially inspired by news of a new police unit to re-open old crime investigations with modern forensic tools, and reports of unprecedented flooding, this story also owes a debt to Steinbeck – 40 years since I read *Of Mice and Men* but Lennie has never left me.

Although the narrator explains Gary's behaviour against a background of childhood abuse, this is only a subtheme. The main theme, the controlling idea, was that the search for truth is conditioned by our own prejudices and fears. In this case, the potential evidence of a twelve-year-old girl not sought in the past, and now, that of an elderly woman which the journalist does not follow up – losing a scoop that could have made his career. And perhaps the revelation that a murder was committed in the room upstairs hastened his departure.

This story could only be told from a first person point of view: by alternating the sister's inner dialogue with her outer responses to the journalist's apparent questions, I could show the truth that was hidden as she recollects events in her mind, and her gradual transition to a point where she is ready to reveal it, because truth is also a heavy burden. 'Hiding' is a recurring motif: the kitten in the shed; the father retreating to his room after dinner; home schooling away from society.

An important subtheme was the different forms in which love may be expressed in extreme situations. In their isolated, lonely lives, the love between brother and sister sustained them: love intense enough for the narrator to murder their father – the origin of their problems – causing the loss of her brother to imprisonment because it was *"for the best"*.

A physical description of the father, though brief, was essential to provide the first hint of menace and make the damage he inflicted later, believable; it also enabled an image of Gary – equally important to the plot – to emerge simply and with few words: *"Gary took after his father physically…"*

I made the narrator a teacher, partly to exonerate the father's efforts at education (no person is all bad), partly as contrast to Gary's wasted life, but mostly so that she was capable of informed analysis of her experience and her 'voice' could convincingly use a phrase like *"modus operandi"*. In a rare moment of illumination, the title came to me early on and quickly: unusual to use Latin for a story title, yet recognizably a strong symbol of crime, courts, investigations, and central to the theme and plot.

Although the arc of the story – the interview – lasts only as long as it takes to read it, the content covers a lifetime, requiring a great deal of tweaking to make the time sequences and plot fit together. A difficult story to write, but the effort was rewarded when I entered it for the 2011 Winchester Writers' Conference writing competition in the Shorter Short Story category where it achieved first place.

The adjudicator commented on its complexity: *"The usual advice is that short story writers should keep their storylines simple…and focus on character…but the story can carry such an intense storyline because the story structure is so very tightly focused."* (I will return to this in the next chapter when we discuss structure).

Two other aspects mentioned in the adjudication were the depth of Gary's character – kind and loyal despite his understandable propensity to violence – and the opening: *"It signals that we are hearing about the narrator's brother, that we are dealing with a journalist, and that the story is going to be about a subject that would appeal to sensation seekers. That's a lot of briefing packed into a short, readable, paragraph."*

[*Modus Operandi* was published in the print edition of *Words with JAM* in June 2012; and in the Winchester Writers' Conference *Best of 2011* – sadly, misprinted without italics and thus lacking the dual narrative].

~~~

Eden's Promise

I feel you nestled beside me in the dark, the quiet warmth of you. There is no boundary where my body ends and yours begins – like the stems of vines twisting together and fusing as one.

You were my first love, Lucy.

I watched you hurry past every day. Your hair, the colour of polished rosewood, swayed with your step. I made you promise, later, never to cut it. I feel the weight of it now on my arm.

You didn't see me but I followed you with my eyes for weeks, until I discovered you worked in the canteen. I had always avoided it; all those eyes and mouths gobbling at each other like worms on a compost heap.

My last term in horticultural college and we met every day when your shift ended, walking together in the hills. You liked the pine forest best, it reminded you of home. Too shy to talk at first, our silences hummed with companionship.

And later, you told me your story; escaping from Kosovo into Albania, then bolting from there, too. My poor Lucy, like a pebble rolled along the beach.

"In the fighting, Martin, all my family ... lost, Mama, Papa ... my two brothers. Just my grandmamma and me, we make a long travel south. We find good village. Is near for Saranda and we growing the flowers and sell on the markets. But Grandmamma, she very old, she die. I am alone then. So afraid."

"You have me now, Lucy. We will be together always."

"That make me happy. Here is free. Is good."

I understand loss, loneliness – scars that turn livid when touched.

When your visa expired you were terrified of being sent back, but I had a plan for us.

"I'll lease some land, Lucy. We can be self-sufficient, grow vegetables and fruit. No one will bother us up in the hills."

"And chickens and bees, Martin? I care with them. I know how."

"Yes, we'll sell eggs and honey, too."

"And I make for you *Tavë Kosi,* I think you like. Is special Albania food of bake lamb and the yogurt. Oh Martin, is like dream. I afraid one day to wake up."

I built this house with my own hands. Made this bed from recycled oak.

You're getting cold. I'll pull the duvet over your shoulder: as soft and smooth as goose down. Your skin tastes of homemade lavender soap, just a trace of citrus.

Clearing the land was sheer joy: brewing tea from nettles we hacked down, watching song thrush cracking snail shells on hard clods of earth, and planting in cycles of the moon.

This is good, sweet soil; we've had bumper harvests. They sell well in the markets. No gate sales. I don't like strangers coming here.

That first batch of chicks you raised made you so happy.

"Martin, is make me want chicks of my own. Now we start family?"

"We're not ready for that yet, Lucy, my love. We are still babes in the wood ourselves."

I laughed you out of it. Children would change everything. We have each other; life here is good. Remember the first time we tried making green tomato chutney in that old pressure cooker – there's still a funny face on the ceiling where we couldn't get the stain out.

How long have I slept? It's light already.

I thought you were happy, Lucy.

Until last night. "Here is too lonely, Martin, I needing people, childrens."

I'm glad you told me. It will be all right now.

See, the sun is reaching in between the curtains – painting us gold, like a blessing.

Let me look at you. Ah, my love, I'm sorry – your lovely neck.

But I couldn't let you leave me, Lucy. You do understand that, darling, don't you?

I promised we would be together, always.

~~~

Story Analysis:

The title for this story went through several revisions. I started with *"Always"* (said to *"lack originality"* in a critique), tried *"In the Quiet of the Night"*, a phrase from a poem that involved death, a reference so obscure that even I have forgotten what it was, and finally settled on *"Eden's Promise"* because it suggested both the love story and the idyllic lifestyle the couple created, although the 'promise' ended up a double-edged sword.

Beginning as a 500-word flash, reworked to 1,074, and finally settling at the present 647 words, the story has quite a history, variations resulting from decisions to increase or decrease back-story for both Martin and Lucy. Because of the final twist, it was necessary to balance justification for the resolution with the danger of signalling the ending too soon.

In its current version, much is left to the reader's imagination, especially in Martin's past, but I'm not sure there is necessarily a single direct cause for his actions: the motivation could be a slow accumulation of factors leading to fear of loss that finally releases the potential of a disturbed mind. In a story this short, the brevity of 'explanations' can place too much weight on one or two factors; I'm wary of simple cause and effect links but I may have erred on the side of insufficient justification. The inspiration for the story was a relationship I knew about which – fortunately – did not end in violence, but my imagination took the basic elements and drew them to an ultimate extreme.

The theme is the power of love to heal trauma and loneliness – as it does initially for Lucy – but also to be terribly distorted by obsession and possessiveness shown by Martin's desperate final act. Love entangled with dire need has unpredictable outcomes: both had painful pasts (Martin's unspecified), yet love restored and strengthened Lucy while unleashing a dark force within Martin. Word choices and imagery – reflecting joy and fulfilment alongside Martin's clearly watchful outsider's view of life – were intended to support this theme as well as create tension.

Eden's Promise has been entered in several open-themed competitions but has never made even the long lists, and has not been offered for publication anywhere. I edited it again before including it here (cutting out more of Martin's back-story), so there is no critique of its present form; perhaps your reading or writing group would like to discuss it – I would love to have your feedback.

~~~

4: Structures (and Plots)

"Where is here?" Northrop Frye.

I'd been thinking about a new story. Carrying so many vivid scenes, delicious words, magnificent images, they grew too heavy, I could barely hold onto them all – I had to put them down somewhere. I could simply let go, tumble them onto the living room carpet, but critical bits could roll under the sofa and be chewed by mice. Delicate phrases would break. Active verbs run away. Where to put them?

That is how I see 'structure': a safe place, a frame on which to hang all these words in a special arrangement that will reveal a particular story in the best way possible. The arrangement – the pattern or logic of the scenes – is the plot. Together, structure and plot enable characters to enact the theme with their 'goings on'.

The structure I start with will determine the way the story is told – its form – but a storyline may demand a specific type of structure: they act upon each other. Another way to visualize this is as the receptacle in which you cook and present your story. You wouldn't simmer a beef casserole in a baking tray, and sometimes the container is almost invisible, like little paper cases for cupcakes where subtle flavour and rise are paramount. It allows for a tight focus, using only those ingredients in quantities essential to the recipe. And the mix must stay within the container – no superfluous words and images dribbling down the sides.

It's more than having a beginning, middle and end – sometimes the end needs to be at the beginning anyway. I find only one rule helpful for structure: there has to be one. Even if someone wins a highbrow literary prize next week for an entry consisting of an amorphous mass of words that don't even make sentences, I will stand by this one canon. The reason there are no others is that the range of structures is limited only by a writer's imagination; their suitability depending in each case on the nature of the tale – the 'holistic' aspect crucial to the short story – and the need to compel the reader to continue to the end.

If you are a reader who does not also write, these last four paragraphs may seem strange to you – cooking pots and baking trays? A reader may be entirely unaware of a story's structure or even that it needs one. When you walk into a building, you go through the doors and along corridors, turn corners or mount steps as they are presented to you in order to reach your destination. You don't stop to notice the construction methods, the angle of a passageway or the internal arrangement of rooms – unless you lose your way, or find the route tediously circuitous.

The second time you visit, especially if you are not in such a rush, you might notice and admire the building – or not, according to your experience. Story structure is what leads you in and through the tale, to reach the resolution at the end. If it succeeds in conducting you smoothly and not leaving you stranded on the first floor, you enjoy the story without noticing how it was built. But a second reading, to understand its architecture and why the author has chosen it, could help explain why, for you, some stories work better than others.

Received wisdom declares that the brevity of a short story requires simplicity. I would qualify that: *something* in a short story has to be simple – whether plot, theme, structure, or number of characters – so that a reader can find a way in and follow it without an apoplexy, but a simple structure can carry a complex plot; the significance of a plain theme may be enhanced by an intricate structure.

In *Modus Operandi* we read a story that could hardly be more complicated – child abuse, a wrongful prosecution, a suicide, three murders, the narrator herself turning out to be one of the perpetrators – yet it worked because the structure is simple, like a single marble column. The entire story is told by one 'first person' narrator in the space of a brief interview – we know the journalist is there though neither 'seen' nor heard directly – but the two veins running through the marble – the dual narrative – enable essential facts of the back-story to be revealed or hinted at extremely briefly, without the need to interrupt with lengthy flashbacks or explanations.

With any other structure, this story would have been considerably longer. Written with 4,000 words, it could form a series of linked columns using flashbacks, perhaps a sequence of scenes from different points of view enlarging on the father, Gary, or even the journalist, but the immediacy of that interview played out in 'real time' would be less: it becomes a different kind of story. And if the journalist was shown directly, as a reader I would be deprived of a source of involvement in imagining his part of the dialogue. Stories have a way of finding their own length; a matter of scale and a further aspect of seamlessness in blending the parts.

The more fiction we read, whether short stories or novels, the more possibilities open up: stories formed around an exchange of correspondence; a series of journal entries; the ebb and flow of a party; an auction (*Getting Rid of Agatha*); two runners competing in a race, each with an inner dialogue of conflict; the process of baking a cake (as metaphor and/or motivation). One structure I've not seen, but would love to try, is the bank statement of a joint account – plenty of potential conflict there.

Structure is a good place to experiment: judges like to stretch the form, looking for originality, and this is often easier to achieve in structure than plot. In her comments on Jenny Clarkson's story *Something* – the winning short story for the Bridport Prize in 2009 – the judge, Ali Smith said: "*Its breadth of social vision, in just over a thousand words, is worldwide.*" It achieves this with a 'third person' point of view: the narration of a job interview in a factory – a structure simple enough to be almost invisible – in which the dialogue of sharply drawn characters conveys a substantial theme.

But among the finalists was an entry by Joshua Lobb formed of 101 numbered sentences – and a long title: *I Forgot My Programme So I Went To Get It Back or 101 Reasons* – consisting of an internal monologue that dodges between past memories and present predicament from varying points of view. Instantly visible and daring, the structure as a list is not complicated and provides an essential access point to a complex piece of writing.

Longer word counts allow more leeway for elaboration, but even 500 words can inspire brilliantly original structures. In the Flash500 competition (fourth quarter 2010) the winning story – *Politically Correct* by Veronica Ryder – an intensely emotional, mealtime conversation between a member of parliament and his wife, covering events from their entire relationship, is formed around the restaurant dinner menu. The structure neatly knits together the couple's situation, the setting, the cycle of the story from entrée to coffee, and their dialogue. You can read it on Flash500's website.

It inspired me to experiment with a story I was thinking through, about an 'eternal triangle' of transsexual attraction within a musical trio. I decided to use the three movements of Beethoven's 'Ghost' Trio as the structure, each movement containing the point of view of one of the three musicians. The result – *Transpositions* – is included at the end of the chapter along with a professional critique.

But why did I put 'plots' in brackets in the title of this chapter when surely it is the hub and driving force of a story? Have I lost the plot?

E. M. Forster, eminent literary critic and novelist, was extremely rude about stories, describing a story as: "*the chopped-off length of the tapeworm of time.*" And as for plot: "*To pot with the plot!*" His invective was aimed at Aristotle's dictum: "*All human happiness and misery take the form of action,*" and the common insistence that every element of a story must focus solely on contributing to a series of actions, causes and effects that repeatedly answer the question: And then what happened?

Forster considered this satisfaction of curiosity through constant "*complication, crisis and solution*" a vulgar form of art. He was speaking as a literary novelist, of course, making the point that, contrary to Aristotle's view, our deepest emotions are hidden. The truly "*secret life*" is not naturally revealed by exterior evidence, not even a sigh – which is as much an 'action' as a word of dialogue, or a thump on the nose. Drama and film can only show emotion visually, through action, whereas the novelist, Forster says, can enter the inner recesses of his character's mind, even find thoughts of which the character is unaware.

Perhaps Forster hadn't read enough short stories, because they can achieve that, too, though not with the languor of the novelist. The use of secret thoughts, even motives unrecognized by the character influenced by them, can relate the theme of a tale more quickly than the acting out of a series of actions and responses. In makes for a different kind of story – a more contemplative tale – and a couple of mine have drawn the comment: "*though well written and moving, this is not a story*". We will look more closely at 'What is a story?' in the chapter on critiquing and editing.

But we write to expand the experience of others, or at least to entertain them, both novels and short stories are written for an audience – unless one is writing exclusively for the closet – as such, they have to be 'readable'. Stories needn't adhere to a standard type – no one size satisfies all – but they do need tension, pace, and incentive to keep reading, however these are achieved. Forster conceded this applied also to novels, but reluctantly, which is why he insisted on a sigh of despair and regret to accompany his famous statement: "*Yes – oh dear yes – the novel tells a story.*"

We can benefit from Forster's insights about access to the inner life, a perspective of particular interest to me, but also from drama (Aristotle spoke as a dramatist), and screen-writers such as Robert McKee. In the article that follows, I have summarized some of the main points from McKee's densely rich advice on plots and story arcs in his book *Story*.

Film shows how much story can be revealed in the simplest movement, or lack of it, and helps us to think in scenes that weave the warp and weft of setting, character and dialogue into the tight cloth required for a small but perfect tale.

"Short story and film are expressions of the same art, the art of telling a story by a series of subtly implied gestures, swift shots, moments of suggestion, an art in which elaboration and above all explanation are superfluous and tedious...Each moment implies something it does not state; each

sends out a swift brief signal on a certain emotional wave-length, relying on the attuned mental apparatus of the audience to pick it up." (H. E. Bates).

Most writers on technique recommend that the overall shape of the plot follows an upward slope made of highs and lows as the protagonist's goal is alternately progressed or thwarted, thus creating tension. The slope continues rising to the climax, near the end of the story, which determines the final resolution, leaving the hero either celebrating his success or drowning his sorrows.

What we have to remember, though, is that the screenwriter's convoluted plots with escalating rounds of challenge followed by success or failure; 'turning points' for acts and scenes; subplots and casts of hundreds, are designed to keep the audience immobilized for two to three hours, their hands poised over the bag of toffees, suspended in apprehension: short story writers do not have that length of time to enthral their readers.

Depending on length, a short story may have room for only one or two scenes. Developing the art of simplicity, and of selectively picking the brains of 'cerebral' novelists as well as screenwriters, is essential. So is the skill of concise writing, addressed in the second article. We can still aspire to making a reader miss his lunch.

It would be a fascinating exercise for a reading group to watch a film and read a novel and a short story all on the same theme, and compare the strength of the message and degree of emotional involvement in each, exploring how it was achieved.

I enjoy the freedom of experimenting, trying what might seem a daft idea – *something* will come out of it, if not a good story. But it's not a good idea for a writer to use a particular structure purely for the sake of being 'extraordinary': it has to chime with the storyline. The question: Why use this structure? is as important to answer as, What is the theme of the story? Why am I writing it? They act in unison.

~~~

Articles:

Structuring the Plot

It's not about rules: it's about process:

The members of my writing group are revolting. Not normally belligerent individuals, they are simply frustrated by finding rules about writing that contradict each other and reading brilliant stories that break the rules anyway. Abandoning rules, we constructed our own workshop to focus on a process that would help us to say what we want to say, the way we want to say it. For ideas, we dipped into Sol Stein: *Stein on Writing*, and Robert McKee: *Story*.

Conflict:

Both Stein and McKee agree that the best plots derive from characters gaining or losing something of critical importance to them (sometimes more than once) – this is their conflict. It doesn't have to revolve around gun-toting gangsters and acrobatic Kung-fu exponents. Conflict is about challenges we face and the resulting hard decisions we have to make in achieving our goals or in holding on to what is dear to us. They may be psychological (within the character's mind); with other individuals (e.g. spouses, siblings, or strangers); with society (e.g. legal or economic injustices), or with the environment (the challenge of a mountain, an earthquake).

Stein says the most common causes of conflict are money, love and power, but whatever we choose, the stakes must be high enough to allow for emotional intensity and a build-up of tension, or why should the reader care sufficiently to continue. From a lifetime of writing and editing, he suggests the six 'favourite' conflicts for readers are:

- Gaining or losing love
- Achieving or failing a lifetime ambition
- Seeing justice done
- Saving a life

- Seeking revenge
- Accomplishing a seemingly impossible task

We turn to McKee: conflicts arise from core human values – qualities of human experience that can change over time between positive and negative, like love and hate, or hope and despair, good and evil: opposites because stories are about transformation, changes from one state to the other. That change – from the situation at the beginning, to the resolution at the end – is the story arc.

The action in a story (what happens to a character and what she does about it) causes change in the core value, e.g. despair for a loved one in danger, turns to hope when a character overcomes her fear, enabling her to rescue the beloved. The change, plus its cause, gives us the Central or Controlling Idea for the story – its theme: we build everything around it.

The Controlling Idea holds the story together to give it purpose and force; helps us to keep the action relevant, and holds readers' attention so that the meaning or message of the story can emerge.

But where is the Plot?

The plot is the writer's choice of events – characters' actions, thoughts, and dialogue – to achieve the story arc and its Controlling Idea. Each event changes something or sets up change for the character, taking her closer to achieving her goal or making it more difficult for her. Each time the protagonist responds to a fresh pressure, an additional new layer of character is revealed, sometimes to her own surprise.

By alternating positive and negative forces in a series of scenes, more tension is created. But the pressures must be significant and, preferably, continue to increase till the story reaches its climax, after which it will end happily (on a positive change); tragically (on a negative change), or ambiguously, e. g. a boy's search for his biological mother is eventually successful, but he doesn't like her.

A film or novel may have five or more 'acts' containing scenes which alternate in highs and lows for the protagonist; a short story may have room for only one strong scene, three at most: the arc is tighter, but the principles are the same.

Our group felt we had found a process: a way to select structures and plots to enact any particular story we wish to share. Into our chosen form we can weave rich characterization; original description and metaphor; purposeful dialogue, and vivid language, all in our own unique voice – we like a challenge.

A good story that arcs round to its inevitable yet unexpected ending has a symmetry and coherence rarely experienced in real life: how infrequently we achieve resolution rather than compromise in our own conflicts – perhaps that is the attraction, for both readers and writers. Stories have to make sense in a way that life rarely does. Such stories are affecting, McKee reminds us, because conflict, sequence, cause and effect – i.e. storytelling – is the basis of humanity and the way the human mind functions.

~~~

Flash Writing

Small is beautiful:

Apart from winning competitions, there are beneficial spin-offs from writing flash fiction: finding one word to replace four stretches your vocabulary; keeping it tight cultivates precision; a small focused target can overcome writers' block, and engineering the twist will develop a devious mind for plotting.

Sometimes called micro or short-short fiction, flash fiction has been around since Aesop wrote his fables around 600 BCE. Here is one of my favourites: *"A vixen sneered at a lioness because she never bore more than one cub. 'Only one,' she replied, 'but a lion.'"* It makes a good comeback for a one-book author.

Flash fiction is increasing in popularity to become a distinctive literary form. Many competitions now include prizes and anthology publication for short-short stories of anything from 6 words to 1,000. Even the Bridport Prize included a flash category for the first time in 2010 – a story of 250 words drawing a prize of £1000.

But perfectly formed:

The challenge is that flash fiction has to be a complete story: catchy hook, distinctive characters, significant conflict and satisfying conclusion. Often, but not always, the story has a twist in the tail – preferably in the last couple of words – that takes the reader by surprise. But you must not cheat; clues to the dénouement must be woven so subtly through the story that the judges – who have seen everything and are as sharp as an editor's pencil – will enjoy being surprised as well.

The other provocation is keeping within the word count; making each word robust enough to carry a maximum of expression, and not being as extravagant with adjectives as I have in the previous paragraph. Imagine you are paying 50cents for each word: seek the best value.

The lower the word count: the greater the challenge. Flash fiction is not an easy option, or just the baby brother of the short story. As with poetry, the need to select a word with precision, possibly to convey multiple layers of meaning, can make a point more pithily and memorably in 500 words than in 5,000. To quote Anton Chekhov, *"Brevity is the sister of talent."*

Read some of the winning flash fiction on competition websites and you will see just how much talent these story writers have. So how do they achieve it?

Cut to the quick:

If you analyse some of those stories, you will see they use the minimum of words to show action and reaction, choosing words strong enough to hint at what they don't say.

I'm stepping off the kerb here, but I'll give an example:

Jason was limping as he slowly approached us. He was on his feet again after an injury on the rugby field but he wouldn't play again – it had left him feeling rather depressed. (33 words)

If we cut unnecessary words like adverbs; observations that are obvious; phrases that 'tell' rather than 'show', and leave a bit to the reader's imagination, we reduce the words to less than a third.

Jason limped towards us – his rugby days were over. (9)

But 'limped' is an unsubtle choice, and suggests flaccidity, absence of tension; it leads nowhere. We could help the reader imagine Jason's feelings by using a less expected and stronger verb that involves the imposition of restraint and so implies a will thwarted.

Jason hobbled towards us – his rugby days were over.

This is a simple illustration; within a story of vivid characters and coiled-spring tension, the power of what is *not* said can be overwhelming. Sometimes, it's the blanks that kill.

Use rich text:

After being this ruthless with a couple of stories, you realize how adjectives and adverbs can gobble up the word count to no purpose. Mark Twain was dead against them. His advice was, '*If you catch an adjective, kill it!*' An adjective may be necessary for precision, but most adverbs can be cut by using stronger verbs. Verbs work hard – holding down two jobs at once if recruited wisely.

Successful flash writers tend to portray characters through their actions, finding visual, active verbs that also keep the story moving to maintain pace; they use dialogue the same way. Another shortcut is the use of metaphor and simile in place of space-eating descriptions.

It is within these layers of rich text and multiple meanings that they sneak the clues to their final twist, and send the reader back to the beginning to see how they did it.

In a tight space, words must play as a team; one idler mid-field can upset the whole game strategy. That's what sustains the flow and tempo of winning stories; pace and tension are compelling. You have only minutes: don't give the judge cause to blink let alone lift her gaze from the page. Cold coffee is not your problem.

Ignite a flash of inspiration:

All this brutality is primarily left-brain activity – analysing, evaluating, and searching – that's why the experts recommend writing freely to let ideas flow uninhibited, then editing as a separate exercise. Hemmingway did it standing up.

'Writers' block' is not in my vocabulary; instead I have the three 'Ds': displacement, deviance and dalliance. I'm cunning with all three, but if my current creation is festering unresolved in a drawer, or mocking me from the screen, focusing on one idea or character and setting a target of just 100 words will stir my 'write-brain' into action.

I take an idea from around my desk – a picture, a book cover, a letter – or whatever I see out of the window. Distracted by a violent storm recently I set to describing it in 25 words – it became the opening paragraph to a new story – *Through the Eye of the Storm* – that was later shortlisted in a competition (you can read it in chapter 6).

Good-to-go for non-fiction too:

Flash techniques apply equally to non-fiction writing. My first experience of stripping down to the kernel was after returning from years of aid work overseas, broke and desperate. I became a gobbeter for a university website – reducing paunchy research reports to their 500-word essence. The pay was so poor I had to hack two a day to pay the bills. Yes, it is possible – whiz through contents, index, headings, conclusions, look for the words 'policy recommendations' and peek at the style.

Now I'm hooked on flash fiction, not just to make judges gobsmacked with my literary nibbles, but because the wordplay, precision and masochistic editing improve my writing and – best of all – I love it.

Here are some flash competition websites with links to winning stories:

www.flash500.com

www.gemini-magazine.com

www.spillinginkreview.com

[*Flash Writing* was originally commissioned by NZ Writers' College as an article for their website, later becoming part of their flash writing course].

~~~

Stories:

Transpositions

Allegro:

Barely dawn but Anton no longer fools himself he is sleeping. The trio is in limbo without a cellist; only two auditioned well. Idly his hand trails familiar curves – they stir...

"Awake, David?"

"Mmm, sort of. What's the time?"

"Early. I'll contact Carla Schultz before we lose her." No consensus, but he daren't risk David's choice.

"You've decided already? On her? Not exactly a bundle of fun, was she?"

"You're being childish, David."

"She hardly opened her mouth."

"She played brilliantly."

"So did Michael. He's a known quantity – you taught us both."

"I remember." They had been too close, those two.

"Ah, a woman is safer, that it? Forgiven, but not forgotten."

"David ... please don't."

Largo:

David nestles his violin into its plush-lined case, his neck is stiff and his left shoulder aches after the week of rehearsing – the constant round of playing, pausing, repeating – enough, if we're not one voice now, it's too late. Luckily tomorrow's competition piece is Beethoven's 'Ghost', seems Carla loves it, too.

He flops onto the sofa, ankles cushioned on the armrest. At least Anton splashed out on a first-rate hotel this time – the Viennese don't let elegance interfere with comfort. Through half closed eyes he watches Carla leaning her cello against a chair, stretching out on the thick rose-toned carpet like a lynx, her tight little arse in the air.

Michael's trio competes tomorrow, too. Mike was tense in the theatre this morning, asking me: "Why did I lose the audition?" Anton makes the decisions, he should know that.

Anton plays in the next room; tumultuous, even for Rachmaninov.

Presto:

Carla touches up her make-up, scowls at her reflection. Passing Michael outside the washroom she nods, unsmiling. That Meikel, he want David, same as Anton.

Rolling her shoulders to relieve the tension, she rejoins the trio as the judges announce the awards.

"Mein Gott!" Carla flings an arm around David's neck. "We won. Fantastisch, no?" She looks triumphantly into Anton's anxious face; his pale skin, it is moist, taut.

"Remarkable how you've blended in with us, Carla," he glances at David. "Truly a transposition." Hands break up the huddle, reaching in to congratulate them, slapping them on the back, leading them off to the bar.

The hotel foyer throbs with carousing musicians – a cacophony of singspiel. Carla drains her glass. Drunk with success she seeks out David. No better time.

"Is too hot. Need a break, no?"

"Good idea."

They jostle their way into the crowded lift; emerge gratefully at the third floor.

The trio's suite is spacious, cool. Carla pushes open the French-windows, stepping onto a tiny balcony. Traffic pulses through blazing city lights below. Taxis swoop to the kerb, picking up waiting prey.

David lifts wine from the fridge, picks up two glasses and joins her, standing so close she smells rosin on his jacket. She conceals a smile of triumph as he nuzzles her neck.

~~~

Story Analysis:

Transpositions was a deliberate experiment to achieve three new goals: write about sexuality; find an original structure, and break a basic 'rule' of writing by telling a very short story through three different points of view instead of one – something the rebel in me had been longing to do.

From the theme – transsexuality creating 'eternal triangles' of uncertainty and change – I found the idea of a musical ensemble. For that, the three movements of a piece of trio music seemed a natural choice for structure and one that I'd never seen before, which also enabled me to let each musician express a point of view without confusing the reader.

To tighten the structure, I made the pace of each story section match the musical movements: a suitably fast and lively Allegro is played through Anton and David's argument; the Largo is slower, more relaxed, sentences are longer, David and Carla rest after rehearsal (a contrast to Anton, working off his anxiety in another room), and for a fast Presto, because I couldn't say what I needed to entirely in dialogue, I used short sentences and words that create an active mood – 'throb', jostle' 'crowded' and 'pulses'. Carla, too, is on a mission. And a small point about language adding consistency and wholeness to a story: David stands so close to Carla she can smell – not his aftershave – but the rosin used on his violin bow.

As far as possible, I used dialogue to introduce characters, suggest back-story, and push the plot, but I won't discuss that further here because I dissect the dialogue from the first movement as an article in the next chapter, which covers voice, dialogue and language.

Transpositions has its own back-story of rewrites, critiques and edits. Originally, it included an alternative ending – another small act of bravado on my part – in the form of a fourth movement, an Encore. The first dénouement in the Presto was as it is above, but the Encore repeated some of the text up to the point where Carla and David enter the suite, when Carla announces 'she' is, in fact, Carl – the alternative twist being not David's dual sexuality, but that Anton's 'safe choice' turns out to be an unexpected temptation.

Unfortunately, this last bit of originality was too much for reader credibility. Having two endings wasn't the problem – I might try that another time – but two critiques doubted that 'Carla' could succeed in hiding her gender in the closely confined life of a rehearsing trio, or even in the wider musical world, and questioned why she would try to do so – there was no motivation. Moral: however devious the twist, it won't work if the plot is unbelievable. Returning to the story a few weeks later, I realized they were right, and deleted all the carefully laid clues to Carla's real gender and launched into yet another rewrite.

I won't exhaust you with all the revisions, though it was an exciting ride, but the trickiest bit is usually the ending. How do you know when you've reached the end of a story? At what point does a reader feel satisfied?

The storyline is resolved when David nuzzles Carla's neck, revealing his transsexuality – a complication the manipulative Anton had not foreseen. But in an earlier draft, I sought to underline the 'eternal triangle' theme by adding two more lines:

"Where's Anton?" he asks.

"Down there with Meikel. You don't see them?"

Cutting these two lines leaves more options open to the reader's imagination – whatever the outcome for the trio, it will be messy – but it stops the story at the point of resolution, forming a stronger ending. Making that cut left me twelve words within the 500 limit, but I resisted the temptation to use them simply because I had them. To paraphrase Bates: a story's polish is complete when one word more, or less, would diminish it.

In its first incarnation, *Transpositions* was unsuccessful in competitions. I have not entered it anywhere in this final form – the trio plays its debut performance here.

~~~

Runnin' the River

"How was it, buddy?"

"Durn near the best prawns and chilli sauce I ever had, Vince."

It was too, with all the right fixin's an all. Plenty green ginger and not so much chilli that you couldn't taste nuthin' else - just like Ma made. She learned me to cook. All the years workin' in restaurants prawns was my specialty; never did tell the boss I dumped his recipes and used my Ma's. Rest her soul.

"Beer?"

I nod at Vince and he ducks out and lobs me a nice cool can. He can be a bit crusty, Vince, but a sound guy. I've known him for ... well, it's gettin' on for 12 years now. You can depend on him. As we say here in Texas, he'll do to run the river with. If you've got a tough assignment, he's the guy to have along. And right now I'm feelin' about as jittery as a long-tailed cat in a room full o'rocking chairs.

How's the time? No sweat yet ... June 10th, now there's a happenstance; big brother Jake's birthday. Bastard. I guess neither one of us got what you might call a real good start – our Pa lit out before we hardly set eyes on him; Ma all wore out working day and night just to keep the shack around us. I don't blame her for the sorry guys she brought home, she was an easy mark, but they sure had a bad influence.

God knows I ain't no angel. I've done dope and a good bit of thieving in my time. Got put in the slammer for it too – twice. But Jake. He was a whole nuther thing. Some guys runnin' dope are as dumb as a box o'rocks. Not Jake the Snake. He was smart and thought he was ridin' high; done it by pushin' high school kids. Kids. Youngsters with no better start than we had. And he pimped the girls he got hooked. He was makin' it all ways. But he took risks when he started jerkin' the suppliers around.

I was goin' straight then. Chef: finger-lickin' good prawns. With Angie, my steady girl – a real foxy lady, but sweet with it. That was too much for big brother. He put the moves on her, used her, would have trashed her like every woman he come in contact with, but my beautiful Angie topped herself. That really choked me up. The bastard deserved everything he got.

"Time to move, buddy. You ready?"

"Sure thing, Vince. Equipment all checked?"

"All good."

There'll be no screw-ups – these guys get plenty of practice. So here I am. Restraints in place, ready to run this river alone. We can't all live honest, that's a fact. But a man should die honest. No judge nor jury ever believed it, but it weren't me as killed my arse-hole of a brother. Wished I had. Whoever did – live long and sweet, buster.

Lord ha'mercy on my soul.

~~~

Story Analysis:

The storyline of *Runnin' the River* is formed around a single scene – eating a meal – during which a narrator thinks about his life, with brief dialogue at the beginning and end: a structure I hoped would be invisible, to emphasise the theme of an unjust execution. To increase that impact, I used a 'first person' point of view in the present tense, and took the risk of writing in dialect to make the prisoner's 'voice' more vivid; using Texan idiom because that state is especially active in carrying out the death penalty.

Media discussion of a current execution in the USA provided the inspiration, and the fact that I had been to Texas, and also worked for several years with a Texan colleague, enabled me to 'hear' the protagonist's speech. I did, though, access an internet site for Texan dialect to check what I was using and find suitable idiomatic phrases.

The story won the Flash500 competition in the first quarter of 2011. I quote the judge's comments in full:

"I was immediately drawn to Runnin' The River because of the uniqueness of the voice and the simplicity of the writing. Here is a man enjoying a meal in a restaurant where he's obviously a well known regular and musing over his life's choices, good and bad. Halfway through we realize he has an appointment to keep, but there's no hurry. The atmosphere is relaxed, even though he admits he's a little nervous. Three short lines of dialogue later the reality dawns like a kick in the stomach. Brilliantly executed, if you'll pardon the pun."

The title is a quote from the text with an appropriate meaning, and although non-Texan readers might not know what it meant, I hoped it was unusual enough to act as a hook.

As a flash story, I had to work at it over and over again to stay within the word count. Clues to the dénouement had to be visible but ambiguous: the featured meal – his 'last meal'– is alongside his back-story as a restaurant chef (the first time I've used food in a story and I had to look up recipes); mention of being in the *"slammer – twice"* was a double bluff I feared might reveal too much. Other small clues: Vince *"ducks out"* (indicating a small space – the cell), and he calls the protagonist *"buddy"* while Vince is addressed by name (suggesting something about their relative status).

Once the basic story was in place, the editing and tweaking – in slots of 5-10 minutes at irregular intervals of days or weeks – continued for several months. The shorter the flash, the longer it seems to take to get it finally right.

[*Runnin' The River* was published on the Flash500 website, and in the first print edition of *Words with JAM* in June/July 2011]

~~~

Tiny Stories

It must be obvious how much I enjoy writing flash fiction – the discipline of brevity, attempting to achieve complete resolution – and it is even more challenging when the word count is exact rather than a maximum, as it was for these three 100-word micro-stories. In this space, structure and plot are minimal; theme and character predominate, leaving a reader with a new idea, a mood, perhaps a question.

They are a useful exercise to stimulate the muse, sometimes providing inspiration for a longer story, but I find the space limitation of tiny stories inherently unsatisfactory and frustrating both as a writer and a reader. These were written for an open-themed competition.

The Window-seat

Tracy moved in on Tuesday. She came from a high-rise. The terrace on this street is nicer; no damp, no ghetto blasters overhead, even a tiny garden. She was lucky. But people can look into your front windows from across the road. She isn't used to that: it unnerves her.

"That sticky-beak in number nine is always sitting at her window," she grumbles, and keeps her curtains closed. To avoid the nosy old biddy she goes out the back, walks down the evil-smelling alley.

Number 9 steps cautiously out of her house and along the path, tapping her white cane.

~~~

Story Analysis:

I was thinking here about the subcultures created by where we live and the assumptions and prejudices they create. Tracy inconveniences herself in her avoidance of 'Number 9' whom she perceives – mistakenly – as a nosy busybody; a theme that could be made into a longer story. I long for her to meet 'Number 9' and find a friend in her. There is so much movement and information required in this story that, most of the time, word choices were made simply to get the plot sequence on the page. Language also had to be simple in keeping with Tracy's 'voice'.

~~~

Lover in Paradise

A jade sea caresses the shore, leaving wet kisses on hot, white sand. Sunlight glances off palm fronds that bend to whisper secrets to their neighbours.

She inhales deeply the warm, sweet spicy air and sees a handsome young man, naked torso gleaming like coffee icing. He approaches her with a garland of white flowers. The breeze carries their erotic fragrance. She recognizes it as frangipani – her favourite. As she walks towards him, slowly, seductively, she hears the faint hum of a bee...no, a distant plane? It gets louder, much louder.

Aargh! She judders awake. Bloody Arthur is snoring again.

~~~

Story Analysis:

The first sentence came into my head and I wanted to use it somewhere. Light, amusing, this 'dream' story was intended as a mood piece – word choices are sensuous – but I saw it as a bit of play, unlikely to develop into anything.

~~~

Last Train

He sits at our table.

His T-shirt is a holey relic imprinted with a month's doss-house soups. Lifting it casually, revealing white flab spattered with red, angry lumps – courtesy of spiteful fleas – he begins rhythmically, meditatively, to scratch. His unfocused gaze hovers on the far wall of the crowded station cafe.

"Let's move," you hiss.

"There's still an hour," I say.

We're starting over: going on a second honeymoon – to Torquay.

"You're always so obtuse." I feel your spittle spatter my face.

You get the Brighton train.

I start on another coffee.

He nods. Passes the sugar bowl.

~~~

Story Analysis:

Inspired by the memory of a 'down and out' man who sat opposite me at a table in King's Cross railway station buffet; another story about prejudice which, in this case, exacerbates existing conflict between the couple, shown by the deliberate misunderstanding of subtext in the brief dialogue – not to mention the hiss and spittle.

With a 'missing' back-story of the couple's antagonism, descriptive words do additional duties in suggesting conflict: *'angry lumps'*, *'spiteful fleas'* and *'spattered with red'* (an angry colour), repeated in *"spatter my face'*. A lot of adjectives but they worked two jobs. Several adverbs, too, but I wanted the first paragraph to feel 'leisurely' to contrast with the tension of the rest – the only bit of structure I found space for.

I chose the title to reflect the couple's attempt to rescue their relationship, a last chance, probably missed. The reader is left to decide.

~~~

5: Voice, Language and Dialogue

"The voice you have when no one is listening." Pico Iyer

'Voice' is a mysterious poltergeist that writers torture themselves trying to transmogrify into the written word – or so it seems. I've been there, gazing up from my little piece of earth at the big shots that 'have a voice'. But I experienced a glow-worm moment: I think I understand it now. Sharing this with you will involve the consumption of more tea and dark chocolate than is good for my health, but I will persevere because appreciating 'voice' is as critical to reading as it is to writing; arguably the most challenging aspect to understand in either activity and probably why it is less frequently written about in detail.

The two commonest statements on the topic are: 'voice is who we are'; and 'it can take a writer, years to find'. The first part explains little but I accept it as a truism from which to build. What I want to know is: if my 'voice' is who I am, why spend years searching for it? – 'I am' already here, have been for a considerable time.

But it is not only writers who have a 'voice.' So let's start with readers.

You no doubt have favourite authors: you read all their books; wait eagerly for each new work they spent two or three years writing, and devour it in two or three days; you guzzle their biographies and autobiographies. There is something about what and how they write – you can't get enough.

Your insatiable appetite for an author is part of who *you* are; you bring your own voice to the reading. It is an active two-way phenomenon; between you and the author is a 'reaction', a chemistry which, to your amazement, is not shared by every other member of your reading group – they each bring a different voice to their reading.

But we can 'go off' an author; feel deeply attached to different authors at various stages of our lives, and sometimes be in the mood for one rather than another, even though we 'love' them both – the chemistry doesn't always work all of the time. Clearly, as readers, our individual voices vary depending on what is happening in our lives. What about writers?

Suppose you are a Ruth Rendell fan – millions of us are – and I give you a book that I wrote, copying her style, with 'Ruth Rendell' printed on the cover. Would you be fooled? Not for long. However carefully I might try to imitate her words, Ruth Rendell as a person is not underneath them, did not generate them – it is not in her voice. Something would be missing.

What if you read a book by Barbara Vine? Whose voice would you recognize? A discerning reader might suspect it is Ruth Rendell's because she *is* Barbara Vine – a pseudonym she uses for an entirely different kind of book. She has other passions apart from Chief Inspector Wexford, which she expresses with another part of her voice – but it still comes from 'who she is'.

So an author can have more than one distinctive inner voice, and a reader's voice is changeable. It's getting tricky. I'd better assemble the key elements we need to weave, one by one, into the 'voice story': the 'voice' every single person has; the 'writer's voice'; the 'character voice'; dialogue, which has a role in all three but is different from each, and language, articulating all four. Have a piece of chocolate to keep you going.

Every person has a voice, expressed not only in spoken and written words, but in thoughts, dress, gestures and actions – the 'who we are' aspect, our persona. I know you don't listen to gossip, but you might hear some, inadvertently, and think: *That can't be true. George would never do (or say) that.* It's contrary to the voice you recognize as George's. But other people will recognize a different persona because we show ourselves differently to the wide range of people with whom we interact.

The 'you' that relates to your mother is likely to be different to the 'you' exchanging experiences with your childhood friend, or your boss. The lawyer standing at the bar in the courtroom may be unrecognizable as he stands at the bar of The Dog and Whistle a few hours later. Our situation impacts our voice, too. I know many people who, through changed circumstances, have manifest a stronger, richer self, their voices previously smothered by a dominant 'other'.

During our lives, we develop new passions, attitudes, experiences, perspectives and memories like a ship accumulates barnacles on its bottom, and the timbre of our voices increases in depth and breadth accordingly. But they are all part of 'I am'.

When you add transient states of mind and the truly inner life to which even we have limited access – although it influences us – it is not so much a distinctive 'voice' we have, but a 'chorus'. At times, more like an ill-matched madrigal choir, each member lustily singing their own part in clamorous disharmony. Truly, we speak in tongues. When a close friend stepped into the frightening maze towards Alzheimer's disease, the saddest feature for me was not the impairment of short-term memory, but the loss of some of those voices from her unique madrigal choir: it alters the persona.

What about 'writer's voice' – how is that different? In essence, it is the same: the particularity comes from our desire to express it principally in the form of the written word – which has its own limitations – and in our seeking experiences, observing and identifying with others, for that sole purpose. By 'limitations' I mean having to work within the linear conventions of written language when at times there seems no word or phrase to do justice to our thoughts. But for some of us, the written word is our most fluent means of expression, allowing thoughts to form more succinctly than through spoken communication. To misquote E. M. Forster's feisty old lady: "How can I tell what I think till I see what I write?"

As a writer, my voice is as much a compound of elements – a personal chorus of voices and potential tones – as any reader's. Perhaps this is what confuses.

Pico Iyer suggests we move beyond those daily voices we use for interacting with sundry 'others': *"At its core, writing is about cutting beneath every social expectation to get to the voice you have when no one is listening...the voice that lies beneath all words."*

From that quiet, or more likely, tumultuous, place we can choose to draw down a particular voice from our inner chorus that will serve a specific passion – as we saw in Ruth Rendell. Whatever we write and whichever tone we use, it will be just as much 'who we are'. *"Wittingly or unwittingly, all stories, honest and dishonest, wise and foolish, faithfully mirror their maker, exposing his humanity...or lack of it."* (McKee).

At first reading, this is a disturbing comment: two stories in this collection include female 'first person' accounts of murderers. Surely McKee is not saying I am a closet killer.

On reflection, I think he refers to the wider treatment given to a story as a whole. It may be necessary to show despicable behaviour if only to vanquish it by demonstrating its consequences, or revealing its causes. We can understand an act without having done it ourselves, or condoning it in others, but to write those acts convincingly requires an identification with character which draws on a darker side of our nature – we may not wish to acknowledge it but we all have one: where dreams and nightmares crouch, along with unresolved conflicts and injustices long forgotten.

To be brutally honest, we cannot know what we might do until the ultimate challenge – a scary aspect of our inevitably incomplete self-knowledge. Is not such understanding something we seek in stories?

Everything we write links in some way to something within us. Using the strength of *"that voice we have when no one is listening"*, we can, for example, write in a different gender because, biologically and psychologically, we have both male and female traits to inform us – if we choose to recognize them – in addition to our powers of observation and imagination.

We can tap into any inner source we choose, construct any kind of story with very disparate characters; if our lives have been deeply immersed in two cultures, we can write from the perspective of either – though not necessarily with equal force. Each voice we elect to use will permeate the page like a watermark; revealed in language, tone, choice of theme, expression of a strong conviction we hold, compassion in the way a story is told, or even in the fact of telling precisely this story in the first place. A strong passion within us, something we care deeply about, will write in the most powerful voice.

And they can only be one of *our* voices: attempting to adopt the voice of a writer we admire doesn't work because we don't have their inner chorus to draw upon. When we are advised to 'know your audience', it means to ask ourselves: For whom am I writing this? It is about selecting an appropriate voice as well as style and content, but there are times when we feel driven to *"cutting beneath every social expectation"* to express an obsession of our own, and hope someone will listen – using every skill we can master to ensure they do. This, I believe, is our most potent voice, although it is not always the most commercial.

As far as I can see, the problem is not so much 'finding a voice', as recognizing and distinguishing between the multiplicity of voices in our inner chorus; taking steps to enrich them, and learning how best to select and express the one we wish to use at any particular time. This, of course, requires the painful process of looking inside ourselves as well as writing – lots of writing – if only a scribble on the back of a shopping list while observing an intriguing customer at the checkout; which brings me to 'character voice.'

We think we are 'creating' characters when in fact we are discovering pieces of ourselves. As we saw in the chapter on character, we can sketch the personality of a protagonist from observation, drawing threads from people we have known and using our imagination, but the composite portrait of deep character – the madrigal chorus of our heroine – comes from within. In the story *Runnin' the River*, the strength of 'character voice' was vital, but 'I am' there also, expressing in the various elements of the story my passion and values – its moral premise – and there are faint reflections from my own character (though not his criminality I hasten to add). Like an actor who walks onto the stage 'all character', yet he brings something of himself to the role. Another actor's performance will never be quite the same.

Both of the stories later in this chapter are written from a male, 'first person' point of view, each very different from the other, and yet my worldview and my own understanding of each of their situations forms the 'watermark' of my writer's voice. And that is where it should stay – in the background. As a reader, I want to 'hear' and believe in the characters; I like the author to step aside and let them get on with their job.

As in real life, a character's voice is expressed through every aspect of their persona – verbal and non-verbal – and it is this show-ing of their true nature through thought, word and deed that enables them to speak directly to us. By 'telling' the reader information instead of allowing the characters to 'show' it, we break the spell of the story's reality by chiming-in in our own voice – not as a water-mark, but like an ink blot on the page.

I need to digress slightly here, to recall the earlier article on 'point of view', and to clarify how this fits in because it is a common phrase with a more limited meaning in writing craft. When we read a story from a 'first person' perspective – the Texan facing execution, for example – the character narrates his own tale because the author has chosen to write in his voice. The Texan's 'point of view' determines what he can see, hear and know from his unique position in the story and his physical situation in a prison cell – he can't see and know everything.

To put it another way: his point of view is where he is sitting; his voice is the expression of his whole person, past and present, while he sits there. As readers, we hear his voice in this story mainly through his inner and spoken dialogue.

Dialogue is an important means of showing both 'character voice' and what is happening, while giving a shove to the plot to maintain pace, so this seems a good moment to weave it into our 'voice story'.

Writers use artifice to make the spoken word appear real because actual conversations contain dreary trivia and are about other people's plots. But dialogue is richly multi-functional; craftsmanship enables us to use it in many ways: to reveal character (through thoughts as well as spoken words); to create and sustain tension (within a relationship for example, by hinting at threats or promises), and to establish facts that turn a corner in the plot. We can also release our own 'voice' by expressing a strongly held conviction through the mouth of our hero (as long as it is within character, brief, and progresses the storyline: not a soap-box tirade). All of this is easier to show than tell, so the first article in this chapter demonstrates what dialogue can do by 'unpicking' verbal exchanges from a couple of stories.

Although language is obviously significant in dialogue – vocabulary and phrasing have to suit a protagonist – choice of images and metaphors throughout a story also establishes mood and atmosphere appropriate to the theme. And it is perhaps through language that our 'watermark' is most clearly revealed, whichever of our voices we are using. We tend to make habitual choices in word usage, and in the symbolism underlying similes, metaphors and objects that appear in our writing – all reflections of our 'inner chorus'.

Not just word choices but syntax – their arrangement into sentences – which determines how ideas flow and hover. And some writers use more adverbs and adjectives than others. I don't let fear of Mark Twain's ghost stop me from using any words available – or inventing some that aren't – if they are right for the story. Adjectives and adverbs may be idle layabouts, but they can be given useful work when the required precision or emphasis cannot be achieved in any other way.

Use of language is our 'style', especially revealing of our voices because how we write is a reflection of how we think and we each have our own patterns of thinking. This applies to everyone, even if all we write is emails and Christmas cards.

You know those plants with sticky burrs that get everywhere, the ones that inspired the invention of Velcro? My brain cultivates these. No sooner do I have an idea than lots of other thoughts get stuck to it. I see them 'all at once', a composite picture in my mind, but words have to go on the page one at a time in a straight line: it's very frustrating. And the written word is one-dimensional – you can't see me waving my arms about and making faces to emphasise a point. Attempting to share my mental image with all those burrs hanging on, my sentences grow dependant clauses, sub-clauses, conditioners like 'although', 'but', 'or', and en-dashes abound – you might have noticed. Punctuation is my lifeline.

But this is how I think; it is my most natural voice, the one I use for writing non-fiction, when I am not acting anyone else but myself. I still have to make adjustments according to purpose and audience: the articles here are in a slightly different tone to these discussions, some were written originally as blog posts; for an academic journal or a popular magazine, I would have to adhere to their 'house style' – some editors are allergic to semi-colons.

This way of thinking and 'talking' is not the way many of my story characters think and talk. I have to get to know them well, understand their minds, and use language craft to let them speak with their own voices. Fiction is harder for me to write than non-fiction, but I find it easier when writing from the first person point of view. I think this is because, if I can reach the stage where I identify with the character, I can write with the freedom as if it were me talking. With a third person perspective I am a narrator looking out and I seem to find that inhibiting. We are all different – fortunately. But whatever our style or genre, written words are how we express it and we have to use language with care.

A key activity in editing short stories (the subject of the next chapter), is to examine each word for its necessity, clarity and precision, assessing its purpose and relevance to what we wish to convey. In this way we sharpen our voice, strengthening it by removing interference – the noise and chatter that doesn't need to be there.

Language flows through everything we have considered here. It is our base of operations, the foundation of our collective humanity and of our individuality. We gain articulacy in written language only through using it: by reading and writing.

This has been a long discussion. Are you still with me? I hope you didn't linger back there and eat all the chocolate – we haven't finished yet. I mentioned the role of non-verbal expression – body language – in the earlier chapter on character as well as in this one. The second article here links these to suggest how one part of the body, the hands, can show not only 'character voice' but aspects of plot.

~~~

Articles:

You Said What? Uses of Dialogue

Most readers love dialogue, they can hurtle through the pages faster, but more importantly, it draws them closer to the action – literally within earshot – to overhear what characters are saying to each other. The appeal is not hearing idle chit-chat, but learning who they are and what they are doing straight from the source.

An approach I find useful is to start by asking myself: Which parts of the story can be told through their mouths? Instead of: What would these people say to each other? I don't want actors gossiping on stage. I want them speaking their lines: revealing my story.

But writing about talking becomes tedious; writing about writing talking even more so. As an alternative, I have pasted below two conversations from short stories we read in the last chapter, indicating beneath each line the contribution that brief utterance is making to the storytelling.

Extract from Transpositions:

Barely dawn but Anton no longer fools himself he is sleeping. The trio is in limbo without a cellist; only two auditioned well. Idly his hand trails familiar curves – they stir...

"Awake, David?"

Dialogue partners the setting here, revealing Anton and David's sexuality in two perfectly ordinary words. Informality is shown by truncating the question: Are you awake? It sounds more natural. After this first mention of a name, we don't need tags – 'David said', 'Anton replied' etc – the exchange flows naturally; we know who is speaking.

"Mmm, sort of. What's the time?"

Unlike Anton, David has slept. Either he is not a worrier by nature, or does not share the responsibility for the trio: character traits which might also have some bearing on the plot.

"Early. I'll contact Carla Schultz before we lose her." No *consensus, but he daren't risk David's choice.*

He answers David's question indirectly and dismissively, a hint of inequality in the relationship. The next phrase pushes the plot: introduces another character and first bit of tension in the sense of urgency. Also it adds to Anton's character traits that he is the one who organizes things – seems we were right about David's lesser responsibility. The final phrase, as internal dialogue, adds more tension: there is usually consensus but Anton is changing the rules, and it creates doubts about David, something else for Anton to worry over and perhaps for us to wonder about.

"You've decided already? On her? Not exactly a bundle of fun, was she?"

We add to David's character that though he is not pleased, he accepts that Anton has made the decision, but grumbles about it – confirming the asymmetry of their relationship and adding tension by showing discord. It may or may not tell us about Carla's character: David's disgruntled and flippant opinion cannot be relied upon.

"You're being childish, David."

"She hardly opened her mouth."

"She played brilliantly."

More oblique responses, this exchange confirms the characters of both, and the comment on her playing is significant to the plot later. Brevity was essential because this is part of a 500-word flash story, but it creates a rapid tit-for-tat dialogue which increases the pace – we want the tension of a row; lengthy invective would slow everything down even in a longer story, unless it contained information that raised the stakes or turned the plot into a new direction.

"So did Michael and he's a known quantity – you taught us both."

The fourth character is introduced and we know he is a cellist, and a good one; as a fellow student he is probably about David's age, and that Anton taught them, so he is likely to be older. It makes sense now that he would be the organizer and dominant partner. Tension and plot thicken because this line has cast doubt on Anton's decision – we now want to know why Anton chose Carla as much as David does.

"I remember." They had been too close, those two.

The ambiguity and hint of threat in those first two words, plus the inner dialogue revealing Anton's jealousy, not only increases the tension, but contributes to plot by suggesting the reason for his action in choosing Carla.

"Ah, a woman is safer, that it? Forgiven, but not forgotten."

Bingo! Jealousy is Anton's underlying motivation, and it seems he is justified because the four last words give us enough information to realize there is a back-story of unfaithfulness by David.

"David ... please don't."

The main contribution here is to a complexity of character: in response to David's challenge, Anton's tone changes from dominance to pleading, revealing that he is the emotionally dependent partner. It doesn't give us any direct information about the plot, but we can sniff trouble ahead.

By analysing any dialogue in this way, a writer can find superfluous words, see where motivation and plot hints could be introduced or strengthened, and include suggestiveness on related back-story that might be enough to stimulate the reader's imagination without spelling it out anywhere. And a reader can gain far more from a text, delving into deeper levels of character, motive and story.

We can imagine this sort of dialogue by putting two characters in a specific and relevant setting and listening through the keyhole. As a reader, I love to eavesdrop, and I don't know a writer who doesn't. And here is the second much shorter example from a 100-word micro-story. It shows what you might convey in only three lines of spoken dialogue and two of inner thoughts.

In this story, a couple sits at a table in a railway station café. A tramp has occupied the same table, and lifts his T-shirt to scratch flea bites.

Extract from The Last Train:

"Let's move," you hiss.

We learn the character being quoted is probably intolerant of tramps. A tag had to be used because no one has spoken up to that point and there are three people at the table, but the '*hiss*' not only tells us how the words were delivered, but that the narrator seems to have a negative attitude towards the comment, or the speaker – to use 'whisper' instead, would have given a whole different meaning and character hint.

"There's still an hour," I say.

It is unlikely that the tramp would have spoken this, so the tag is not necessary in that sense, but it provides the symmetry of 'you said/I said' to point up the rejoinder that deliberately ignores the sub-text of the other speaker as to the reason for moving: there is underlying tension here.

We're starting over: going on a second honeymoon – to Torquay.

This suggests problems in the past but the inner voice of the narrator is optimistic, and gives vital plot information – where they are going and why.

"You're always so obtuse." I feel your spittle spatter my face.

The choice of '*obtuse*', while apt anyway, was made especially for its spittle-delivering qualities. The use of '*always*', like 'never', is argumentative and again indicates a history of conflict. The spittle comment is not needed as a speech tag, but it up-grades the speaker's anger and paints a visual picture of the scene.

You get the Brighton train.

The narrator's inner dialogue describes an important action in the plot, and the one word *"Brighton"* tells us there will be no second honeymoon (the significance of *"Torquay"* earlier).

In both extracts, questions in the dialogue are not answered directly, people do often respond at a tangent, but it can be especially useful to show not only antagonism, but that a character is hiding something, lying, or attempting to mislead in some way – all potential ways to add tension and develop or progress a plot through dialogue.

When I'm reading, 'overhearing' dialogue brings me into the scene and portrays a great deal in a neat, concise way, but unless it tells me about the characters or leads me into the next bit of the story plot, it has no purpose and is an annoying diversion.

~~~

Hands Up for Character

Our inner chorus of 'voices' express themselves through our whole body – sometimes against our wishes – and they give effective signals, even when we can't be seen: if you smile on the telephone it can be 'heard' in your voice. Rather than skim superficially over the whole range of body language, I have focused in detail on one part of our anatomy – hands – because I think that makes it easier to transfer this kind of thinking, to the eyes, for example, or to posture.

~~~

Hands that clasp, caress, entwine; gnarled as tree roots or as soft as down – how can we use them to draw characters?

Only we humans have the rotating and opposable thumb that allows us to make tools and weapons with such potential for creativity and devastation – and to hold a pen. More significantly, our hands are garrulous communicators; gestures undoubtedly played a role in the evolution of language. Try talking while sitting on your hands (appropriately, a metaphor for inaction).

They are eyes to the blind and tongues between the deaf or mute, and our hands can send unintentional messages our faces have learned to conceal – a 'handy' way for writers to show inner conflict or deceit, but I am jumping ahead.

Since our prehistoric ancestors stencilled their hands onto cave walls, hands have come to stand for the whole person. Once anatomically accurate drawings were made, in the fifteenth century – by Albrecht Durer and Leonardo da Vinci for example – a hand could also represented individual personality. And in 1882, a French anthropologist and police officer, Alphonse Bertillon, used detailed measurements of hands as a means of identifying criminals, later developed into fingerprinting – providing signatures for the non-literate and familiar to any modern traveller.

In art, drama, dance, music and literature, hands are a means of revealing story, expressing feelings and transmitting information. But meanings vary with time and place. It is a tradition that in ancient Rome, 'thumbs down' signalled death for a gladiator: in modern Greece, 'thumbs up' bears the same insult as 'two fingers'. All cultures have myths and taboos of one form or another relating to hands, most commonly to do with left and right and rules for what you can or cannot do with each.

In the Philippines, a father blesses his son by touching his forehead. Christians receive benediction by the laying on of hands; Muslim's wash their hands in symbolic cleansing of the soul before praying, and in parts of Papua New Guinea, mourners show grief at the death of a close relative (and thereby declaim their innocence in the cause of death), by cutting off the top joints of their fingers.

Hands – *manus* in Latin – have a firm grip on the English language, giving us 'mandate', 'manoeuvre', 'manifest', 'manage', and 'handsome' (originally meaning 'dexterous' and thus also 'right-handed'.) Our hands are into everything: in a hand-shake, a handkerchief, or a finger of gin – and that is before we start on palmistry and telling the future. One could write several volumes about hands; someone probably has.

Shakespeare used hands to signify inner states of mind, most notably using Lady Macbeth's 'hand-washing' while sleepwalking as a way to show her feelings of guilt – the 'blood on her hands' after Duncan's murder – and her famous lines in Act V, Scene 1 of *Macbeth*: *"Here's the smell of the blood still: all the perfumes of Arabia will not sweeten this little hand."*

John Steinbeck also used hands as symbols. Lennie's hands in *Of Mice and Men* are referred to as 'paws' because, in his impaired mental state, he could not control the instinctive violence they could inflict, yet those same hands could tenderly fondle the soft fur of a rabbit – a deceptively simple way of portraying the complexity and conflict within Lennie's character. But Steinbeck goes further, using detailed physical descriptions of hands to sketch individual personality: George's hands are neat and deft; Curly's wife paints her nails with red varnish, and so on for all the main characters.

And I wonder: did the tender but work-rough hands of Oliver Mellors – Lady Chatterley's lover – snag the fine fabrics of his upper-class paramour?

So how can we 'get a handle' on all of this to enrich the way our characters show themselves in our stories? I'm sure you have thought of many already, but here are a few random suggestions, some of which could have different meanings depending on story context (as with most body language).

Physical description of hands can:

Indicate states and status – skin texture (coarse / smooth / lined / scaly) may show age; social status and/or occupation such as physical labour (and may contrast with a character's inner desires or abilities – an interesting conflict); habitual activities such as gardening, lifestyles (by choice or coercion), and health.

Colour of hands can show ethnicity indirectly (there is no melanin in the palm of the hand); brown spots show aging; blueness around the nail bed in infants can signal imminent death; suntanned/pale/manicured/paint-spattered hands, painted or bitten nails, all tell different stories. Also, hennaed, tattooed, bejewelled and scarred hands can hint at status or class in various cultures and sub-cultures.

Conditions that are reversible or progressive could be used to define changes in time or situation (and provide a potential progression or turn in the plot).

Structure (swollen joints / veins / slender or stubby fingers / missing digits) may show age; health; foreshadow aptitudes; feature in a character's self-image or past, and even identify them after death.

An example from a story we have already read: *Modus Operandi*, in which hands indicate character but also foreshadow the plot with a hint of menace. *"A big man, too – he had to duck under doorways. His hands were as wide as dinner plates. To see those long fleshy fingers you'd realize the strength that was in them."*

Signal emotional states – surface (moist / dry / warm / cold) singly, or in various combinations and situations may show fear, excitement, detachment, calmness, openness, eagerness, and health or sickness, as well as changes in these emotions. Where hands are placed, and their posture (gripping / relaxed / flaccid / flexed / held together or apart), can characterize similar emotions and help to reveal inner states.

Movement of hands can:

Demonstrate relationships – who touches whom, how, where, and how does the recipient and any observer react; open palms (invitation / innocence / acceptance); clenched hands (denial / anger / frustration / tension / withdrawal); how a character's hands move (hidden or overt gestures) when different people are addressing them or approach them; use of sign-language may signal deafness, or conspiracy in silence.

Show emotion – by wringing / clenching/ rubbing of hands; waving; a whole gamut of gestures from beckoning to 'giving the finger'; fidgeting; fumbling; twitching; chewing/sucking nails and fingers; picking at the quick of the nails; tremor (excitement / fear / or sickness – Parkinson's disease, delirium tremens), or by complete stillness. And have you ever watched a woman gently touch a beautiful object she cannot afford to buy? It is a specific kind of hand movement – a caress without possession, or hope.

Sudden change in habitual movement or immobility of the hands can be particularly potent in showing a character's reactions. I knew when my mother was especially excited about something because she would shake her hands while telling me about it. An aunt was a worrier: she constantly scraped the sides of her thumb nails with her finger nails – the tips of her thumbs were permanently red and swollen.

Hand movements can show skill, too: the discerning shopper squeezing fruit; the seamstress assessing fabric between finger and thumb, and the disarming laxity with which a virtuoso cellist appears to hold the frog of her bow.

Another possibility is demonstrating inner conflict/confusion or deceit – some have already been mentioned, but if you wanted to emphasize it, you could do so through dissonance between what the hands are indicating and what the eyes, face and/or dialogue say, or your character might cross her fingers behind her back when she lies.

Both description and movement of hands can also portray setting and environment and a character's response to them:

For example, the effects on exposed hands of hot or cold climates or working conditions; exploratory feeling with the hands may signal blindness, but also ambient darkness; different cultural methods of greeting with the hands can depict period and place: hand kissing / handshaking / 'high-five' / backslapping, or palms pressed together as in Thailand – the height of the hands indicates relative status of the one being greeted.

~~~

Stories:

Red Like My Shoes

"Once upon a time, there was a beautiful princess."

"And she had long, golden hair, didn't she, Daddy?"

"Yes, Suzy, she did." They know every detail, Suzy and Amy; it's their favourite bedtime story. Mine too.

"Like my hair. It's not very long yet, but it's growing."

"More story, Daddy." Amy, the three-and-a-half-year-old, doesn't like interruptions to the telling, unlike Suzy who loves to put in the finer points, new ones each time. She's just started school and become very wise; Amy sometimes feels a little oppressed by her own lack of status – only at play group.

"Every day, the princess put on a lovely satin dress of the brightest ..."

"Blue," says Suzy. It was "Red-like-my-shoes," last night.

"All right, the brightest blue, and went into her garden to feed the two white doves that were her special friends. She would spend all day with her doves among the flowers, and the honey-bees, and the tiny fluttery birds that sang and danced around them. Then one day, the princess plucked a rose from her favourite bush ..."

"A pink rose, Daddy."

Colours fascinate Suzy, just like her mother, perhaps one day she will be an artist, too. She draws well. The kitchen walls are covered in her daily offerings, we'll need to expand into the living room soon. Amy is more into music and dancing. They use music a lot in her pre-school group. Sometimes they ask me to play the guitar there. I give them short classical pieces and I'm astonished by their wide-eyed enchantment.

"Go non, Daddy." Amy is drowsy already.

"But the stem of the rose had a sharp thorn that pricked her finger, and she fell into a deep swoon. Nobody could wake her: not the honey-bees, not the birds, not the little white doves, not even the gardener who looked after all the flowers."

"And the magician comes," Suzy whispers. Sometimes it's a wizard. Once it was a gnome – I think that was inspired by a project she did at school that day.

"Yes, and the magician said, 'There is only one thing to do. I must take her to the grand palace beyond the sun.' So they laid the princess on a palanquin studded with jewels, and mounted it on a magnificent white horse with gleaming silver harness, and they rode away beyond the clouds, beyond the sky, beyond the sun."

Amy is asleep. Suzy is struggling to keep her eyes half open.

"Daddy?"

"Yes, darling?"

"The sunbeams ..."

"Of course. Well, the princess was so sad to leave her special friends, she sent sunbeams down for the two little doves because she loved them very much" – and the gardener, too. "Time to sleep now, Poppet."

"Ni-nigh, Daddy."

"Night-night, darling." I kiss them and leave the door ajar; they like some light from the landing.

Fairy tales. But how else could we bear to share our grief?

~~~

Story Analysis:

Structured around a single scene, the story of how this little family faces its terrible loss is played out through the telling of a fairy tale, and is told almost entirely in spoken dialogue with only brief internal thoughts from the narrator. The tale he tells contains the plot information we need in order to understand, at the end, what lies behind a seemingly routine bedtime story.

A writing friend told me she had to work quite hard to grasp the meaning of that last line, but that gave the message – the healing power of story – greater force for her. As a reader, I like to be involved in doing some of the working out for myself; as a writer, achieving balance between opacity and transparency is difficult. How hard or easy you found the story depends, I think, on the chemistry between your voice and mine.

The intention in telling the story through dialogue was to differentiate the three characters while revealing inner voices that would suggest how they each cope with their tragic situation. I will explain what I was attempting to show with each one.

Suzy, old enough to speak in full sentences but with the phrasing of a five-year old, identifies herself with the Princess – her desire for long hair, her red shoes – making the story her own by interrupting Daddy to put in her choice of colours. She is aware that the story has special significance. In some deeper level of her mind she recognizes the Princess as her mother, and in the same way, she understands who the two little doves are. The repetition of the fairy tale with its loving symbolism of sunbeams, reassures her with its continuity – she prompts Daddy, fighting sleep to ensure he misses nothing out.

Amy is only three-and-a-half-years old; she speaks seldom and in fragments. She, too, feels the story has special significance and prefers it without interruptions, urging Daddy to continue. She finds reassurance in the fairy tale's frequent retelling, although she is too young to grasp the deeper meaning; lulled by familiar words, she falls asleep before the end.

Daddy expresses three voices, which we can envisage as part of his inner chorus. Unspoken dialogue – his thoughts – show the responsible adult carrying a new burden of single parenthood, considering the differing natures and needs of his two daughters, and playing a wider role in their lives by his participation in the preschool. Through the simple, repetitive language of his storyteller voice, he seeks to explain to the children what has happened to their mother, and to comfort them with the assurance of her continuing love. In a third, brief and deeper inner voice – *"and the gardener, too"* –

he identifies himself with the fairy tale, recognizing it sustains him, also.

And the 'writer's voice'? The hardest part to explain because we are not privy to our whole mind, but as far as I am aware, there is nothing in the story that relates directly to my own experience. It must have emerged from a deep place – *"when no one is listening"* – because it came to me, almost complete, while I was driving. That occurs rarely and I can't recall what was happening in my life at the time – nothing particularly dramatic or I would have remembered – but the underlying theme and tone reflect my own values. Although the story was not planned and structured in any deliberate way, it was edited and tweaked, especially the language; analysis came later.

[*Red Like My Shoes* was twice shortlisted in Flash500 competitions.]

~~~

Spinning on Two Wheels

Mashed up pumpkin was down my Teeshirt, on the carpet, even on the wall. "I'll leave you two to sort it out, Jason." Mum laughed as she went off to work. I guess she remembers how it used to be.

I'd only been back from the spinal unit a few days – lots of new stuff to handle and I couldn't cut it. When you're dead from the waist down your guts don't work properly; you plan 'bowel days' and dose up the day before. It had worked. I was expected to be pleased. "I couldn't do anything right before, now I get six bloody gold stars for shitting on time." I was yelling like a rousie, enjoying the power of my voice bouncing off the ceiling. She winced and bit her lip. I wanted to hurt her. I hated myself for that. She was my mum for Christ's sake. She got up nights to turn me so I wouldn't get pressure sores – like some decrepit old geezer – and then did everything else for me during the day. Why didn't she shout back? She used to give a good enough tongue-lashing before the accident.

I don't think Mum knew quite what to do with me. No problem with the practical side; she'd given up her part-time job at the old people's home to be my carer, but where was the tough hug "get-that-mess-out-of-here" Mum? She would've shifted a mountain if it got in your way but she didn't take any lip and you wouldn't want a passing clip from those powerful hands. Now, it was like putting my foot on the brake and finding no resistance: I hit the wall too often. I hated her for being like that, doing what she had to do. I hated myself. I had plenty of hate to go round, and to spare.

I broke off with my girlfriend – well, fiancé – we were supposed to get hitched in October. I knew Trace still came round to see Mum. I heard their low voices nattering in the kitchen. I didn't care. I didn't want to see her. What was the point?

Dad was the only one who didn't get my shit. He's a builder, runs a few steers on the property, too. In the house he's a calm presence; big – fills the doorway but all muscle – and quiet. He never wastes words. Does what's needed – lifting, pushing, fixing, with no more than, "OK, son?" He's like a roof truss, Dad. Stops the whole shambles falling in. I know a bit about roof trusses – I'd just got my chippy's certificate before hell came knocking.

I wonder no one ever said: "It's your own bloody fault, Jason." because in a way it was, but knowing that didn't help. The irony is it was going to be my last stint on the speedway. Mum hated me driving at meets and usually had a go at me beforehand. Trace never said much but didn't go with me. Anyway, I'd decided to give it away. It's not cheap, and we were saving for a deposit. Trace was working harder at it than I was and that didn't seem right. But I was determined to have a final race to remember and I'd got my eager mitts on a super production – a WRX Subaru – the sideways, on-boost cornering of that car is really something else. The track was dry, hard, and fast and I still don't know how we got into a three car pile-up. Talk about carnage. The other two lucky buggers walked away. They said it was a freak accident. Yeah, freak is what I felt like.

They let me leave the spinal unit earlier than usual because I wasn't responding, co-operating or whatever. There were people there worse off, it's not that I thought I was the only one with a problem – I'm not that much of a dick-head. They tried to give me counselling but pain shared is pain doubled as far as I can see. I was glad to be home, but I was a real mess for a while, despite all the drugs – post trauma something or other they said. Dad had already made alterations in the house – widened doorways, put in ramps, grip bars – a wheelchair changes your whole environment.

But things improved once I started rehab. The trainer was Bennie – a real hard case. He'd been a rugby coach and took no shit from anyone. His favourite saying was: "Get to know your body, if anything moves, use it, be it only two fingers."

According to the doc it could have been worse. "You've sustained a C7 injury, a crushed vertebra," he said, "It's causing compression on the spinal cord but it's not severed – that's something." In plain language, I couldn't move my legs: no one was sticking their necks out to say whether I ever would. Bennie worked on strengthening my upper body and trying to get back some confidence. It was proving a hard slog, but as the weeks went by I felt my body, at least, was beginning to get somewhere.

Then one day Trace walked into the living room. I knew it was her because I'd seen her car turning into the drive. I was sitting in my wheelchair watching a video and didn't turn around.

"What do you want, Trace?" I hadn't yet made much progress as a reasonable human being – still rejecting everything to do with my old life though I hadn't found a new one. Being Trace, she rode out my welcome and I can't remember what was said at first – not a lot. I'd destroyed what we had; made us almost strangers. We'd been going out since high school; went everywhere together and shared a wacky sense of humour. We even looked alike: tall and big-boned, the same dark, curly hair out of control most of the time. There'd never been anyone else. She was the best. But I felt like dead meat then; it changed everything. Then she started on about the wedding. The RSA hall had been booked a while back – you had to do that, it was a popular venue.

I still didn't look up from the screen, "Well, you can bloody cancel it."

"I can cancel the wedding, Jason, no problem, but I'm not cancelling the baby."

I spun the chair round and looked at her. Jesus Christ. I couldn't even stand and she was throwing a kid at me. I hadn't seen her for months; I hadn't known and I couldn't take it.

"Mine, is it?"

Without a word, Trace lunged forward and slapped my face. I must have just stared at her, because after a while she said, "I'll leave you to think it through, Jason." and let herself out through the range slider. I watched her get into her old Colt and drive off. She must have come straight from work; she was still wearing her blue jacket from the pharmacy.

Bloody terrible thing to say. I could have cut out my tongue. I hadn't meant it. I was just kicking out – yeah, right.

Truth is, that would have been the best news going before I became such a useless pillock.

I was so pathetic during rehab that afternoon Bennie knew something was up.

"What's the matter with you, Jason, you've not got both oars in the water, mate?" I spilled out the whole story. He looked at me hard for a while, nodded and said, "Right, grab the bar, Jason, lift your arse out of that chair, you've got a big game coming up."

The following day I saw Trace parking in the yard – Mum went out to feed the chooks. Before she was hardly through the door, I was spinning my wheels towards her, "Jeez, Trace, look I'm sorry, I didn't mean–"

"I know that J, that's why I slapped you – to wake up the real Jason, and I'm not sorry." She laughed; so did I. I'd almost forgotten how. I asked her about the baby. I was still getting my head around that – our own kid. "Two more months…we'll work it out together, Jason."

It was a bit scary, wondering how we'd manage everything, but I felt like I'd won the first division prize. Those two months I didn't see much of Trace – working in the gym like my life depended on it. I was aiming to start a furniture-making course at the rehab centre.

That feels like yonks ago, and now I've got young Tobi on my knees, trying to shovel mushy food into his mouth. He spits it out and throws it around – thinks it's all a game. He's a lively little sprog – my son.

I've got a job, but I still train with Bennie: nobody's promising I can chuck the chair one day, but as Bennie says, "Cut out the dags first, mate."

We haven't done the wedding thing yet. I want to stand beside Trace for that.

~~~

Story Analysis:

The whole story is told through the inner recollections of one character acting as 'first person' narrator, including his memory of brief dialogue spoken by four other characters. Each piece of dialogue plays a specific role.

The mother's words at the beginning provide the narrator's name and gender, and indicate the presence of another, unidentified person. The doctor's diagnosis of Jason's injury establishes a key plot element. Bennie reveals more about the challenges involved in Jason's rehabilitation and marks turning points in his progress, and Trace's lines move the plot to a new level and direction: the announcement of her pregnancy; her understanding of Jason and intention to stand by him, and the fact that the baby is due in two months – urgency that spurs Jason's efforts.

Jason's 'character voice' during the early part of the story is that of a young man traumatized into a state of self pity and hatred of everyone, including himself. He has occasional insights: correcting himself saying "*girlfriend*" when she is his "*fiancée*" – no longer denying the more serious loss of an imminent bride – and when acknowledging that his body, but not his attitude, had made some improvement.

His inability to cope comes to a climax in his response to news of the baby: "*Mine, is it?*" Up to that point, no one had challenged his behaviour, acting as if he was not responsible and could not be expected to alter it. Trace's slap treats him as the old, pre-injury Jason, making him rethink his situation. He reconnects with a deeper self that wants to create a future with Trace.

After this crisis, the tone of inner dialogue changes to optimism as Jason prepares for fatherhood by undertaking training and finding a job so he can support his new family. Delighting in his son, he seems to have come to terms with his condition, but the ending is ambiguous: he has yet to face the fact that he may never be able to stand beside Trace.

Language, especially the choice of metaphors and phrasing, provided the key not only to characterization, but to tracing the arc of the story as Jason's physical and mental ability to cope increased and his 'voice' changed.

At the time I wrote this story, I was giving rehabilitation massage to a client who had sustained more severe spinal injuries than Jason – a much older man at a different stage of life – but that situation provided more than a story idea and technical knowledge about dealing with disability on a day to day basis. I was aware of my own inner conflict between sympathy (which can diminish its recipient) and the role of a therapist expected to offer a degree of challenge to a patient, albeit with compassion. Empathy was more value than sympathy – to both of us.

The process of working through this – almost like absorbing a new culture, developing an additional voice– generated the story and the need to write it. The voice of young Jason was shaped from observation and reading, especially on speedways, but also from inner doubts of my own capacity to cope with severe disability.

[*Spinning on Two Wheels* is set in New Zealand, accounting for the words 'rousie', 'RSA', 'dags' and other local details. A longer version, with some cultural reference edited, was selected for a shortlist of twelve by the 2010 H. E. Bates Short Story Competition and published in their anthology.]

~~~

6: Critiquing and Editing

"To avoid criticism, say nothing, do nothing, be nothing."
Anon.

I remember vividly the first time I received group feedback on something I'd written. My short story being dissected on the table included an act of revenge by one of the characters. Although it was a subplot in the main theme, some people saw my character as spiteful and unsympathetic; it stopped them seeing beyond that to appreciate the rest of the story. With a brave smile, I covered my bristles with: "Thank you for pointing that out."

At home, my first thought was: *They misread the story, didn't understand it.* While I waited for the kettle to boil for a soothing cup of tea, I had a second thought: *They picked up on that because their interests are different to mine* – acceptable, but disappointing because it was important for the story that the character be seen as sympathetic. As the teabag dangled, dripping over the mug, a third thought emerged from somewhere deeper: *But they got that idea from the words you wrote on the page.*

We don't always say what we think we say. If I wanted the storyline to be unambiguous I would have to do some editing: strengthen the character's good points; make the revenge appear more justifiable, or change some plot details.

None of us likes to be criticized – to have faults exposed, receive censure – so it is a relief that we can use a fancy French word, 'critique', because it relates specifically to creative works and has a subtly different meaning: to analyse. To analyse *critically*, yes, but that includes reasons, explanations and the 'good' as well as the 'bad'.

I learned an important lesson at that first workshop: to give myself time to convert a reaction into a considered response. Not all comments are of equal value – we can critique the critique. Effective critics avoid judging from the basis of their own style or genre preferences. It is not helpful to criticize the chef's lamb curry because you don't like the flavour of turmeric – and anyway, you're a vegetarian. An important point for readers and reviewers to remember.

Nor do suggestions necessarily lead to changing what has been written – sometimes feedback is contradictory – but all comments are worth thinking about as clues to how our words are received and interpreted. The least helpful are those that begin: "*What you ought to do is change the gender of your protagonist and have them living in a squat...*" Essential though it is to know what 'doesn't work' for others, critiquing is not editing: that is a different process in which specific changes to any story element may be suggested, and it requires professional training and experience.

An understanding of critiquing, and even editing, is useful to readers whether or not they also write. Who reads a book or story and has no opinion on it? Knowing what to look out for and how to express it, not only increases reading pleasure and impresses dinner guests, it adds value to the communal experience of a reading group. When members agree on basic criteria to consider while assessing what they read, discussion becomes focused and deeper, insights more enlightening; less time is frittered away talking about the pizza someone ate last night and what it cost to take their dog to the vet.

If you have friends who write – and most reading groups contain writers, even if they are still in the closet – they might ask you to read a story and say what you think about it. The reactions of as many readers as possible is valuable to a writer – we don't only write for each other, although at times you'd be forgiven for thinking so. And having come this far inside stories, you may have an urge to write yourself – a few reviews perhaps? Why not?

There is an art in giving feedback: begin and end on a positive note; focus on the writing, not the person; explain reasons for your view, and ban words like 'ought' and 'should'. Mutual feedback between fellow scribblers is so important I have included an article in this chapter suggesting a method for critiquing without turning friends into enemies. It's a useful framework for reading groups, too.

Writers need to hear views that are as unbiased as possible: family and loved ones are notorious for boosting our egos rather than our self-knowledge. That is not always the case, though, as Chekhov's rueful comment in a letter to a friend reveals: *"People close to me have always disparaged my writing and have never ceased to give me well-meaning advice not to abandon a proper profession for scribbling."* Counsel that still resonates only too loudly.

Chekhov's own advice to his elder brother Sasha, a writer and journalist, is unsparing: *"Boot out your depressed civil servants! Surely you've picked up by now that this subject is long out of date and has become a big yawn?...don't let anyone get their hands on your stories to abridge or rewrite them...do your own rewriting...rewrite five times, prune constantly...You're a good writer, you could earn twice as much as you do and yet you're living off wild honey and locusts...all because of the crossed wires you have in your noddle."*

When we receive comments from someone whose opinion we especially value, it can influence our whole approach.

Chekhov feels a huge lift to his morale when he receives feedback on one of his own stories from Alexey Suvorin – writer and owner of a powerful publishing empire – and responds with gratitude: *"I have been writing for six years, but you are the first person who has gone to the trouble of making suggestions and explaining the reasons for them."*

It created his first *"impulse towards self-criticism...but I still lacked any faith in my ability to write anything of real literary worth."*

A few weeks later, an encouraging letter from an eminent writer and friend of Dostoyevsky, Dmitry Grigorovich, initiated a turning point in Chekhov's writing career. Grigorovich assures him that he has talent, but he must take it more seriously, working harder at each story. Chekhov replies: *"Until now I have approached my writing in a most frivolous, irresponsible and meaningless way. I cannot recall a single story on which I spent more than a day...I've been writing my stories like reporters churn out pieces about fires: mechanically, half-asleep, caring as little for the reader as for myself...I do intend to stop writing against short deadlines"*

Like many writers, then and now, Chekhov had family responsibilities and needed to earn a living at a day job – he was a poorly-paid doctor – balancing, in the limited time available, the financial benefits of dashing off stories he could sell to a magazine with the desire to develop his writing skills.

Most of what I understand about my writing came from critiques that made me examine my work more closely from a reader's point of view. A good professional critique service (which is generally cheaper when attached to a competition) will give feedback on each story element – theme, structure, character, plot and dialogue – showing where you need to expend most effort. And it raises two key questions: For whom am I writing? – and, What is a story?

Two equally experienced authors and writing teachers commented on the story *Veil of Innocence* (included in this chapter). The first wrote: "*This is not a complete story.*" The second described it as: "*A kind of magic.*" Their views are not incompatible: the former was critiquing the piece as an entry to a competition; the latter, simply responding as a reader. Competition stories are not all the same – far from it – but each competition and individual judge applies certain criteria as the basis for assessment in a similar way to a publishing house. The answer to: What is a story? – depends considerably on the eye of the reader and is closely related to the question: For whom am I writing?

For all his years of practice and scholarship, H. E. Bates concluded that, because of its "*infinite flexibility…the short story has never been adequately defined.*" And he offers no finite answer of his own. Bates compared Chekhov (after he took his writing more seriously), with Maupassant – both equally passionate short story writers and popular in their own time – discovering a major difference in their attitudes towards, and relationships with, their readers.

Maupassant is more direct: he fills in the details, gives his stories clear conclusions, requiring less participation by the reader. Chekhov takes it for granted that his audience will fill out the picture for themselves: actions may be only hinted at, and much of 'what happens' takes place after the story is over – in the reader's mind. We can read both and make our own choices; definitions are less relevant in the context of simple reader enjoyment. And tastes change: both may seem slow and dated to a modern reader accustomed to a fast-paced life and hi-tech media – it is themes, truths, not forms, that are time-less.

Both authors wrote for a range of publications with different editorial requirements, and wrote other stories for their collections, targeting their work in each case to appropriate audiences.

I've learned to gain the most benefit from feedback by thicken-ing my skin, not my ears – listening carefully to everything – but remembering who I am and why I write. That has to be clear before I can edit and give a positive answer to the question: Is this story ready to fulfil its purpose?

Self-editing is like weeding the garden: you never seem to reach the end of the job. Some writers hate it, others love it. A different mind-set is involved than when writing; I find it helps to go to a dif-ferent place (in my case a tree house), and to read from a printout – for some reason it seems easier to pick out problems from the page than the screen. Everyone has their own pet methods of editing; I make several 'passes' looking for different things – my brain can't cope with noticing everything at once.

I read straight through to get a sense of story while looking for plot holes or things that don't follow logically, and to check if the end-ing is a natural consequence of what went before. A second pass looks to see if theme is reflected effectively through the story and the lan-guage. Another concentrates on characters and where they might be strengthened.

More slowly, I examine each sentence, cutting what isn't essen-tial – especially when working to a tight word count – checking each word for precision, allowing some leeway to include one that 'sounds' better in rhythm or tone. Finally I check for typos and punctuation, the latter becoming a form of torture by indecision. Then I read it aloud, listening for any of the above problems.

And that is only the first edit. I find stories need time to mature (although, in reality, it is my perception that sharpens), so they rest – somewhere among the debris on my desk – until I repeat the process days, or even weeks, later. After that, minor tweaking can recur over several months. I have been criticized as a procrastinator. In retaliation, I wrote a piece in praise of procrastination – included as the second article here so that you may use it in your own defence.

~~~

Articles:

How to Critique and Still Stay Friends

Listening to honest comments from fellow scribblers is one of the most effective ways of improving our writing, but how do we prevent it damaging a friendship?

Accepting a critique doesn't mean slavishly changing our story to follow others' suggestions; they are only opinions, and anyway, if we invite comments from several people, their perceptions may vary.

But it does give us a reader's perspective and it can raise issues that we are too involved in the work to identify for ourselves: a contradiction in the plot, a character that seems vivid to us but no one else finds believable, or the deviously hidden twist at the end...that they guessed after the second paragraph.

Some professional critique services are excellent, but for short stories they are a luxury few of us can afford very often. Most on-line writing groups provide free mutual feedback, but not everyone feels comfortable receiving this in an open forum. And while we may need that biased praise from family to keep us slogging on, it's not going to sharpen our prose or strengthen our story structure. Writing buddies giving mutual feedback is the obvious answer. The problem is: however constructive the criticism, and however philosophically we try to respond, it still hurts to have our creations picked over and found wanting. It can strain a relationship.

When our small Scribblers group started to bring first drafts of short stories for critique, we found some common criteria for assessing and commenting on each other's work – benchmarks we could refer to. They help us focus on priorities and avoid getting bogged in details. More important perhaps, they are a neutral presence, an impersonal framework. They provide a dialect for 'talking story' rather than 'talking personal'. And for all these reasons, they form a useful structure for reader's groups, too.

The criteria we use are from the Writer's Village competition website http://www.writers-village.org John Yeoman generously agreed to my reproducing them here. He uses these guidelines to judge entries for Writers Village short story competitions, based on a total potential score of 45 points for each story. (Most competitions use something similar). We don't use the scoring in our Scribblers group, but we find the following criteria, with John Yeoman's notes, extremely helpful:

Does the story emotionally engage the reader?

A maximum of ten points go to the stories which engage me emotionally throughout. I read many entries that are impressively clever. They dance with ingenuity, wit or wordplay. But they are cerebral exercises, not stories. That said, a truly witty story may win high points. Laughter is an emotion too!

Is it original?

I then award up to ten points for a story's originality. True, there are just 36 story plots or themes, according to Georges Polti (1916), but there's always room for a new twist on Cinderella, Bluebeard's cupboard or Romeo and Juliet. Point is, the twist has to be fresh.

Is the first paragraph imbued with power?

The quality of the first paragraph gains a further maximum of eight points. Does it compel me to read on? I am seriously under-whelmed by shock openings along the lines of 'I pulled the trigger. The punk fell dead'. Yawn! What gains my vote instead is the intrigue or enchantment of the opening lines.

Does the story have a sense of form?

Another eight points in total are allocated to the story's sense of form. It has to show a coherent progression, a plot structure involving conflict between characters (or entities represented as characters) and a satisfying conclusion.

Many a fine story lacks 'closure', of course. It may leave the reader with untidy loose ends or an unresolved mystery. It might even appear, at first glance, to be a collection of vivid but disjointed impressions (Joyce's Ulysses comes to mind.)

But the story still has to be rigorous in its construction. I have to feel: nothing could usefully have been added to it or cut. It's a 'whole'.

Is the language well handled?

I then allot up to six points for the originality or deft use of language. A story does not need to dance with spry metaphors or turn somersaults in its syntax. Indeed, an outlandish tale often gains great emphasis by being told in the most prosaic language. But clichés, clumsiness and lazy expressions are a no, no.

Is the grammar, punctuation and presentation professional?

A final three points are given for the professionalism of the presentation. I have no problems with the odd misspelling or typing error. (I make enough of them myself :)) But I do shudder at the systematic misuse of apostrophes!

~~~

I use John's list for self-critique of my own stories as well as in our writing group. A reading group could use these as a starting point to develop its own criteria for a deeper appreciation of any short story or novel, or to provide an outline for constructing reviews.

~~~

In Praise of Procrastination

Impatience, not procrastination, limits our stories.

When I started writing short stories, especially flash fiction, I would spend a week drafting a story, editing and re-editing it and tearing out my hair because it wasn't 'coming right'. I usually left it for a week or two to cool off before working on it again, giving it a final 'polish' before submitting it to a competition.

At one time I had eight or nine stories competing and a pattern emerged. I could guarantee that within 30 seconds of pressing 'send', inspiration would strike as to how to make it a better story. I was being too impatient.

'Procrastination' receives a bad press. Thomas De Quincey clearly considered it the ultimate crime:

"If once a man indulges himself in murder, very soon he comes to think little of robbing; and from robbing he comes next to drinking and Sabbath-breaking, and from that to incivility and procrastination." (*Blackwood's Magazine,* November 1839, "On Murder Considered as One of the Fine Arts").

If procrastination is interpreted as doing absolutely nothing, obviously, that's what it will achieve. That is 'negative procrastination'. But it also means to gain time, to prolong – which makes space for thinking and for two other processes that I am convinced are critical to creative writing: 'story fermentation' and 'incremental editing' or tweaking. This is 'positive procrastination' and I adopted it as a new way of working.

Stories have their own gestation period; they need to mature, ferment, but not simply be left alone in a dark drawer. In reality, it is our relationship with the story that is evolving because our understanding, inspiration and creativity can change almost by the hour, depending on what is happening to us and within us. And this is where incremental editing comes in.

I let print copies of my stories scud around my desk, reading through them at odd moments, maybe deleting a line, changing a single word – probably swopping a weak verb for a stronger one – or changing punctuation. Each small change can open opportunities for a further one next time I look. This is not rewriting; it's tweaking, and it can go on intermittently for months until I can't see anything further to change. Only when that is the case for several days in a row do I press the 'send' button.

This happened with the first of my stories to win a first placing, about nine months after I wrote the initial draft. The changes were small but significant. I think it was Maupassant who once described a morning's work as "good" after his entire output consisted of placing one comma and later removing it.

Tweaking works well for short stories because they take only a few minutes to read. And critically reading a short piece of my own is

a productive way to tune in to a writing session; it can even crack a stubborn fit of negative procrastination.

~~~

Stories:

Through the Eye of the Storm

It wasn't the storm that bothered her but the stirring of memories kept safely cocooned in a drawer of her mind, except on nights like this.

Hard, cold rain hammered the glass. Wind screamed through crevices to escape the relentless force driving it on through the darkness. A typical west coast winter, Marjory tried to blot it out – radio in the background, a good fire in the woodstove, a pile of class reports on the table beside her. Only a few days to the end of term; after thirty years she was teaching the offspring of earlier students. She could retire in a couple of years but she didn't want to do that – there was comfort in continuity and it kept her in touch with what was happening in the community.

On a better night she might have gone to the cinema in town; she sometimes did on a Saturday if they were showing something good – it wasn't far. The string of houses extending from the town along the coast was like a necklace, hers the pendant hanging off the end; in relative isolation before the next scattering of cottages began.

She was near the road, but no lights were visible from her place – certainly not on a filthy night like this.

"Settle down, Jessie, it's only the storm." The dog paced back and forth between her own piece of worn rug by the fire, and the door, whining and flicking reproachful, milky-eyed glances towards her mistress. Her mustering days were over but the old collie's prescience was undimmed.

Her concentration disturbed, Marjorie put another log on the fire. She would finish for the evening and make a pot of tea. She didn't have to leave the heat of the fire: the kitchen was part of her living room. The internal wall had been removed years ago for convenience, and to make it easier to keep warm in the winter. She had changed nothing else. Her hand rested for a moment on the well-polished surface of the table – all her furniture was old fashioned, she lived in a time warp, but that suited her.

Sudden drumming on the roof was almost deafening. Hail. Big stones by the sound of it; the ones hitting the metal chimney added a descant of sharp, tinny pings.

Marjory was plugging in the kettle when a crash from the veranda penetrated the storm's racket. Jessie's simultaneous barking, almost a howl, made her shiver. Damn, that'll be the big blue pot she was planning to put plants in for the spring, must have tipped over in the wind.

Turning on the outside light, she looked through the porch window. Caught in the glare, a crouched figure held shards of broken pot, beside him, a young woman dazzled by the light, stared unseeing at the window. A pitiful sight. Buffeted and pinched with cold, rain making rivulets of their hair.

They looked like stranded tourists. She pulled open the door and shouted above the wind's roar, "Leave that, come inside. Quickly."

Jessie hustled up to the couple, tail swaying. "Get away, Jessie. Lie down."

The man was slight, thin, even in his overcoat. Shy, dark eyes, blinked away the rain still dripping from his head, neat brown hands gesticulated as he stammered an apology.

"Car...in deep drain," he seemed to struggle with fatigue and lack of the right words. "Phone...everything we lose. Walk far in the dark." Looking down to see water from his coat pooling on the floor around him, he took a step back.

Marjory put out her hand. "Never mind that. It'll dry. Take off your wet things. You both look frozen."

The woman, scarcely more than a girl, stood with her arms clutched across her body. Wet hair hung like black curtains around her face, strands sticking to her skin. Silent tears mingled with the rain – from relief, exhaustion, or both. She seemed dazed.

Marjory helped her unbutton the front of her coat, and stopped. For a moment she couldn't breathe. Ebony eyes looked out at her with a dull, unfocused gaze. She caressed a cheek with the tip of her finger, felt the quivering beneath her hand. "Dear God, we must get the child dry and warm."

"His name, Ashane..." the girl appeared to emerge from a trance. Marjory led her to the couch where the young mother began, deftly, to remove the baby's wet clothing, murmuring endearments in a language Marjory did not recognize.

The child was breathing but seemed unnaturally quiet and list-less. The faint blue tinge on the tiny fingernails was a bad sign, but he looked old enough to survive if they could get him warm quickly. She hurried to the end of the passage, choking back a sob. Yanking open the door of the airing cupboard, she tugged out towels, flannelette sheets, a soft wool blanket, rushing back to help dry and wrap the small shivering figure.

As they watched the baby and dried themselves by the fire, Marjory learned who they were. They'd been lodged in Wellington since emigrating from Sri Lanka only a few weeks before. Dilvan had secured an engineering job in the town. He was bringing Kusum and the baby down to look for somewhere to live when their car skidded off the road, tipping over into a storm drain.

Marjory went to make up the bed in the spare room, find arnica for Kusum's bruises, and take pumpkin soup out of the freezer to put in the microwave. Preparing food would keep her busy, Jessie hadn't been fed either. She must do that.

When she returned, Kusum was crooning softly, rocking from side to side as the child fed at her breast. Dilvan sat beside her, holding a blanket around them. Marjory watched the tableau. A band tightened around her chest. She turned away and looked at the plastic container in her hand, wondering for a moment what it was doing there.

Marjory lay on her bed, bone tired and wrung out by emotion but too far from sleep to undress. The baby would be fine. They'd made a nest for him in a drawer of the old chest, placing it on the floor close to their bed. They were young, resilient; a good night's sleep would put them right.

She could no longer restrain the memories that surged through her mind. They lapped over her in a familiar, weary tide.

Granny Findlay's sixtieth birthday – June 23rd 1984 – a Saturday and they had planned to spend the day with her. When the day arrived, Marjory was still recovering from flu, "Stay home in the warm, love," Ian insisted. "I'll take wee Alec to see his gran." Granny Findlay doted on Alec; still adjusting to widowhood, she handed the family business over to Ian and focused her life on her first grandchild.

Thin rain had fallen most of the day while Marjory dutifully dosed herself with *marupa* and rested. But the wind strengthened as daylight faded and had built up to a full storm. Expecting them back any minute, Marjory was half watching the Billy T James show on the television while she kept a meal warm for them in the oven. She barely heard the banging on the door over the din of rain on the roof. The local Bobby stood on the veranda, his bike propped against the wall, his helmet slung over the handlebars.

"Come in by the fire, Dick, you're drenched…"

He stepped inside but stayed by the door, water running off his uniform pooling on the floor. He hesitated, seemed unsure where to begin, but finally his voice came, thick with emotion.

"…heavy timber truck…hail on the road…both…"

She hadn't really heard the words, all she needed to know was written on his face. While she stood in the middle of the room, unmoving, still staring towards the door, Dick had pitched across the room to silence the sudden burst of laughter from the television. He stayed, then, making her drink tea. Granny Findlay had not survived that final loss.

Marjory slid off the bed and listened at her open bedroom door. Silence. The storm had passed. She crept into the small room beside her own, closed the door and switched on the light. She didn't need it – every detail was etched on her mind: the family of fat little ducks stomping across the curtains, the white painted chest of drawers, a mobile of wooden fantails they'd bought on holiday, and the lem-on-washed walls she had stencilled so painstakingly while she grew heavy, waiting her time. She laid her hands on the rail of the empty cot, leaned in to smooth invisible ruckles in the quilt Granny Findlay had made, and felt the deep cavity within her.

Turning to the chest of drawers, she picked up the framed pho-tograph of the three of them – Ian holding Alec up to the camera, a grin of fatherly pride as broad as Golden Bay, her arm around his neck. Replacing the picture with a trembling hand, she slowly slid open the top drawer, methodically lifting out neatly folded baby clothes, lemon, white, blue, until she had a small pile. They were fresh; she kept them laundered. She stood and surveyed the collec-tion.

Replacing everything carefully in the drawer, she pushed it shut and rested her arms on top of the chest. Ashane should be sleeping in here. They can stay until they find a place of their own. She'd talk to them tomorrow.

Picking up the faded photograph, she switched off the light, closed the door, and returned to her bed.

[*Through the Eye of the Storm* was shortlisted in the NZ Writers' College annual short story competition in 2011]

~~~

Story Analysis:

So much inspiration for stories emerges from ordinary living and interaction with others. I discovered that two new friends had both lost children more than twenty years ago. The loss left a permanent imprint on their lives; writing the story was my attempt to understand their experience.

Although I usually find a 'third person' point of view more difficult to write, I used it here because I felt a strange inappropriateness in writing in 'first person' about a tragedy I hadn't had to suffer and come to terms with – I hadn't earned the right. But this may simply be a rationalization. Perhaps I was afraid of something and should have tried harder, challenged myself further – I might have found an entirely different voice. However, I used what we described in chapter 2 as 'close third': the narrator is almost 'invisible', making comments like '*They looked like stranded tourists,*' which 'feel' like Marjory's own thoughts. To have written, 'Marjory thought they looked like stranded tourists' would have taken the reader one step back from her.

I structured the story with the flashback in the middle to show two levels of Marjory's grief: her recollection of the past accident appears to explain her agitation at the beginning as she helps to revive Ashane, but the scene in the nursery reveals a deeper scar that has led her to keep her dead baby's clothes freshly laundered for over twenty years – as fresh as her pain.

To create a contrast within a character made vulnerable by her bereavement, I made Marjory a teacher whose manner in dialogue is direct, even a little bossy. And I used dialogue to reveal news of the fatal accident in the flashback to show Marjory's shock in the fragmented way she heard and remembered Dick's words.

Successive editing – mostly cutting – reduced the original story from 2,000 words to its present 1,615, and I switched the first and second paragraphs to provide more of a hook at the beginning: starting with the weather, though significant, looked too much like, "*It was a dark and stormy night.*" The title journeyed from *The Nest*, to *A Breeze Through a Window* (a line from the ending, later cut), finally arriving as *Through The Eye of the Storm* to reflect Marjory's emotional experience as well as the young couple's ordeal.

I'm still not sure whether the last line should be cut. My intention was symbolic: removing the photograph 'freed' the room for Ashani as she had freed herself, not from loss, but from some of its restriction on her life. But the story is resolved in the line above or even the line before that. When I read like a writer, I want to cut the last sentence. When I think like a reader I want to keep it, to have a small space to wind-down and see the character settle after her moment of realization. What do you think?

I have no professional critique for this story so you might like to do one yourself, using John Yeoman's criteria. It might also be a useful exercise for writing or reading groups learning to develop critiquing skills.

~~~

Veil of Innocence

It's all right to travel alone. I've done it before and I'll be twelve next month.

It's not long since children were sent all over the country with labels round their necks, escaping the Blitz. Our neighbour, Mrs Gladwynn, told me that. I was a baby and stayed with my mother.

Mrs Gladwyne brought me to the station for the Liverpool train – the first part of my journey.

I'm lucky to have a window seat with a table. People stand in corridors. Some sit on battered suitcases. I don't like just sitting. I brought the tray-cloth I'm making for my mother – in cross-stitch, blue and yellow.

An old man next to me is sleeping. His lips make funny wet purring noises when he breathes. Two dark young men opposite, talk to each other in a foreign language. One wears a blue pendant. He smiles, pointing at my embroidery. "What you make?"

They save my seat when I go to the buffet for a drink and a sandwich.

"Where you family? Next carriage?"

"No, my mother is in hospital. I'm going to my auntie and uncle in the Isle of Man – I was born there."

They stare at me as if I've said something rude. I spoke slowly, but perhaps they haven't understood.

"In our country, sister no travel this way. Is no good."

"What is your country?"

"We are of Arabia."

Geography is my favourite subject so I ask lots of questions. They are brothers, but it is the younger one, Malik, who knows some English.

It is late at night when we arrive at Liverpool. The old man wakes with a snort. We all shuffle off the train.

"Where you go now?" Malik asks.

"To the Steam Packet terminal – the ferry leaves at five in the morning. Other passengers will be waiting there." They talk rapidly together, gesticulating wildly. They can't leave me here, Malik says, I must go with them to their cousin. They will take me to the boat in the morning. "You same our sister. We make safe for you."

A broken window in the terraced house is boarded-up, paint peels from the door. The room is bare and smells of old shoes. Rattling at them in their strange tongue, flicking glances at me, their older cousin seems cross.

They sit me in the only chair at one end of the room; they lie on mats at the other, a lighted candle set in a saucer in the middle. It's a hard wooden kitchen chair, but I doze. The short night passes.

In the morning, I'm surprised that Malik boards the ferry, too. A long rough passage makes me seasick; he finds me a bunk, brings me water.

Docked at Douglas, we move with other passengers towards the gangway. "Where you family?"

They're waiting on the quay. I wave at them. "By the barrier, see?"

But Malik is not there.

In my pocket is a small blue stone.

~~~

Story Analysis:

An autobiographical story: the only fictional element is finding the small blue stone (from Malik's pendant) in my pocket – it is there to give tangible form to a sort of grace I received from the experience of that journey which has kept the memory so vivid. Everything else is exactly how I remember it. The full meaning emerged years later when, reminiscing, it occurred to me that Malik had paid for a ferry passage he could ill afford simply to keep a stranger's child safe; a stranger whose perceived neglect was unthinkable in his own culture.

Society has changed so much over the last fifty years. We have lost trust, become fearful; with some justification, certainly, but I feel our lives are depleted as a result. I wanted to remember what we had lost.

But real life doesn't necessarily make 'a story' as McKee describes it: the dramatization of a truth by challenges and outcomes played out and resolved through a plot. We noted earlier that stories provide a clarity and logic rarely found in our own lives. Stories are 'more than' reality. Without a plot, a tale is an anecdote rather than a story and this was the point made in the critique of this piece when it was entered in a competition. "*The child goes on a journey and arrives safely. We get a sense of a different age…but other than that, there isn't any storyline."*

The critique was positive about other elements: *"The writing is good, the characterization of the young men and their dialogue is excellent,"* But the narrator did not come alive in the same way: *"How does she feel in this strange house? What is she thinking? Her lack of reaction distances the reader from her emotions. In fact, throughout the story, not at any time does she display any emotion."*

Rereading the piece, this is certainly true and I realize the story is actually about something else – a deeper personal truth. A traumatic childhood gave me knowledge beyond my years, including the fact that more harm may come from within the home than outside. I was watchful, even fatalistic at that age, but I was curious and I liked people – at least, the ones who passed my child's instant judgment.

You may view the story differently, but it was a thorough and helpful critique that showed me the importance of establishing the purpose of what I write, and for whom. I could rewrite the story, creating plot and structure to enact the theme. But my voice – the one *"that lies beneath all words"* – rebels: the experience is a snippet of my life, part of who I am. One alternative is to use it as memoir – if I ever find the courage to write one. Another is to include it here, to share with you.

My writing group brainstormed the title; a combination of two ideas provided *Veil of Innocence*, describing the child's innocence which the Arabian travellers recognized as clearly as if she'd been wearing the veil, as even very young girls do in some Muslim societies.

~~~

7: Maintaining Momentum

"Go, and catch a falling star." John Donne.

To refocus on some thoughts from earlier chapters: for readers and writers alike, stories seduce us for a few moments into another world, perhaps an alternative identity. Storytelling evokes collaboration, too. We may think a writer creates a story which a reader consumes and that we do both on our own, but neither is strictly true. Each is part of a paradox.

As a reader I might interpret a story in a different way to another reader, but also find meanings that the writer did not intend. Our minds blend what we read with our existing knowledge and experience, weaving it into our own narratives; it becomes part of our inner chorus of voices. A story is not complete until it has been read. Which stories, or more likely, particular scenes and characters, do you remember from years ago, even from your childhood? Why have they stayed with you?

If you reread some of your old favourites, you might see the hero as less sympathetic, or find a different theme in the story because you now bring a more mature comprehension to the reading.

We may not like a tale, or reject what we understand as its underlying premise because it conflicts with the stories already in our minds – our own and other people's narratives – but the way a story touches us can linger for years; whether enjoyed or hated, it can change our lives, or at least, our attitudes to life, which is much the same thing.

The other paradox is that we are never alone when writing any-more than we are when reading. It's not simply that both provide the company of 'characters' – although they can seem a strong presence – but we are social animals: people who influence who we are, sway what and how we write and read. Titles leaning on our bookshelves and lurking in our e-readers reflect what teachers, parents and peers have considered a 'good read'. Others represent the market's definition: the bestseller on which we all feel obliged to form an opinion. And conscious of the audience behind the computer screen, what writer doesn't want to produce a bestseller?

All of these thoughts contain more than passing interest because they open up possibilities for expanding the skills and enjoyment of both writing and reading. They offer ways of maintaining momentum.

Slippered and cosy in our comfort zone, our perspective on life can be limited by these habitual influences. We gain enormous benefit from putting on galoshes and venturing into the rain – splashing through puddles, making mud pies. Connectedness in our world seems askew: a bank draft and a tin of pilchards have far more freedom of movement than people; and ideas – however accessible the internet – are only free if others are listening. In practice, understanding of the 'other' seems the most fettered of all. And yet we connect in some way almost daily.

At least one item you bought this week was made by a Chinese factory hand. When you last spoke to someone in a call centre, she was probably in Bombay – on a fourteen-hour shift in an overcrowded office with no fire escape. Your favourite restaurant is likely cleaned by immigrant workers and your palm oil grown by African labourers. These people are part of our lives, but what do we know of their stories? Increasingly, their voices are out there to be read and appreciated. As readers we can broaden our vision by seeking them out, as writers we can diversify and enrich our own stories by recognizing these other identities.

The African activist and writer, Chenua Achebe, who died 21 May 2013, is better known for his novels, especially his first – *Things Fall Apart* – but he began his writing career with concise, powerful short stories. Not many: he published only one collection, *Girls at War*. He wrote in an essay that it falls to the writer to "*create…a different order of reality from that which is given to him.*" His context was the colonial definition of Africa and African-ness but it poses an interesting challenge.

As readers, and writers, do we have a duty to care? – In the former role, through adding new voices to our book shelves; in the latter by using our skill and the undoubted power of story to give voice to those who are not heard? The choice is plentiful: their number is huge, their situations varied. It is a way of asking ourselves why we write – a significant question because what we write is part of who we are.

In its original plan, this chapter was to include mention of time constraints, breaking through writers' block and other writerly concerns, but I realized that the number of existing articles, books and blog posts on these topics probably exceeds the word count of this book. Besides, putting this collection together has made me recognize that if we have something we need to say, we will find a way to write. And if we really want to appreciate life fully, we will make time to read.

But a few other ideas on momentum for story writing are worth sharing; approaches I've been trying myself lately. The first one is to take a fresh look at your stories and set new goals for them. For example, returning to 'old' stories, editing or rewriting them from where you are now as a person and accumulating what might become a collection – grazing in a tattered ring file of my early scribbles inspired *Inside Stories*. Another possibility is to pick out a story that has development potential – characters that might do far more with their lives, for example – and consider expanding it into a longer story or a novel.

You could keep a journal to develop a habit of observing and writing – a single sentence is better than none – or to make a few notes on what you read. I confess my own weakness here: unless reading specifically for review, I forget to write anything down and often cannot recall the title, or even the author, accurately after a few weeks – I will try harder. Recording experience is one way of engaging, going out to meet the muse.

Another is to change your routine: take a different route to work; visit shops, parks, restaurants that you've never been into; read or write a genre you haven't tried before, or, on a holiday weekend, instead of clogging the roads with your car, get in a bus or train to...anywhere – you will meet new people, expand your experience and enrich your chorus of voices. And don't forget to take your notebook.

Joining a reading or writing group can provide mutual encouragement, enlightenment and feedback – if necessary, start one. And why not create a combined readers' *and* writers' group? – critiquing and discussing your reviews as well as members' own writing? Reviews could be submitted to a local newspaper, or your group could start a blog. For further activities, any chapter in this book could form the basis of a workshop for either group. And then there are writing competitions, a regular indulgence of mine.

I've been lucky in a few contests but winning was not my main motivation. Closing dates offer deadlines that concentrate the mind wonderfully; specified themes can spark ideas (although I prefer open themes); they incite you to exceed your reach and tap inner reserves, and even a brief comment from a judge can spur renewed energy to tweak and polish a story until it shines. To goad you, the first article here details ways to get the most benefit from competitions; the second considers different ways and purposes of reading.

Sometimes, though, we write a story because it has special meaning for us; we love it for its own sake – lack of competition or publication potential does not diminish it. One of the stories in this chapter, *A Man of His Word*, is one such story. And the last piece before I leave you – a brief account of my own writing journey – taught me not to take myself too seriously. Both reading and writing should be fun.

~~~

Articles:

Make Writing Competitions Work for You

You know that sinking feeling just below the diaphragm when the competition entry you groomed to perfection fails to bring home the prize money? Then you read the winning story and secretly think yours is better? You may be right: selection is a subjective process and a different judge might have chosen your story. But these thoughts only rub salt into lacerated pride. A different judge could choose your story if you enter another competition, but there is more to gain from writing competitions than winning. I went through a lot of salt learning that, so I'm sharing it with you.

Go for the feedback:

Choose competitions that offer optional critiques to further develop your talent. You have to pay extra but they can be excellent value, cheaper than regular critiquing services and the feedback is straight from the source. Watch out for the ones that offer only a tick list: they are less helpful. But even a sentence can give you a vital clue to future success; I learned that titles for stories are important through an informal scribble from a judge. Up till then I'd given them little thought.

Go for the anthologies:

Not only big international competitions, many regional or locally based contests publish anthologies of the top 10 or 20 entries as well as the winners. Some pay a small fee for inclusion in the anthology (if you didn't win prize money), others may only give free copies, but it can lead to that first publication. Look for small independent publishers who regularly produce anthologies based on writing contests – these are promising openings to get your nib in the door. Check first that these competitions tell you who is judging; specify prize money and closing dates; and have a reasonable entry fee. Sometimes, 'free competitions' with no details are simply a trawl-net for free copy which the organizers then sell.

If you are part of a writing group, why not suggest the group publishes its own anthology? Everything is now possible with electronic publishing and print-on-demand.

Smile if your story is shortlisted:

It is easier to win or to have an entry shortlisted in local competitions, but be bold, have a go at the big ones. To be shortlisted in a major contest is significant recognition and worth putting in your bio. The judge's final choice is unavoidably subjective but a story that is shortlisted is *capable* of winning. For the really big competitions it's a morale booster to be on the long list. Say your story was in a long list of 40: if there were 900 entries, as a percentage, your story would be in the top ... um ... well, an encouraging result. We should celebrate being shortlisted and long listed, it means we are facing in the right direction and can polish a bit more before sending it off to a different judge. It could win next time.

Grab Attention for the Right Reasons:

Trying to catch the judge's eye with pink paper, even if it is handmade and incorporates African elephant dung, will only attract the attention of those in charge of the waste-paper basket – it will be disqualified. The first thing a reader sees on your entry is the title – that's what needs to be spectacular. It must relate to the content in some way and should be intriguing, perhaps an unexpected or unique combination of words, a metaphor, a question. We should be reading lots of short stories anyway as a source of inspiration, so pay special attention to their titles.

Strive for Originality:

I prefer open-themed competitions, but those with specified themes can be a stimulus to creativity, might even jolt you out of writers' block. Note, though, that a few hundred other competitors are all working to the same theme: enough to send any judge into a vegetative state. To ensure your entry is original, list as least ten ideas around the theme. Ignore those and write four more. Cross these out. Make a large pot of tea; the next idea to emerge is probably the best one to use.

And remember, originality does not mean making your own rules – follow the guidelines and avoid getting your story binned.

A positive approach to competitions is a bit like marathon running: it helps you keep in training, and the challenge of the race brings out that extra sparkle you didn't know you had.

~~~

Reading Between the Lines

Reading used to be considered a dangerous practice. If the 'lower classes' started doing it they might begin questioning the social order, and young girls would get 'ideas'. How right they were to worry.

No doubt you give consideration to *what* you read, though you probably don't give much thought to *how* you read. Why would you? We read all the time for one reason or another – most of us take it for granted. But we had to train our brain to read. We have an in-built, genetic capacity for language, but the writing and reading came much later – we have to learn them.

How we were taught to read can influence the way we respond to different types of writing. As a child I was deeply affected by a teacher's careless remark in a school report that I was 'on a low reading plateau' – imagining myself some kind of insect scratching in debris left by those who had reached the summit. I don't think this term is used anymore.

It wasn't that I was slow to read, but that I read slowly. Words were a form of magic; I loved the sound of them and how they felt in my mouth. When reading to myself, I didn't move my lips to form the words but I pronounced them silently in my head. This now has a respectable name – sub-vocalization – and it reflects the method of teaching to read by breaking up words phonetically.

Apparently, when we read – however we read – minute electrical charges are exchanged between the brain and the larynx; these are stronger in people who read sub-vocally. It is something to do with the evolution of language and the fact that we first learn words orally. This brain-larynx connection is present in some degree however fast we read.

The other main teaching method is sight-reading: recognizing the shapes of whole words and even phrases. Reading this way is faster – sometimes called speed reading – and overwhelmed by homework, I had to learn it at high school. Even that wasn't rapid enough when I reached horrendous university reading lists. I learned to skim – gulping whole paragraphs to find the gist of the text, selecting which, if any, would be read in detail. I still use this system for research and for reading the local newspaper.

Had I finally reached the summit? Not exactly. It turns out that each form of reading has a different effect on our comprehension, imaginative response, and memory; which would explain how education ruined my enjoyment of reading for years. It seems that translating visual material into 'sounds' in our mind – slow or close reading – results in greater flexibility and duration, allowing us more effectively to integrate new material with existing ideas while enhancing emotional engagement and memory. The good news is: we can choose how we read.

Bombarded with texts on our iPhones and screens, swept up in the escalation of modern fast life, a counter insurgency is under way: The Slow Book Movement launched in 2009 by writer, I. Alexander Olchowski.

Creative writing is multi-layered. When we rip through an exciting novel, desperate to know what happens, we risk missing other themes and values the writer may laboriously have woven into the tale, never mind an appreciation of the author's style. This applies even more strongly to a short story.

In the limited space of a short story, words and images often perform several tasks at once. Each word has been thoughtfully chosen; perhaps its sound as well as its precise connotation was selected to suggest atmosphere, setting, or a character trait without adding additional words; it may contain a deeper layer of meaning. As with poetry, sound and rhythm are an integral part of experiencing the wholeness of a short story; a pleasure we miss when we speed read or skim. And their brevity enables us to enjoy this level of reading and rereading without taking up a whole weekend: a mere fifteen minutes can be surprisingly rewarding.

It is no coincidence that writers read their stories aloud while editing.

~~~

Stories:

A Man of His Word

I don't know how long George will be, 'e couldn't say. But he'll be cross if he finds me sittin' here in the cold. I knows what chill and damp can do. Best heave myself out of this chair an' get the heater goin'.

He wouldn't be cross for long, though, George. That time I was really mad at him and used his toothbrush to clean the bathroom taps – 'e laughed like a drain when I told 'im. Trust 'im to see the funny side.

First time I clapped eyes on him 'e was jokin'. I was workin' in the big furniture place in the High Street. My first job. I'd to keep the displays all spick and span. He come in delivering stuff while I was polishin' kitchen appliances. "That kettle work does it?" he asked.

"Yes, 'course it does."

"Well, you plug it in, sweetheart, and I'll nip out for some ginger nuts." Cheeky devil. It weren't his usual route, he was standin' in for a pal, but he must have changed that 'cause he come in every week after that. It weren't long before we was courtin'.

Well, this won't do. Better get some tea on. "Do you want to go out, Bisto, pet? Yer never got a walk today, did yer?" They won't let 'er in the Post Office, so she 'ad to stay here while I was out, "didn't yer, pet? There yer go."

Don't know how we'd be without Bisto. We got 'er from the RSPCA more years ago than I can remember. The name suits 'er. With them short little legs she sticks 'er nose right up in the air and sniffs to see what's goin' on – like them kids in the advert.

I got 'er some nice tidbits from the butcher in the market – 'e always finds 'er summat – scraps of ox heart today. She never gobbles 'er food like some dogs, she's a dainty eater. Gazes at me with them soulful eyes as she chews each mouthful.

There's Bisto scratchin' at the door to get back in. Oh, my bloomin' joints is rusted up summat shockin' today – nights are gettin' cold. That always sets 'em off. "You weren't long, pet, bit parky out, is it?" I suppose she feels the chill with her belly so close to the ground.

What a show of stars tonight, not a stitch of cloud on the sky – looks like a giant birthday cake with all the candles lit and the lights turned off, like the cake me and George had for our golden wedding when we was livin' at East Street. All the neighbours was there and we was dancin' in the road. George got so tipsy that night we'd to carry 'im to bed. Not a regular heavy drinker, my Georgie, not like some of 'em round 'ere.

The families in that old terrace had been renting them 'two-up and two-downs' for generations. If you ran short, anyone'd lend a cup of flour or sugar. We'd sit on our front steps on fine days suppin' tea and waggin' our tongues. There'd be all the youngsters growing up and havin' their own kids; always a new baby's head to wet. Not for me though, as it turned out. I took it bad but George said it didn't matter; I was enough for 'im anyway. That's nice. Forever smoothin' things over my George – some would say it's better to face up to life but I reckon it all depends. Any road, that was before everything turned to dregs.

Wish George would hurry up. "I'll be back soon, Maisie-girl, you got my word on that," he said, and he's always a man of his word. One time, 'e went up north for work – there weren't nuffink round here then – said he'd send me a postal order every week: 'e never missed. That's George.

Terrible long queue at the Post Office today. When they're busy like that they can get a bit shirty – depends who's on duty. When I came over with a funny turn waitin' in line last week, one of the girls came round to the front and found me a chair to sit down. She's a kind girl. It ain't their fault about Bisto: it's the manager, 'e don't let no dogs in.

'E came out of his cubby-hole to talk to me once – frowned through the end of his nose at me like I'd turned up late for school or summat. We'd got this letter sayin' that pensions was to be put into a bank account. We don't have one: we've barely enough to last the week never mind puttin' any away – it's not even the full pension we gets. I got so worried I went to see 'em; had to go on my own 'cause George was workin'. But after some argy bargee the manager said it would be all right so long as we'd a permanent address. We was still livin' at East Street then.

"Is that permanent?" he asked, squintin' at me over his specs.

"We been there more'n forty years, how permanent do yer want?" I didn't mean to snap but 'e fair got my dander up. That were a while back now though.

I hates bein' stuck in a crowd of people – makes me nervous. When it was my turn this mornin' I got one of the older blokes, he's been there a long time, 'e should know me by now but 'e was scowling at my book so long it made me queasy.

"Hmm … this isn't right, missus. I know East Street. It was demolished to widen the road a few months back," he said, "I can't pay the pension without a permanent abode. You'll have to do a change of address form."

"Oh. … you do it for me, then," I said, "my hands is stiff." They were, too, I could barely hold onto the trolley. So 'e gets the form out and I tells 'im, 59A, Station Road. It's tiring – all that worry and ker-fuffle.

It seemed a longer walk back than usual today. I was plannin' to go up the welfare – it's got some fancy new name but I forget – they might give me a chitty so I can get summat for this chest; it sounds like a nest of mice scratchin' around down there. Maybe some of that red stuff George had when 'is cough was bad – it worked a treat. Labourin' on building sites ain't much of a lark when you gets older, and I reckon it's all that pesto from demolishing them old council flats what does it. I need ointment for my leg too. Bloomin' thing won't heal up and I've been ever so careful with it. George said, "Now see you look after yerself till I gets back, Maisie-luv." I'm doin' my best but it ain't easy. It's too late to traipse all the way up the welfare now, even if I 'ad the strength.

It upset me, that business in the Post Office today, brought on another funny turn after I left. I'd to sit on the windowsill outside the Co-op till it passed. It was so chilly this mornin' I put on both my coats and them fluffy boots I got from the Sally Army, but it was hot inside. Should've felt better after goin' to the cafe for Welsh rarebit, I always likes that on a Thursday, but I couldn't finish it– Bisto can have what's left.

When we was first wed I could only make things on toast – cheese, beans, eggs. It didn't bother George. I never learned to cook in a family like most girls 'cause I were dumped on the church steps as a baby. Like Bisto. Her in the dogs' home: me in the kids' home. When I told George he said, "Don't never say dumped, Maisie-girl. You was a donation, that's what." Daft bugger. Always makes me laugh.

"You wasn't 'ere then, Bisto, but that's what 'e said."

It was working in the school kitchens learned me to cook. Dinner ladies we was called. Ladies. I liked that. I liked making puddings best. Must be nearly 30 years I done that. Nuffink changed much, could've done it in my sleep. But standin' on hard tiles all day does real mischief to yer legs – yer gets them bellicose veins. It ain't much good for yer feet neither. By the end of the shift my plates was barkin' summat rotten. Soaked 'em in hot water and Epsom salts, I did. George rubbed 'em for me.

I'm worried now them Post Office people will come ferreting around 'ere and cause trouble. They kept the pension book, said it 'ad to be vertified or summat. I could get it back next week. I feels naked without it. George told me to keep it safe. "Whatever else you do,

Maisie-girl, 'ang on to that there pension book." It's all goin' round doin' my head in.

I need to stay 'ere till George comes back. It weren't really a lie – about the address – the house is number 59, but they knocked the back out. Funny, that: they left the front standin' there with nuffink behind it but this old shed.

Rain drips through the roof in one corner but I keeps a bucket there, and I stuck plastic over the broken window – it growls when the wind gets up. That used to frighten Bisto; she'd whine and crawl behind my legs. A rolled-up old blanket along the bottom of the door keeps out the draught and it makes a cosy spot once I gets the heater goin'. Lucky find that was. Someone's doin' up that old terrace at the back of Woolies and there's been loads of stuff left out on the pavement for anyone as wants. I reckon its needing a new wick though, the flame's all lopsided, but I doubt yer can still get 'em. It's a real comfort, the warm smell of an oil stove. Reminds me of ripe apples when they've been kept a while. Makes yer drowsy though.

We're right behind the railway station. I likes hearin' the clangs and rumbles and farts of the trains. Sometimes me and Bisto sit on a bench there, watching all the people come and go. They're all carrying summat around, on their backs, under their arms, in their hands – on their minds too, most of 'em.

When they demolished our street we found a basement room not far from 'ere. It weren't nice sharing the lavvy with God knows who else, but the funniest thing was all them people goin' past with no bodies. You could tell the time of day by the feet – workin' boots first thing, then comes the polished shoes and high heels. Mostly trainers after that.

Any road, we weren't there long – couldn't keep up with the rent. After we moved out we was sleepin' in the park behind the library, George, me, and Bisto, tucked in under the wall of that old bandstand they don't use no more. But we weren't the only ones. George didn't like that so 'e found this place, knew it from workin' on the site. He loosed a few planks in the fence and we was plannin' to move in till we could find summat cheaper to rent.

Then George got that pneumonium.

I wouldn't go to none of them hostels. I likes my privacy and they wouldn't take Bisto any road.

It's goin' to be a raw night – feels like the coldest we've had so far. Best leave the heater on tonight, it's full. Liftin' that can didn't half give my shoulder gyp.

"Come up 'ere, Bisto, luv ... that's it, yer likes a cuddle don't yer, pet? I reckon we're both ready for a bit of shut-eye."

Should've tried to get a new wick today.

Bloomin' thing needs turnin' down ... can't bother gettin' up again.

Ah… Georgie dear...

~~~

Story Analysis:

Maisie has waited a long time to come on stage: I mentioned seeing 'her' in the post office queue as a source of inspiration in chapter 1. I didn't know the woman's real name and had never spoken to her on my brief visits to Brighton. My mother knew her better and some-times chatted to her in the street – usually about the small mongrel dog that accompanied her – but I know nothing of her life. The story here is entirely from my imagination, supplemented by my own memories of watching feet pass by a basement window; hearing the rattle of plastic stuck over a broken window, and feeling the warm comfort of an oil stove.

Maisie occupies a special place in my affections because she is one of those whose voices are not heard. Not to be pitied: her resilient feistiness and capacity for love that sustains her to the end, rule out such negative sympathy. She is among the old and poor who are 'players' – endlessly creative and resourceful in their struggle with the constant attrition of poverty – in a game stacked against them.

Given her situation and who she is, the story's ending is inevit-able. Sad, but not unhappy for Maisie: to die in the belief that Georgie's spirit has returned for her. What else could we wish her? – A straight-backed chair in a council care home without Bisto?

There are many like Maisie and George: men and women with long, hardworking lives behind them, battling with the challenges of a changing and fast-moving society that thrusts them to the margins of survival. And their numbers are increasing with 'austerity measures' that safeguard the accumulated wealth of those in power, not only in Europe but in America and elsewhere. This was my intended theme, although you may see others to do with loneliness or love, for example, or the value of delusion in coping with a harsh reality.

In a story told entirely through internal monologue, maintaining reader interest can be difficult. In terms of modern stories, 'not a lot happens', although the small incidents are significant to Maisie's precarious position, so I showed their importance by focusing on her character and circumstances.

As usual, the opening and ending required most editing and tweaking. George had to be introduced in a way that enabled the reader to believe in his return for as long as possible. The end had to be clear without spelling it out unnaturally – being a 'first person' point of view I had only her thoughts, no description of her was possible. Dying in the 'first person present tense' is tricky; I've only done it once before in fiction. I very nearly did it for real some years ago when I had severe malaria while working in Papua New Guinea, but that's another story.

[This is the first time *A Man of His Word* has been published. Maisie's voice will be heard].

~~~

Last Call

I grumbled, under my breath, at your rambling telephone calls in the middle of the night. You'd forget the twelve-hour difference between us – afternoons were the longest and loneliest hours for you.

After your neighbour's call, I spent whole nights sustained by strong coffee, getting through to the hospital, tussling with bureaucrats, finding a nursing home. Then that daunting twenty-five hour flight.

But when I walked into your cosy room filled with treasures, my fatigue evaporated in the radiance of your smile. You could no longer walk far. No more ambling in the park with the dogs, stopping to buy ice cream at the green and white striped kiosk. "Chocolate cone please, dear, my favourite." But always too impatient to eat it right down to the end. No more Saturday mornings wandering through the street market, tasting the grapes, exchanging banter with the barrow boys. "Wotcha, 'ere comes the dog lady," they called to each other but not without affection.

Age and arthritis subdued your body but not your spirit. "Let's go to the market, can we?" We borrowed a wheelchair from the nursing home and together, mother and daughter, battled a course through the narrow cobbled streets of the crooked old town. We laughed so much you nearly capsized in the doorway of the Yellow Shop – your regular haunt, where you chose notebooks for writing your poems.

We sifted old photographs, reliving our memories and slotting them into the shiny new album we bought. Fumbling with the pages you cursed softly, "Oh damn these swollen, clumsy fingers." Too tired to talk anymore, we sat in silence warmed by love.

Our 'goodbyes' were brief, denying them significance.

Then that last call: the urgency, the scramble to get a seat on the first possible flight. You looked so small and frail, your fine brown eyes closed. I know you tried to wait for me. Bless you.

Now I can't tell which is worse – wondering if the phone will ring in the middle of the night or knowing it will not.

~~~

Story Analysis:

Last Call began as a response to a competition for a 350-word 'piece of prose' but became far more than that. Strictly speaking it is not a story, although I tried to show enough character to engage the reader's emotions in what is the narrator's personal expression of grief and regret. It also hints at the issue of dispersed families in a global society and the difficulty we have in trying to bridge that inter-vening space.

A writer friend wanted to give me suggestions to turn it into a 'proper story'. This could certainly be done but that is not its purpose. For me, it is complete. Sometimes we don't realize we have written only for ourselves until a piece is finished – we can still share it; per-haps it will resonate for someone else. I've always thought that my main reason for writing.

I don't know if the Yellow Shop remains behind London Road, but if it does, it might still have a good selection of notebooks.

~~~

Scribbler's Progress – my writing journey

My most productive period as a storyteller was between the ages of three and five years.

I hid for hours in the bathroom, squabbling with my characters. Sebastian was there too: we were inseparable. He sat on the floor, ears pricked, tail wagging as if he understood every word. Being an only child, he was my sole critic for a long time.

Then one day, the relatives came for tea. There were frantic pre-parations. Clothes, used tea bags, half-eaten gingerbread men – all the things normally within easy reach in the living room – were stuffed into cupboards and drawers; the table was wiped and draped with a lace-edged cloth I'd never seen before.

My face was washed, ears inspected, hair tugged painfully into bunches, but I didn't mind: I would have an audience at last.

Uncle Alec gave me sixpence and I decided, at that moment, I would share with him my best story. When a stab of indigestion briefly silenced Aunt Maude I seized my chance. Engrossed in my first character, it was a moment before I realized Mummy was hissing in my ear, "Empty your mouth before you speak." Driven to tell my story, I spat the mush of peas and fish fingers back onto my half empty plate and kept going.

But they weren't listening anymore. It was then that I learned how important presentation is in storytelling.

There were other setbacks in my journey as a writer. One in particular occurred after I began high school. We learned geography. I loved geography – all those exotic places. I knew about some of them already: my great grandfather and two uncles had been missionaries in China, and Africa, and great aunt Lucy spent years in India and came back a yogi. We didn't talk about her though: she grew strange plants at the bottom of her garden.

When my first assignment was on Africa I was ecstatic. I wrote about a man taking a river steamer into the deepest jungle to recover from a broken heart – it was my heroic phase and I'd seen *The African Queen* – he became a missionary, living among the lepers but died tragically, shot by a madman. I sweated over it for days; checked all my spellings and everything. I put it on Mr Rime's desk on Friday afternoon and waited modestly all weekend for the recognition I was sure would be mine on Monday morning.

I was devastated to see '*1/10*' and '*this is not an essay*' scrawled across the page in red biro.

It was much later that I understood the word 'genre' and the absolute necessity of researching your market.

I didn't let it undermine my confidence. In fact, a year or so later, Graham Greene's *A Burnt-out Case* was published and I did wonder at the time whether he had somehow managed to read my geography homework.

But the way before me was more treacherous than I knew.

I soon found myself thigh deep in the quagmire of knowledge. The burden of footnotes, citations, bibliographies, examinations, and parabolic curves, sucked me back into the gore with every step until I had to abandon my stories by the wayside to avoid sinking into oblivion.

Eventually I scrambled clear of the swamp. The path narrowed, passing through a cleft in the rocks and suddenly I was engulfed in a seething, yabbering river. At first I was tossed about and dragged below the surface, struggling for breath. But once I learned to swim, the turbulence was exhilarating; the scenery we swirled through intrigued me; and I was fascinated by my fellow swimmers: like me, gasping and striking through the current.

There were respites – still pools and shingly banks where I wrote journals, features, even books about my work and travel – but there were no stories.

As rivers do, it slowed its pace approaching the sea. Before it sluiced me out to the final destination, I waded ashore and trekked to the hilltop of tranquillity from where I could view the distance covered. Here I rested. And here I planted a forest and watched it grow.

During those quiet years, slowly, stealthily, the characters sought me out and insisted on their stories. I had grown accustomed to the stimulus of colleagues, events and storms in canteen coffee cups, to fuel my writing. Now, my characters demanded the creation of their own world, but there are no colleagues in the workplace of my mind. I can share the reality of my imagination only through the written word. Where would I find the inspiration and feedback to satisfy my characters?

The way revealed to me is long but passes through sweet meadows.

I enrolled in a writing course; my friend enrolled too – my first travelling companion. We found another aspiring writer in our small community, and then two more. We are unofficial: no 'business stuff' to gobble time; no pecking order; a band of word guerrillas ambushing the world of letters. When one wins a competition, or is published, the euphoria is multiplied, and we are caring critics of each other's tender creations.

We write different kinds of stories in distinctive styles but we are all readers who understand the struggle to find the right words.

To see my story through the eyes of another can release that lightning moment of insight.

Our lunchtimes together are too short: we have to talk with our mouths full. There is a delicious *déjà vu* in that for me. And as Sebastian has long since reached the celestial kennels, I value instead the sharp ears and wagging tales of my fellow travellers.

Our band of scribblers is starting its writing journey in a small town whose motto is *'where journeys begin'*. We each have different ambitions and our fingers have to tap those keys alone, but companions on the journey can enrich the whole person that is the writer and encourage those fingers to tap their way to new heights.

THE BEGINNING

~~~

References

- Achebe, Chenua (2010) *Girls at War and Other Stories*. Penguin Modern Classics.

- Achebe. Chenua (2011) *The Education of a British-Protected Child*. Penguin Modern Classics. [Collection of essays].

- Ascham, Roger (1904) *The Schoolmaster*. Originally published 1570, this edition is available to read on-line at the Gutenberg Project website. [Heading quote to chapter 2].

- Bates, H. E. (1988) *The Modern Short Story from 1809 to 1953*. Robert Hale.

- Bartlett, Rosamund (Ed.) (2004) *Anton Chekhov: A Life in Letters*. Penguin Classics.

- Bellow, Saul (1993) *Something to Remember Me By*. Penguin. [A collection of three stories].

- Bridport Prize, (2009) *The Bridport Prize*. Redcliffe Press. [Judges' reports and winning and placed short stories and poems].

- Donne, John (2000) *Songs and Sonnets*. Originally published in 1633, this modern e-text edited by Anniina Jokinen is available to read on-line at www.luminarium.org/editions [Heading quote to chapter 7].

- Forster, E. M. (1976) *Aspects of the Novel*. Penguin Books.

- Frye, Northrop (1977) "Haunted by Lack of Ghosts" in David Staines (Ed.) *The Canadian Imagination*. [Heading quote to chapter 4].

- Gioia, Dana & R. S. Gwynn (Eds.) (2006) *The Art of the Short Story*. Pearson Longman.

- Hensbergen, Gijs Van (2001) *Gaudi: a biography*. Harper Collins.

- Iyer, Pico (2013) "Voices Inside Their Heads", in *The New York Times* April 11.

- Maupassant, Guy de (1934) *Short Stories*. Translated by Marjorie Laurie. Everyman's Library.

- McKee, Robert (1999) *Story*. Methuen.

- Michalko, Michael (2011) *Creative Thinkering: Putting Your Imagination to Work*. New World Library [Heading quote to chapter 1].

- Munro, Hector Hugh (1993) *The Complete Works of Saki*. Wordsworth Classics.

- Polti, Georges (2007) *The Thirty-six Dramatic Situations*. Book Jungle.

- Stein, Sol (1995) *Stein on Writing*. St. Martin's Griffin.

- Steinbeck, John (1983) *Of Mice and Men*. Bantam Books.

- Twain, Mark. Quotes in the Introduction: "*Quite true…*" letter to Bruce Weston Munro 15 March 1887; "*It is so unsatisfactory…*" in, *My Father Mark Twain* Clara Clemens (1931) Harper and Brothers. Sourced from www.twainquotes.com/reading.html

- Young-Bruehl, Elisabeth (1994) *Global Cultures: A Transnational Short Fiction Reader*. Wesleyan University Press.

Acknowledgements

Companionship in writing and reading comes in many forms and there is a host of people I would like to acknowledge, but I want especially to thank those who have been unstinting in their encouragement and generous with their time in reading all or parts of early drafts of *Inside Stories*. Alphabetically: Stavros Halvatzis; Lorraine Mace; Jane Rusbridge; JD Smith; Joe Stein; Ernest Swain, and Sue Uden.

From Apes to Apps

How humans evolved as storytellers and why it matters

Trish Nicholson

collca

Introduction

One of the fascinations of science is the endless scope for reading between the lines, scratching at the edges of what is known, to ask new questions and speculate on what might be – the 'what if' questions beloved of story writers. This essay is similarly speculative, extending from published research to pose an original perspective on the part played by stories in our human evolution. We all know that stories of all kinds are extremely important to us, but this is not a work of literary criticism, nor is it a manual on writing stories. It is a study of human evolution which casts storytelling in a dominant role in the development of our ancestors' capacity to think, reason, imagine and relate to others – all the things that make us human.

In writing *From Apes to Apps*, I also want to celebrate a new trend towards collaboration between various branches of science. Into this nutshell is gathered and distilled relevant current research in biology, psychology, archaeology, neuroscience, linguistics, and my own field, anthropology, to explore plots and heroes in the story of how we evolved with a brain function based on storytelling.

To explain complex ideas briefly is more difficult than writing at length, but I have kept this short and used language accessible to everyone because the thrust of my message affects us all. The way our ancient ancestors interacted with their challenging environment in the African savanna, resulting in our brains being wired for narrative, has important implications for us in our new digital environment. To quote from the last chapter of this essay:

"In some respects, we are returning to the immediacy and malleability of oral traditions: stories mutated through different tellers and a plethora of listeners.

And yet, this freedom is more apparent – perhaps more virtual – than real. Larger presences making more noise with even better technology are also telling their stories, filling the air with narratives they want us to accept."

Why does it matter how our storytelling brain evolved? It depends who is constructing our story.

~~~

Prologue

If Story could write her autobiography, it would go something like this:

"In the beginning I had complete freedom – it was wonderful. Though young and not yet fully formed, I roamed everywhere, became involved in everything. I was even entrusted with important matters of life and death. This soon developed my strength and character. But my emancipation did not last. It felt like a good thing at first – the writing – it was exciting to be clothed in lines and dots and curlicues, even though they weighed me down at times; to be independent of infallible human memory seemed like a promise of immortality. And so it might have transpired had not the human desire to possess and control begun my enslavement. I was captured many times, fought over by those who claimed to own me, misrepresented and misquoted, sometimes hidden-away until I despaired of following my mission ever again. My true nature was not understood ..."

In this book I set Story free, untie her bonds of definition: fiction is often nearer the truth than non-fiction; short stories may be long on meaning; long-form, short on value. In this study of the evolution of storytelling, all forms of narrative – ultimately, even wordless narrative – are the stories by which we live, and die. No, it is more than that: they are the stories we are composed of; it is story that makes us human. In the famous words of poet, Muriel Ryukeyser: *"The universe is made of stories, not atoms."*

A realization appreciated also at the other end of the planet by the less famous:

> *This story e coming through your body*
> *E go right down foot and head*
> *Fingernail and blood...through the heart*
> *And e can feel it because e'll come right through.*

(*Story About Feeling*, Bill Neidjie, Aboriginal Australian)

And now, I will tell you the story of stories.

~~~

1: Did we talk our way into being humans two million years ago?

In this tale, we are the protagonist, the main character: it is our own story. To understand the world as narrative, to imagine the unknown and unknowable through metaphor, is the essence of being human. Our thoughts on *'life, the universe and everything'* we express through story.

To begin at the beginning, or as near to the beginning as science can take us, we need to start with the words – the evolution of language. For many scholars, language is the defining aspect of the human species; its evolution, the first Act in an epic being written with many plot turns and a cast of hundreds, each with their own script. In recent years, researchers in cognitive science, biology, archaeology, anthropology, psychology, and linguistics have started to collaborate in searching for the roots of language, but theories and alliances change constantly.

The whole field of study is in flux, revised scenarios roll in like new weekly episodes of a soap opera and with as much gossip and disagreement. Clashes between points of view are inevitable when thought and language are both the tools *and* the objects of enquiry.

In *The First Word*, a recent study tracing the twists and turns of research into the origins of language, Christine Kenneally writes: *"Ideas are frustratingly anchored in the heads of individuals, and each of these individuals has his own version of any one thought. They all agree on some of the implications and none of the others. And everyone has a slightly different set of assumptions, not all of which he is conscious of or willing to admit to."*

But every good story is based on conflict and its resolution, and each storyteller must choose his or her own way of telling a tale. There are different ways this story could be told: we make plot choices and pick our way through the controversies to get as near as we can to understand when, how and why, thought and language conceived story.

By 'language' I mean the capacity to initiate and exchange messages with original content and meaning; beyond the repetition of a set menu of signals like the variations in tone and rhythm of bird calls, or the choreography of a honeybee dancing the wealth and location of a pollen lode for his fellow workers. All primates communicate with sounds and gestures, but even the Great Apes lack the physical and mental equipment to generate the inspired and inventive utterances of humans.

There is no limit to the use we may make of words or the ideas we might seek to share with them. In this sense, ours is the only species to have language. Brain scientists describe language as a 'cognitive specialisation': a capacity wired into our mental software and supported by structures within the brain; a feature unique to human biology, and passed on through our genes.

The idea that the right side of the brain offers creativity and imagination, while the left side provides analysis and structured thinking – popular for years in management training – is an oversimplification. Although two locations – Broca's and Wernicke's areas – are particularly important for language, and for most of us are situated on the left side of the brain, either side may dominate during certain processes. Both expressive communication and thinking are whole brain activities: neural circuits for language are located in other places in the brain and cross-referenced with areas controlling sight, hearing and movement.

For an idea of the complexity of the wiring, imagine a diagram of global road, rail, and airline routes superimposed one on the other. Information is passed from one specialized nerve cell (neuron) to another, by the flow of chemicals (neurotransmitters) along connecting fibres called axons; each neuron having thousands of connections to others. V.S. Ramachandran in the *Tell-tale Brain* shows how these interconnections link our ability to recognize sounds and sights, and to think, gesture, and talk about them simultaneously. To communicate effectively, we synthesise this mass of neural stimulation into meaning.

The combination of hand gestures with speech may be appreciated in its most vivid form among excited Italian waiters, but it is a universal feature of human communication. Try talking with your usual fluency while sitting on your hands. Once we began to walk upright – about four million years ago – our hands were free to gesture and make tools as we explored the open grasslands of East Africa. Although it no doubt made a more exciting life, it was a more dangerous one, where communicating became important not only to give warnings and instructions, but to create relationships for co-operation.

Even before we spoke words, when we exchanged little more than grunts and yelps, and the emotional coos and calls of courting suggested by Darwin, gestures would have been important to our survival, enabling us to point out dangerous predators lurking in the undergrowth, and give silent directions to hunting companions creeping up on the next meal.

Such hand language almost certainly preceded spoken words but has evolved with them as an essential part of spoken communication. That the soundless conversation of hands can be in complex and grammatical forms is seen in the sign language of the deaf, and in communities with taboos on speaking, for example in silent religious orders. And to see the speed with which hands and arms can communicate, you need only watch the bookies at Newmarket racetrack.

Even in conjunction with gestures, spoken words do not have to carry the burden of understanding on their own: we use a variety of visual and audio clues to give us context, innuendo and double meanings. Studies of 'conversations' between mothers and their newborn babies, show how much can be mutually communicated without formal language. Other clues come from the immediate situation, or memory of past encounters.

When the !Kung San forager groups in southern Africa travel through the dense Mongongo nut groves, they listen out for the sound of mortars used to grind meal; a welcome indication of human presence they associate with the conviviality of the campsite. They call it: *!gi kokxoie* – 'mortar speech'. Amid the cacophony of the modern world that constantly assails our senses, we become selective as to what we see, hear and feel, but still these stimuli 'speak' to us and enhance our comprehension of written and spoken words.

Our early ancestors, too, would have drawn upon a wide range of clues to communicate with each other, but at some point, the flexibility and portability of spoken words gave them an edge in portraying deeper meaning; they multiplied in our heads, combined and became language.

We are born with an uncanny facility for language; able to express relationships between thoughts and objects with our first utterances. With this genetic tool kit we learn to expand our vocabulary with exposure to speech, and to sharpen the pertinence of our words with the stimulation of our environment. Any parent recognizes the significance of the transition from, "Why?" to "Why not?"

Those who have laboured to learn a foreign language, or given up the struggle in favour of shouting louder, may laugh at Noam Chomsky's suggestion that part of our genetic tool kit is a Universal Grammar. This is not grammar as we learned it in school, but a fundamental set of mental keys to analyse the words we hear, make sense of them, and generalise to make new phrases. Children are born with this capacity.

Specific sounds and words, their order, arrangement, and pattern of combinations, may be different in each language, but all arise from the presence and manipulation of this basic set of language keys, hard-wired into our brains. A rarity among linguists: almost everyone agrees on this issue, it is now a base from which other research reaches out:

> "..the babel of languages no longer appear to vary in arbitrary ways and without limit. One now sees a common design to the machinery underlying the world's languages, a Universal Grammar." (Steven Pinker: *The Language Instinct*).

What they disagree on is whether this language kit came as a pre-packed complete genetic outfit unrelated to anything else as

Chomsky claims, or whether it accrued over time, based on existing primate capabilities to communicate, and involved some form of proto-language.

Steven Pinker believes it was a gradual process and that, not only grammar, but basic concepts from which we build language and the way we describe and communicate ideas, appear also to have evolved as a universal feature of our mental wiring. Pinker explores this at length in, *The Way the Mind Works*. In the equivalent of a tweet by comparison, it is this: the basis of our language and thought is a small suite of concepts allowing us to think and communicate about space, time, matter, and causation – the four fundamentals necessary to survive our prehistoric environment. The words we use to express these four dimensions, we extend, by metaphor, to the totality of our human experience.

For example, with the concept of space, and movement within it, we *'bring forward'* a meeting as if it were a solid object, and go *'on'* holiday as if it were a shape in space. We develop our own personal sets of metaphors that have particular significance to us, as well as understand common metaphors in our own culture – so frequently used as shorthand that they become clichés like *'leave no stone unturned'*.

Metaphors are significant in storytelling: they can tap our inner thoughts to enhance our understanding of the story and elicit emotional responses – from Cinderella's slipper as a metaphor for her true fitness to marry the prince, to a literary allusion to rain, such as *'the sky wept'*. Storytelling is universal: it should come as no surprise, then, that research indicates one of its most important components – metaphor – to be part of our genetic heritage: a mechanism for thinking embedded in our mental software.

According to Pinker, these fundamental thought modules evolved as our ancestors grappled with the problems of survival in a challenging and changing environment: they conferred an advantage for the thriving of the species. Our early ancestors were contending with natural cataclysms and climate change on a vast scale: ice sheets repeatedly advanced and retreated across Europe, floodwaters scoured the land, volcanoes erupted, and the earth moved. Our first protagonists had to overcome such conflicts in their quest for existence. Only species whose capacities gave them a natural advantage in adapting to these conditions survived.

How do these adaptations take place and end up adjusting our cognitive software?

During reproduction, our genes make slight copying errors; genetic 'typos' called mutations. Many are insignificant, some are fatal to the organism, but others may turn out to be beneficial. Natural selection acts upon genetic errors to make small incremental changes – selecting those that confer some advantage for survival, i.e. enable the organism in some way to reproduce more successfully than its contemporaries, and thus pass on genes containing the advantageous change.

By this long slow process, involving many thousands of generations, complex systems can evolve. As evolutionary biologists point out, this process can account for everything else about us, so it is reasonable to assume it applies also to the internal wiring and structures that give us the capacity for language.

Human evolution is an epic in many episodes still being written and revised. Thankfully, we do not need the entire back-story: it is not the specific age of language that is important in our tale – with a time scale so vast and data so sketchy, what is a millennium more or less? – instead, we seek insight into the nature and lifestyle of our ancestors at the time when they could have told their first stories; an activity that could have contributed to their own social and cognitive development.

For this, our tale needs more characters; not only linguists and cognitive scientists, but scholars of all the other disciplines that now collaborate on the nature of humanity – evolutionary biologists and psychologists, archaeologists and anthropologists. Despite this synergy rapidly progressing our understanding, we do not yet know exactly how or when language evolved. The search is a bit like Darwin's definition of a mathematician, *"...a blind man in a dark room looking for a black cat that isn't there."* Unfortunately, the soft, juicy parts of culture, all the animations that would indicate use of symbolic thought and language – stories, songs, rituals, dances, and doodles in the sand – leave no lasting trace.

This lack of evidence, while making it impossible to prove their existence, is no proof that they did not exist in some form, even among the Hominids – our earliest ancestors – a few millennia before modern humans. Terence Deacon's *The symbolic Species*, puts it more succinctly: *"Absence of evidence is not evidence of absence."* It is worth remembering this as our story unfolds.

~~~

2: The stories told by stones and bones and what they don't say

What we do have are heaps of stones and a few bones. Archaeologists and anthropologists can extract an astonishing amount of information from both, but there are limitations. Even the famous "Lucy" – the four-million-year-old partial skeleton, *Australopithecine afarensis* who walked upright – just might have been a "Lucas": teeth and bone conditions prove 'she' was a young adult, but the missing sixty percent of the skeleton leaves indications of 'her' sex down to size only, a calculated guess.

Important bones for predicting language use are the size of the brain case; spaces inside it that could accommodate the major organs of language (Broca's and Wernicke's areas), and the hyoid and other small bony parts that control manipulation of the tongue and voice box.

In order to pronounce the full range of vowel sounds, the position of our vocal apparatus has evolved lower in our throats than other mammals. As a result, food and drink pass over the trachea before we can swallow them: the reproductive gains from the use of language were clearly far greater than losses from choking.

Based on reconstructions of what the soft body parts required for language might have looked like in early humans, speech scientist Philip Lieberman, suggests that humans before about 50,000 years ago did not have language because the position of the larynx and pharynx would not have allowed the full range of vowel sounds. This assumes that complex thought could not be communicated effectively with limited vowels – a debatable point.

Fully modern humans – Homo sapiens – have been around for at least 200,000 years; we cannot know how they spoke or what they said to each other, but if Lokele and Yoruba drummers in West Africa can send messages – not merely signals – with only a two-tone drum, without consonants, let alone vowels, we may be underestimating the ingenuity of our ancestors.

The Lokele, like the Yoruba, have a tonal language in which each syllable is in a different pitch, enabling 'talking drums' to simulate the rhythm and intonation of the spoken word. Complex conversations can be transmitted between drummers 40km apart; leather strips around the drum are tightened or released to control the pitch. So effective a means of communication that plantation owners in America banned 'talking drums' in 1838 for fear their slaves would use them to incite rebellion.

And this sparks an intriguing idea which might already have occurred to you: was it the tonal quality of the language that enabled drums to mimic it so well, or the tone of the drums that influenced the sound of their language? Unfortunately, we will never know: drums are another piece of soft culture made from perishable material unlikely to survive enough millennia.

Going back to our question as to whether our ancestral cousins could hold a meaningful dialogue without a full set of vowels: they probably could, and it might well be a case of Mark Twain's comment on Wagner's music – Neanderthal's language was better than it sounded.

Neanderthals are not known as innovators, in fact they have had a bad press, but they did develop knapping (chipping at stone to make points) into an art form. Faceted flakes started to develop around 300,000 years ago, but Neanderthals perfected the technique and worked out how to fix their beautiful, multifaceted flakes to wooden shafts (with bitumen): now their hunting parties could go for big game. What hunters are not going to brag about the quality of their spears, and impress the women around the camp fire with stories of mammoths "this big"?

But to return to our bones: there is no doubt that brain size has been steadily increasing over the last three million years from the first increase in Homo habilis – the earliest tool maker – with a brain capacity of 640cc, to that of modern humans at around 1400cc. For comparison, chimpanzees, our closest related primates, have an average brain capacity of 400cc. From the point of view of calories, and the effort involved in collecting them, the brain is an expensive organ for the body to maintain, and an increase in head size obviously adds risks at childbirth.

The brain would only continue to evolve if it enabled a species to function more successfully, giving it a reproductive advantage to survive and even spread to new territory. Natural selection cannot work on potential qualities; it can only select for features that are being *used* advantageously. If larger brained humans were succeeding better than others, so that their genes predominated, leading to a gradual increase in size, then that brain capacity was already being used. Clearly, something significant was taking place.

Size does matter, but the dimensions of the brain case are only part of the story: Einstein's brain was smaller than the average, and Neanderthal's brain case was larger than ours. Like everything else, the reasons for enlarged brains are debated, but the ability to think and communicate effectively would have been an enormous advantage.

And what about the stones? What can they tell us about this period? Stone tools ranged from simple flakes and points, to hand axes, and later, more elaborate razor-sharp spearheads and hafted blades. The existence of a feedback loop between the sophistication of stone tools, and brain development, is a theory widely accepted among anthropologists. An interesting anomaly, though, is that one of our ancestors from 1.5 million years ago – Homo erectus – had a brain size close to that of modern humans: beyond what scientists consider necessary for the quality of his heavy hand axes and his livelihood as a forager and hunter.

Erectus were around for several hundred thousand years, probably the first of our species to migrate out of Africa because they are found also in Asia and Europe, so if they weren't beefing up their tool kit, what were they doing with that enhanced brain power? Were they playing Sudoku in the sand with all those basalt chips they whittled away to fashion their axes?

A more plausible scenario is that their curiosity and ideas became more complex, stretching their powers of communication beyond gestures and calls, leading to the use of specific sounds with group consensus on what they meant: words and the beginning of language. Language enabled our ancestors to structure their thoughts so they could be shared with others. Ideas and words gearing up each other would build out cognitive powers. The advantage of narrative – stories – in this process is that a story is a structured sequence of actions showing cause and effect; it can help us to understand how things happen and to explain it to those around us.

If their tools provided a good living for all those years, why should they have shared our obsession with output and concentrated on tools rather than other things? They didn't know we would be here, classifying their progress according to our own values. There is more to life than work, and it is tempting to believe that H. erectus was also aware of this cliché, and his 'excess' brain capacity was the result of feedback from developments in thought, language and other soft parts of culture, even singing courting songs and telling stories, rather than his flaky tools. As we have seen, this possibility is difficult to prove.

Finding shards of decorated pots creates a buzz among archaeologists like an excited hive of bees. Not simply the style of pot, but the pigments, symbols and patterns, even smears remaining from its contents can reveal a huge amount about the culture of the people who made it. If, at some stage in their long history, Homo erectus had woven baskets from some decomposable material like reeds, treated them with vegetable or animal fat, and decorated them in distinctive symbolic designs using plant fibres, feathers and the juice from berries, we would find no trace today.

Anthropologists often cite the simplicity of stone tools as evidence of minimal culture, but clubs, traps and nets, catapults, fishing gear, shelters, garments and bags, as well as ritual objects, toys, and musical instruments, can all be made of perishable materials. They still are, by modern indigenous people's following a hunting and gathering lifestyle; peoples whose language and stories are no less subtle than our own.

The vocabulary of different languages may focus on specific aspects of importance to a society: scores of words to describe the nature of snow, dozens to explain the behaviour of game, or none to count beyond "many" because it is not needed. Despite this difference, Marvin Harris points out that all languages currently spoken in the world – some three thousand – possess a common fundamental structure; with only minor adjustments in vocabulary they are *"equally efficient in storing, retrieving, and transmitting information and in organizing social behaviour."* He quotes anthropologist and linguist, Edward Sapir, who wrote, in 1921: *"When it comes to linguistic form, Plato walks with the Macedonian swine-herd, Confucius with the head-hunting savages of Assam."* A bold statement at the time, vindicated by subsequent linguistic research.

At this point, we can draw breath and a general conclusion: thought and language could gradually have evolved in complexity, while cultures changed in small increments, for many more thousands of years than previously assumed – we may have been talking to each other in some form for two million years.

There was plenty to talk about in addition to the weather and the neighbours: the location of good foraging grounds, derring-do of hunting exploits, and whether to explore the other side of the ridge. Once verbal language became more important than gestures, our hands would be free to work and talk at the same time, to demonstrate tool techniques – or how to weave a basket. And somewhere along the line, we started to tell each other stories about how to sustain the good things in life; what to do about the fearful things we didn't understand, such as where the sun went at night, and the things we still don't know, like where a 'person' goes when they die.

But most of all, our stories helped us to understand our fellow humans, to compare our behaviour with that of others – both known and not yet met – and to form an inner consciousness of ourselves as social beings and as individual personalities.

To do this, we had to use those basic concepts of space, time, matter and causation that ensured our survival, extend them as meta-phors, and begin using words and objects as symbols for more complicated ideas, like abstract thoughts and invisible forces.

Because cultural objects and performances are so often short-lived, anthropologists use ritual burial as an indicator of complex culture and use of symbols. It is safe to assume that the ritual, and the beliefs, myths and stories behind it, had taken some time to develop: it was not a sudden whim one dreary morning for someone to set the corpse in a particular position, or select specific objects to go into the grave – such rituals presume previously considered purpose and meaning. New discoveries of these burials pushes further and further back, the time when our ancestors were creating symbolic worlds through narrative to cope with the known and the unknown.

The earliest irrefutable evidence of ritual burial was found as recently as 2003 in Bouri-Herto, Ethiopia, and dates from 165,000 years ago. Other evidence of trading in shells from distant areas and of designs cut into ochre pieces – found in Blombos Cave in South Africa – date from 77,000 years ago. For such trading, craftwork, and shared symbolism, a means of passing on knowledge and ideas, and a degree of social organisation are necessary: these require complex thought and language, with or without a full complement of vowels.

These were exciting discoveries because evidence of complex cultures remains sparse until about 50,000 years ago. Digs from this period onwards are rich in carvings and cave paintings as well as new tools like knives and needles. Some scholars interpret this period as a 'great leap forward,' even suggesting some significant genetic event to account for it. But whether this marks a true revolution in human activity, or reflects the allocation of research funds to digs in favoured areas, is an open question. There is always more to find; many regions yet to be investigated. Fate and chance play a role in this, as in most stories.

There were no 'light-bulb moments' for humanity: the conscious awareness and cognitive skills required for complex social interaction, for trade, and the use of material symbols, would have taken many thousands of years to emerge. It is clear though, that around 50,000 years ago, the rate of change speeded up. By that time, migrations had spread across continents: not only Europe, but to North America and Asia, and were newly arriving in Australia and parts of the Pacific such as coastal Papua New Guinea.

Successful groups competed for resources, encroaching on the less successful – like the Neanderthals – pushing them into marginal areas and eventually to extinction. The last known presence of Neanderthals is around 28,000 years ago in the Middle East, where they had co-existed, and probably inter-bred, with Homo sapiens for 30,000 years.

What drove this rapid change is one of the most intriguing questions in current research and a significant plot twist in our story.

~~~

3: Did story power drive the creation of complex societies?

The most widely accepted explanation for the rapid diversity in human activity in the last 50,000 years, is that the effective use of language and the growth of complex cultures, together contributed to our cognitive development in a feedback spiral of evolutionary change. More efficient tools make better use of food resources enabling a larger population to be supported, more people requires more elaborate social organisation and clearer communication about a wider range of issues. And food surpluses, however irregular, release time and energy for other creativity.

From this potent mix, earlier talents for art, ritual, dance, music – and stories – undoubtedly flourished, becoming a powerful means of community and personal expression.

I will take our tale even deeper into the scholars' lair, and suggest that storytelling was itself a significant stimulus in the feedback spiral of cultural and cognitive complexity, resulting in our ancestors' brains being adapted for story as much as for language. To be convincing, we must show that stories could confer sufficient adaptive advantage on storytellers and their communities to enable them to survive more effectively, to reproduce more successfully, and thus pass on their genes to successive generations – to us.

How could stories have this kind of impact? We can learn much from the traditional cultures of present day hunter-gatherer societies who have adapted to comparable conditions faced by our early ancestors and – before colonial contact – with similar tools and artefacts. Not that societies like the Inuit, the !Kung San, or Aboriginal Australians are in any way fossilised cultures, on the contrary, they have survived because they are dynamic, adaptive to changing conditions, even enduring the tsunami of colonisation, albeit much altered. They are also diverse, but they share certain organisational and cultural features that emerged as they wrested a foraging livelihood from a testing environment – as our ancestors did.

Territory where food resources are variable, according to seasons and locations, is more effectively utilised by small mobile groups. Richard Lee's detailed study of the !Kung San in southern Africa indicates such mobility requires social organisation that allows for accumulation and passing on of complex knowledge; flexibility in group membership, and accepted systems of food distribution – all requiring shared values of mutual support, and communication and negotiation skills.

We are essentially social animals. Perhaps the two most important cognitive activities associated with living in small groups are: trying to work out what the other person is *really* thinking (and likely to do), and deciding whether or not to subdue an instinctive selfishness in order to co-operate for some greater or longer term good. Our capacity for relating to our fellows doesn't mean we can do so without conflict. We are in competition for food and social attention not only with our neighbours, but with our mating partners, siblings and parents – an on-going contest that has fashioned many a good story.

Adaptations to hunting and foraging in social groups had ample time to lay the foundations of our language and cognitive capacities: our ancestors followed this lifestyle for around three million years; settled agricultural life is a mere blip on the time-line that began only 10,000 years ago. During those three million years, intricate knowledge of place, weather, resources, other species, and each other, would have been essential tools to ameliorate the effects of their environment in order to survive. More than that, this knowledge had to be shared and remembered for it to be passed down to succeeding generations – what more effective method of transmission than stories.

Hunter-gatherer societies have been given a stereotyped image. The balance they achieve with the vagaries of their habitats is sometimes interpreted as stagnation, stuck in a rut, some kind of time warp, but new archaeological finds in south-east Turkey are revealing extraordinary feats of complexity requiring inspiration and leadership that could be repeated elsewhere if we knew where to look.

The concept of 'simple' foraging societies is being turned on its head by Klaus Schmidt's current excavations at Göbekli Tepe. Carved megaliths forming seven circles over a twenty-five acre site, and dating back to about 11,000 BC/BCE, were built, extended and renewed over a period of two thousand years. We are accustomed to ancient ruins of settled agrarian cultures, but according to Schmidt, this was a spiritual centre erected with the technology and economy of nomadic foraging societies: it would make it the earliest known 'temple'.

If that was the case, apart from sheer physical effort without metal tools or the wheel, several hundred construction workers would have to be fed: a massive burden of extra hunting, foraging, carrying and processing. Why they built these structures is not yet known – may never be known – but the imagination that created these representations of gods, natural forces, ancestral heroes, or whoever they were, and the motivation to complete and sustain such an undertaking, can only have come from the sharing of narratives – myths and stories – that incorporated these ideas.

By 'shared', I do not mean to imply any particular process to achieve consensus: it is possible these narratives were imposed by a powerful cult or charismatic individual, perhaps supported by claims to religious or other specialist knowledge. We are not even sure whether they were temples or, as some have argued, elaborate communal houses. Either way, they presuppose stories, narratives that inspired them and contained the knowledge to build and use them. What is important to our story is that the economy of Göbekli Tepe appears to be that of hunters and gathers, but their culture was far from 'simple.'

If this level of symbolic and cognitive ability was present among hunter-gatherer societies in 11,000 BC/BCE, it could have been present in groups with similar material cultures much earlier. Either we have failed to find them, or they chose, perhaps, to invest their efforts in the performing arts, exploration, trade and migration rather than grand buildings.

Erecting edifices is something we tend to see as a mark of human progress. In the long term view of our species, such activity may prove to be quite the reverse. Writings on human evolution frequently use words like 'progress' and 'advance' – suggesting a step up, a promotion – when what they actually describe is 'change'. Earlier human-like species were not following a destiny to become better humans and failed as not quite good enough to become H. sapiens. They were simply doing their own thing. Those who died out either did not adapt to environmental changes; lost the competition for resources, or succumbed to some epidemic disease – probably a combination of all three.

This egotistical view of modern humans as being at the top of the tree, what Richard Dawkins calls *"the conceit of hindsight"* is hard to eradicate. Already we call our most recent selves *H. 'sapiens sapiens'* – 'even smarter than the smart one', assuming we are on an evolutionary escalator rising towards some ultimate point of glory – perhaps to become *H. sapiens sapiens ultimus,* ('the superlative species')?

Considering our current performance in dealing with a changing planet, it would be more realistic to recognize that 'ultimate' also means 'final', the end of the line – *Homo sapiens sapiens (failed)*? In the overview of human evolution, our species is a newbie; it is an open question whether we will last as long as H. erectus, for example. Rather than reducing us into swallowing more antidepressants, this possibility should goad us into using our wisdom to become better adapted.

But edifices aside, the Göbekli Tepe research raises another intriguing idea: if stories were potent enough in foraging societies to drive the building of such megalithic centres, could story power have instigated the move towards settlement and agriculture?

It would have made the building process so much easier. Edward Banning – who believes Göbekli was also a residential site – suggests the people who built it may have begun to grow some of their foods, if only on a casual basis. This could have been a common practice for a long time. Semi-nomadic forest-dwellers in Papua New Guinea plant a chance crop, of yams for example, before moving to new hunting grounds, returning later in the year to harvest whatever has grown.

It is entirely feasible that the stories creating the beliefs and driving the desire to erect these extraordinary structures, also led to experiments in agriculture to increase their food supply – construction workers have big appetites.

Stories have the power to clarify description, enhance memory, and give instruction as well as to enthrall and inspire. We remember numerous stories or parts of stories heard since we were toddlers. We may not have realised it at the time, but many of these stories contained cautions and rules for living that inform our moral sense for the rest of our lives. And the more appealing, emotionally captivating, and entertaining the stories, the better and longer we can recall them.

Information on the nature and location of food sources, from a bush of berries fleetingly in season, to the spoor tracks of game or the differentiation of poisonous from edible plants, are critical to the survival of hunter-gathering communities. Knowledge of techniques for killing prey, and for travelling safely through gathering and hunting grounds – possibly through a 50-100km radius – are also essential to their well-being, and would have been equally so to early humans.

Among the desert communities of Central Australia, stories of 'the dreaming' integrate people with their past, their present, and the land. With the future, too, in that knowledge of the land and all its inhabitants – including their creation heroes – incorporates the means to ensure their sustenance. Large parts of this knowledge and responsibility are 'women's business'. The *jukurrpa*, for example, is both a story of creation in the distant past, and a present force that locates individuals within society and within the land.

"In the jukurrpa was established an all-encompassing Law which binds people, flora, fauna and natural phenomena into one enormous inter-functioning world." (Diane Bell).

On a practical level, the rituals and stories of 'the dreaming' safeguard and transmit the knowledge and behaviour necessary for their continuance. The gestures, rituals, and dances that are part of these stories provide rich and unforgettable portrayals of complex and vital cultural memory.

Our ancestors operated in small, semi-mobile camps in a similar way to modern hunter-gathers, and their social organisation would have become as sophisticated. Such groups develop systems for ordering obligations and expectations between themselves, for differentiating their own group identity from others, and for co-operating with other groups for trade, peaceful passage – or not – through each other's territory, and the acquisition of mates from outside their own gene pool.

For example, every culture has rules of kinship, often extremely complex. They may be as much geared to establishing rules for living together peacefully and productively as ensuring mates come from a different gene pool – social definitions of kin, even close kin, are not always limited to blood relations. Larger groups may divide into clearly identified and named sub-groups, with rules to establish within which sub-groups young males or females can seek mates.

Exogamy – a social rule requiring a marriage partner to come from outside ones own group – is found in most cultures. In the absence of the written word, what better way to record, explain, and remember the intricacies of such systems than by stories. Some features of ancient folk tales defy interpretation except by reference to ancient kinship rules whereby young people move away – often reluctantly – from their own hearths to undergo changes in status or identity, and to forge new alliances.

In families that follow Maori traditions, children learn from an early age to recite their *whakapapa* – their genealogy. It includes the name of the mountain and river that identifies their location; their *hapu* (extended family group); their *iwi* (tribe), and names their ancestors and their marriages, deeds, and migrations back to the *waka* (canoe) on which they first arrived in New Zealand hundreds of years earlier. Stories heard and repeated throughout childhood encourage acceptance and compliance with group rules in adulthood.

Early human communities were egalitarian in the sense that they had no structured hierarchies of classes, castes, or ruling dynasties – food resources would have been insufficient to sustain such systems. Not that everyone would be equal in every respect, nor that they lacked leaders or individuals held in particular esteem. It is more likely that persuasion, charisma, articulacy and the recognition of special knowledge were the means to influence and guide group opinion and behaviour. Doubtless there was sorcery and magic, too. Through acquisition of such 'soft' power, leaders emerged whose agency depended on their knowledge and their eloquence in expressing it.

These were people with wisdom to resolve conflicts; others with skills to lead productive hunting parties, and yet others with knowledge to heal sickness, confidence to lead migrations, or insight and imagination to temper the terror of the unknown with explanation. Their power was 'story power' – they were the first storytellers whose stories captivated and swayed their audience. Through stories, the audience confers authority on the author. We associate 'author' with the written word – the published written word – but it means originator, promoter of ideas and action and it shares a common root with 'authority'.

Authority can control violence within a community, or channel it for defense and attack – life was not all sweetness and light for our early ancestors anymore than it is for modern foraging societies. Indeed, with force, power may be taken whether or not authority is conferred, but power has always been bolstered by the control of narrative. Official histories are written by the victors. George Orwell was acutely aware of this. The government of Oceania in *1984* invented an entirely different language – 'newspeak' – through which old ideas could be eradicated by the simple expedient of having no words for them.

Military and political colonisers in every period have sought to replace indigenous languages with their own, demonstrating the same fear of the power contained in others' stories that lead oppressive regimes today to burn books and imprison their writers and poets. Stories create identity and continuity from an historical or imagined past to a concept of future – possibly a very different future.

It is hard to believe our earliest ancestors looked at the stars, observed the cycles of sun and moon, and did not ask themselves who these glowing bodies were and what drove them. The mystery of creation, and rituals to mitigate the effects of natural forces, are the stuff of myths and stories in every culture. It is unfortunate that in our information-oriented age the word 'myth' has taken on a derogatory sense as being the opposite of a fact: we use it as a way of saying something is widely believed but is untrue. This misunderstands the nature and purpose of myth.

Myths are a form of story that embodies intrinsic truths: personal, social, moral, environmental – even universal. They often involve gesture, song, images and other elements of performance as well as narrative, giving them emotional reach far beyond a directory of facts; their power lies in enactment, repetition, and infinite variation. Myths contain deep truths: they are not stock market reports or scientific treatise.

Creation myths often revolve around conflict and its resolution – the essence of every good story – reflecting the struggle that life has always been for our species. We might even call ourselves 'Homo conflictus'. The Shilluk people of East Africa relate how the sun and moon quarrelled and so forever live apart; we have our own 'Big Bang' creation story. Of course, scientists use different methods and have many more rituals and rules, but they address the same questions that gave rise to the first shamans, soothsayers, and spiritual leaders: all strive for better stories.

Another aspect of humanity important in story, but rarely mentioned by the evolutionary sciences, is fun. Did early humans have a sense of humour? Did they tell stories to entertain each other on long dark evenings when firelight flickered eerily around them on the walls of their cave? Apparently they did. We already know from biologists that certain experiences release in us dopamine – an enzyme that gives us that warm fuzzy feeling of pleasure – and that laughter is essential to our general well-being, but recent investigations by neurobiologist Robert Provine, confirm Charles Darwin's belief:

laughter is a universal, in-built characteristic that we share with the apes.

And it may come as no surprise that despite its benefits to our personal health, the prime evolutionary role of laughter is in creating and maintaining social relationships. So a capacity for fun, too, is incorporated in our cognitive structures, and as laughing requires no vowels, even Lucy might have shared a joke four million years ago. If our ancestors told jokes and made their stories funny and entertaining, they may also have recognized the practical spin-off: fun and laughter promote understanding, acceptance, and retention of information, even if few teachers appreciate the fact.

Each one of these benefits of storytelling – from food to fun – could account for sexual advantage for those who told the best stories. These informal yet influential leaders would attract the most desirable mates, and so pass on their genes to successive generations. Combined, these benefits make a formidable force.

But could they be sufficiently advantageous for storytelling capacity to create a feedback loop toward further cognitive development, in a similar way that tool making did? Did more and better storytelling play a major role in the sudden flourishing of our species over 50,000 years ago?

Basic modules of thought and language had already evolved; all that would be required over several thousand generations would be the evolution of additional pathways (synapses) between neurons. This is not a difficult task. The true extent of brain plasticity has been one of the most inspiring discoveries in neurological research in recent years, and we are still learning.

At this point in our story, we follow a brief sub-plot because there is another major theory about how human cognition – the capacity to perceive, think, imagine and remember – has evolved, and we need to see how this relates to Story's conception.

~~~

4: Are genes really the heroes or did culture grab the action?

In his book, *The Cultural Origins of Human Cognition*, Michael Tomasello is not convinced about learning, language, thinking and so on, being hard-wired as modules which have evolved, by natural selection, within the human brain. His main objection is that in the period since humans separated from the Great Apes (probably 4-5 million years ago), there has not been enough time for this process, especially since the most significant developments in cognitive skills seem to date only within the last 200,000 years with the emergence of Homo sapiens, modern humans.

Instead, he suggests that the differences between ape and human thinking skills have been the result of 'cultural transmission' – changes in behaviour and cognition caused by social interactions. Cultural transmission is a recognized phenomenon in biology: it includes a range of behaviours where imitation, learning or instruction, enable the young of a species to carry out species specific acts, for example, birds mimicking their parent's songs, or chimpanzees learning to use sticks as tools by watching adults. It is a complex process that works in different ways in separate species and is often only triggered by other, instinctive behaviours.

The two critical aspects for Tomasello's theory are that (a) cultural transmission is a much faster process than genetic transmission by natural selection, and (b) various cognitive skills already possessed by our non-human primate 'ancestors', would have provided the basis for Hominid and Homo brains to evolve into what we now define as Homo sapien cognitive abilities – including language, tool-making, reasoning and imagination.

The question is: if other species, including apes, also have cultural transmission, how did it happen differently with our species that we are the only ones with these distinctive cognitive skills?

According to Tomasello, the turning point, sometime in the last 2 or 3 million years, was when humans evolved the capacity to identify with other humans, and to perceive them as thinking beings with intentions, like themselves. This conscious awareness enabled – indeed necessitated – complex forms of communication, like language, to understand the other's motivation and potential action. In other words: to empathize with fellow humans so that they could interact effectively. How and when conscious awareness evolved is as much a black hole in this theory as it is in all the others; the ultimate question, answered only in stories.

But from that stage, cultural transmission in humans became a more complex affair: basic discoveries and inventions could be repeated in multiple locations, remembered and passed on through generations and across peer groups; others could add their own ideas to improve tools, expand local knowledge, or determine ways to influence the behaviour of others. Some scholars have called this process 'sociogenesis' – a sort of brainstorming together with the social organisation to implement ideas.

The ability to accumulate, develop and spread skills, thoughts and information in this way is what Tomasello calls the 'ratchet' effect, a feature of human cultural transmission that is not present in other species. He makes no claims as to when this process began (other than '*sometime in the last 2-3 million years*'), but suggests it could account for the significant developments and results of human cognition – the 'great leap forward' – over the last 50,000 years. Whenever it started, what better 'ratchet' mechanism to develop memory, understanding and narrative skills than storytelling, especially when stories involve gestures, actions and other elements of performance? It is still the principal driver of cultural transmission.

Tomasello's research is based on the study of primate behaviour and evolution (the species, or phylogenetic approach), and on the progression of individual human cognitive skills from birth (the ontogenetic approach). The idea that there is some connection between these two processes, that one might be a reflection of the other, goes back to early Greek science.

It became a doctrine in the nineteenth century, championed by the German naturalist Ernst Haeckel, that ontogeny is a re-play of phylogeny: that the language and cognitive stages a human infant goes through from birth, are the same as the species followed in human evolution. Who is not familiar with the consequences of upright mobility in the young, when a toddler begins to demonstrate the destructive forces of a hunter-gatherer?

This idea was ridiculed and rejected by later scientists, but there remained a nagging seed of intrigue to stimulate the interest of modern biologists – sufficient for Stephen Jay Gould to write a history of the whole debate in 1977, and suggest there is still potential in digging deeper into this general concept; a challenge that Tomasello has taken up, although he does not state a direct relationship between phylogenesis and ontogenesis.

It is a feature of scientific enquiry to focus narrowly in order to delve deeply – lifting a manhole cover, groping a way down into a labyrinth of passages, caves of treasure, and dead-ends. Those on the surface, taking the broader view, need to consider where these passages might connect underground and emerge through other manholes. It is more than likely that neither the natural selection of brain modules, nor cultural transmission, account entirely for the development of human cognition: it is far more plausible that both have played significant roles.

More collaboration between disciplines is needed to find where these narrow passages connect, and a promising opening is the recent discovery by a neurophysiologist, Dr Giacomo Rizzolatti, of what have been dubbed 'mirror neurons' in the frontal lobes of monkeys, and his assertion that they exist also – in a more complex form – in humans. What role do they play in our story?

'Mirror neurons' are cells in the brain that become active when the body makes a movement, like grasping an object. Each neuron, or group of neurons, is specific to a particular movement and corresponding set of muscles. But this is more than simply a motor control system – a hand to brain connection – because those same neurons will 'spark' when we watch someone else make that movement. When we see someone pick up a spanner, our mirror neurons 'fire', sending messages to our own hand muscles as if we were doing the action. When apprentices say: "Show me, I learn best by watching," they are talking more science than they know.

This development in our brains would have boosted our learning capacity, enabling us to learn new skills and to pass them on – accelerating, perhaps even initiating, Tomasello's 'ratchet effect'. It forms a link between the two opposing theories: 'it's all in brain modules and genetic', and 'it's all in culture and learned'. But even more exciting, and controversial, is Rizzolatti's further claim: an additional dimension of mirror neurons in humans allows us to perceive the *intentions* behind the action – we can empathize, read the other person's mind. When someone lifts that spanner, we know whether he will use it to tighten a nut, or whack us over the head.

If further work proves this to be the case, it shines a spotlight into that black hole of 'conscious awareness' and empathy on which everything else human appears to depend, in particular, the ability to form relationships and social groups.

Naturally, a finding with such far reaching potential to re-write much of what is already known has attracted critics that point out plot-holes. For example, the interpretation of another's intentions from body movements may be as much a reflection of our own thoughts as those of the person we are observing. We can also be misled by a host of other clues past and present: if the man holding the spanner is dressed in mechanic's overalls we may miss the fact that he is a psychopath cunning enough to disarm us by appearances.

But to recognize that others have intentions – inner states of mind that may be the same as, or different to our own – was a crucial step even if we frequently misread them. 'Getting it wrong' often makes the best story plots – another way stories allow us to 'rehearse' social interactions without actually getting hit on the head.

Of particular importance to our tale is the strong possibility that a set of mirror neurons triggers emotions, and could explain for example, why, when a good storyteller 'shows' us the fear or joy of a character, we feel that same emotion even when we know the story is fictional. Stories are a powerful medium to engage and enhance that all important ability to empathize – something we look at further in the next chapter.

Without claiming they answer all the unknowns in our evolution, Ramachandran has suggested that mirror neurons were a necessary, decisive step in our development:

"...once you have a certain minimum amount of 'imitation learning' and 'culture' in place, this culture can, in turn, exert the selection pressure for developing those additional mental traits that make us human."

And from what we have learned so far, we can cast storytelling in a dominant role in 'culture.'

So, returning to our story arc, let us say it boldly: storytelling is as much a part of the genetic heritage of our species as language, thought, and tool making. We can go further, and suggest that storytelling drove our later evolutionary changes, forming a feedback loop that enhanced our cognitive abilities. Stories have made us: we are all born storytellers.

Without story we might have become smarter than the average Great Ape but we would not have become human. As individuals we have conscious awareness of our own identities, but we are essentially social creatures, as such we have been fashioned by stories – our own, and other peoples. The conception of story – the opening paragraphs, if you like – was set in the harsh physical environment and tentative social organisation of our early ancestors, but our environment, physical and social, has been transformed even within our own brief Anthropocene era.

We've read the back-story, but what are the implications of all of this for us now: what is happening in the middle part of the story?

~~~

5: Our story software is all in the mind, so 'mind the gap'

Modern psychology lends support to the notion that storytelling is deeply embedded in the brain's engineering: the workings of our minds, both conscious and unconscious, are based on narrative – we can only understand the stimuli around us as stories. Mind is the product of the brain much as a weaver can produce an exquisite shawl from her loom: extraordinary variety is possible within the limitations of the loom's structure. If we think and dream in narrative, it suggests that our brains are structured to weave narrative.

What enters our senses – our experience – we relate to ourselves as a story, but the fact that we dream, even fantastic and disconnected dreams, shows that our minds do more than simply absorb sensations like blotting paper: a process intervenes.

There is a part of the brain that formulates stimuli of all kinds into narrative, takes it in, assesses its worth, categorises and uses it immediately, or stores it for use with other narratives for future thought, dreaming and action – all in a nanosecond. This tiny gap between what we receive from our senses, and the story we make of it, is what Tom Stafford identifies as the opportunity for 'narrative escape':

"That we can make-up a reality at all, even an unstable one, shows that our minds are not just sensing machines. Core to what the mind does is tell stories about what is likely to happen, or could be happening. It is this ability that is left to run wild during dreams."

The 'narrative escape' is that moment in the mind when we can either create our own narrative of what is happening and what the implications are, or accept and act on the narrative someone or something else is giving us. Because of the complexity and sheer volume of multiple stimuli we receive, most of the time we believe and act on the narratives we receive from others. Trying to cope with the mass of messages coming through all our senses, our attention spans are getting shorter, but we are not necessarily becoming any smarter.

Stafford discusses experiments carried out in 1961/2 at Yale University by social psychologist Stanley Milgram. In the scientific atmosphere of a laboratory staffed by white-coated technicians, volunteers were instructed – in the interests of completing an experiment, an unspecified scientific enquiry – to administer a series of electric shocks rising to 450 volts, to another volunteer they could not see, but whose cries of pain they could hear. Although they were not comfortable with the situation – sweating, stuttering, aiming anxious glances at the lab-coated attendants – 65% complied, both men and women equally.

Designed to test how obedient people are to what they perceive as legitimate authority, the experiment was, in essence, an attempt to understand compliance with the Holocaust.

In reality there were no electric shocks, of course, the screams were those of an actor. But for 65% of the volunteers, ordinary citizens of New Haven, the narrative they were exposed to, the story of scientific authority in which they were immersed, crossed over that split-second gap and evaded the 'narrative escape', resulting in actions they would have thought impossible.

This experiment has been replicated in other countries a dozen times over a 25-year period with the same results. Our minds are made of stories: we are built to believe and obey them – a significant majority of us are, at least.

In his book, Milgram comments: *"The social psychology of this century reveals a major lesson: often it is not so much the kind of person a man is as the kind of situation in which he finds himself that determines how he will act."*

In the 50 years since Milgram's research there has been a revolution in communications, media, and publishing; storytelling as a mode of influence, as well as entertainment, has attracted the attention of social media, business corporations, politicians, and, more recently, scientists. We know we can feel deeply affected emotionally by stories, even by ones we know to be entirely fictional. The psychology of fiction is a small but expanding research area at a number of universities, notably in the USA and Canada. Even research from a totally different angle – psychopathology – throws light on the role of story in the human condition.

In a good thriller that hooks us into caring about the characters, our pulse increases and our muscles tense with fear as the heroine is stalked down a dark alley by the villain; we get a surge of relief when she escapes, and smile with contentment when she finally finds romance – we feel and exhibit genuine emotional responses to what characters are experiencing. This is empathy: the power of identifying oneself mentally with a person or object. We know it is fiction – a made-up story – but still we identify with the character and *involuntarily* feel their emotions within ourselves.

But there are some people who cannot empathise, who have no sense of feeling what others feel, and may consequently perform acts of cruelty that the world calls 'evil', and Professor Simon Baron-Cohen calls 'zero degrees of empathy':

"Zero degrees of empathy means you have no awareness of how you come across to others, how to interact with others, or how to anticipate their feelings or reactions."

Baron-Cohen is an experimental psychologist working in psychopathology, and in autism. His findings show that we all have different degrees of empathy, with a major clustering somewhere in the middle, but those at the extreme negative end of the continuum – with zero degrees of empathy – exhibit a range of personality disorders, including borderline and psychopathic personalities, and their brains function in a significantly different way.

"...scientists have managed to study their brains, which are definitely different in much of the empathy circuit. First there is decreased binding of neurotransmitters to one of the serotonin receptors. Neuroimaging also reveals underactivity in the orbital frontal cortex and in the temporal cortex –all part of the empathy circuit."

(Neurotransmitters are chemicals in the body that act as messengers between nerve cells and play a major role in mood and behaviour. Serotonin is a neurotransmitter associated with feelings of calm and wellbeing).

It is not surprising to discover that the brain has an inbuilt capability for empathy: it is the cognitive capacity required, along with the elusive 'conscious awareness', to enable our early ancestors to begin what we – with hindsight – call the human trajectory, and the area of enquiry where future mirror neuron research may have the greatest impact on our understanding.

Without empathy we could not have formed stable relationships to negotiate social groupings, co-operated in food gathering, or defended ourselves from the possible ill intentions of others in any more complex way than other primates. Storytelling clearly had a role in learning to understand these other, essentially social, human creatures around us and in passing on accumulated wisdom (as it still does).

Local gossip reveals not only what the neighbours are up to, but whether or not their actions comply with social mores – moral lessons the listeners should heed if they wish to be accepted in the same circles. It may be stretching the point to say that regular watchers of *Coronation Street*, *Neighbours*, or *The Bold and the Beautiful* are actually indulging in moral philosophy tutorials, but in a sense, they are.

Before going any further, it is important to make clear how 'empathy' differs from 'sympathy'. Sympathetic words and deeds show support and caring to someone else, even though we may not fully understand or share what they are feeling.

What brain scientists call 'empathy', is the capacity (probably via mirror neurons) to recognize the emotions and intentions of others – to work out what is in their minds. It is emotionally based knowledge, we feel it, but it is information, and does not automatically result in any specific actions. It need not, therefore, lead to sympathy: empathy can be used to outwit others as well as to cherish them. Not all branches of psychology and cognitive science agree on the exact definition of 'empathy', but this is how I use the term because it reflects more realistically the inherent conflict in our sociability. We do not always 'play nicely'.

That reading fiction can fulfil a fundamental need for social connectedness, and increase the ability to empathize, was the result of recent research by Dr Shira Gabriel and Ariana Young of Buffalo University. Their undergraduate volunteers had more fun than Milgram's subjects. One group read wizardry extracts from J K Rowling's *Harry Potter and the Philosopher's Stone*; the other, reading a vampire-rich section from Stephanie Meyer's *Twilight*. During subsequent testing, volunteers expressed attitudes and feelings of association akin to belonging to real-life groups, leading Gabriel to conclude:

"The current research suggests that books give readers more than an opportunity to tune out and submerge themselves in fantasy worlds. Books provide the opportunity for social connection and the blissful calm that comes from becoming a part of something larger than oneself for a precious, fleeting moment."

As might be expected, changes in attitudes and feelings can subtly affect behaviour. A different set of experiments (led by Sarah Coyne at Bingham Young University) found that subjects who had read stories involving violence were more likely, shortly afterwards, to respond to provocation with aggression, either physical, or social ('relational') – by harming the provocateur's reputation, for example. This does not mean that reading thrillers turns us into thugs or murderers, but having specific scenes – narratives – in our minds, can influence our subsequent behaviour towards others.

Stories can be equally effective at increasing empathy that may lead to compassion. Pro-active, helpful behaviour was expressed by volunteer subjects after reading a 'feel good' story in experiments carried out by Dan Johnson, at Washington and Lee University.

Further support of our need for social connectedness in our appreciation of stories is the suggestion from Keith Oatley that fiction grabs our emotions and enters our consciousness more readily than non-fiction.

"I think the reason fiction but not non-fiction has the effect of improving empathy is because fiction is primarily about selves interacting with other selves....We can think about it in terms of the psychology of expertise.

If I read fiction, this kind of social thinking is what I get better at. If I read genetics or astronomy, I get more expert at genetics or astronomy."

This fact is not lost on journalists: increasingly the old 'pyramid' structure of an article that starts with a bare – preferably startling – outcome is replaced by opening paragraphs that name a local person and his or her feelings about the event before broadening out to facts and wider issues. This blurring of the boundaries between fiction and non-fiction encourages empathy through a personal and social perspective that enlists our emotions, drawing the facts along with them, to become part of our own inner narrative. How many of us have learned more history through well researched historical novels that we did from staring at a blackboard in school?

One way and another, we gain a huge amount of pleasure through our empathy circuits, but before the serotonin and dopamine kick-in and start making this feel like a free lunch, we need to be aware that, like all benefits, there is a cost; in this case, our vulnerability to manipulation – that belief and compliance problem we came upon earlier. And this applies to non-fiction works as well as fiction. Researchers at the University of North Carolina, Dr Melanie Green and John Donahue, found that the beliefs and attitudes of their subjects had changed after reading articles given to them, whether the texts were fact or fiction. But there was another surprising outcome.

Much of the material in the non-fiction article used in the experiment was fabricated. When this was explained to the subjects, their opinion of the writer plummeted, but tests showed that their change in attitudes, after their first reading of the article, remained the same. Being later told it was untrue did not lessen the initial impact of the text – its effect had become embedded. Empathy with the main character in the article – Jimmy, a child drug addict – may have been the strongest factor in that process.

The article, "Jimmy's World: 8-Year-Old Heroin Addict Lives for a Fix" written by Janet Cooke, was published in 1980 on the front page of the *Washington Post* and awarded a Pulitzer Prize before it was found to be largely fabricated. In particular, 'Jimmy' did not exist.

How many of our own attitudes and beliefs are based on untruths, and if we knew what they were, could we change them? It seems that is far harder than we might suppose: our ability to empathize, and believe what we feel, appears to be stronger than our cognitive capacity to think and reason. Perhaps we need to evolve a little further before earning the title 'Homo sapiens' – 'wise guy'.

At this point, we need to draw together the threads of our story so far, before we begin to lose the plot.

~~~

6: Why does it matter? It depends who is constructing our story

Stories – other people's narratives – affect our emotions, our attitudes, and may spill over into our behaviour, especially in the short-term. They feed our fundamental need for social connectedness, for understanding others of our species, and for belonging. We are primed to believe and obey the stories we receive. We can add to this what most educators already know: the more of our senses involved in the process, the more effective is the engagement with our consciousness – the internalizing of narrative, accepting it as our own.

It is fair to assume that the ancient oral traditions of our ancestors used movement, sound, ritual and other elements of performance in their myth-sharing and storytelling much as indigenous cultures and many professional storytellers do today.

And perhaps the capacity for belief and obedience had adaptive value in forming and maintaining stable social groups during our evolutionary history: a society of 'Chiefs' without any 'Indians' would not remain stable for long.

We have traced the significance of all this in our cognitive development as humans wresting our survival from the pre-historic savannah, but what does this mean for us in our new digital world of instant global communication, trans-media storytelling, and widespread personal use of social media?

No longer is it only the local storyteller, the village leader, or the shaman whose stories enchant us. And it is not simply reading books and magazines, or watching films and television that are giving us narratives: mobile apps in our pockets allow us to tune-in to the planetary chatter of Twitter streams, YouTube and all aspects of the media 24/7, everywhere and anywhere. The social and geographical boundaries that defined cultural groups and their stories have been blown away in the ether and caught up in the world-wide web.

Ours is a world of multiple stories which penetrate our senses in ever more effective ways. The technology of trans-media storytelling lets us click our way through pictorial and auditory elements of narrative intermingled with the text. With some formats we can interact and select alternative plots with different outcomes.

We can be involved and participatory, putting our own personal narratives and received gossip on Twitter, Face-book or YouTube; create our own blogs, self-publish our own stories through an increasing array of e-publishing platforms without the traditional gatekeepers of agents and publishers. And texting on our cell phones has even invented a new language – almost a form of proto-language – without vowels or grammar. In some respects, we are returning to the immediacy and malleability of oral tradition: stories mutated through different tellers and a plethora of listeners.

And yet, this freedom is more apparent – perhaps more virtual – than real. Larger presences making more noise with even better technology are also telling their stories, filling the air with narratives they want us to accept. Political spin-doctors use story techniques to create their own fairy tales to lull us to sleep – '*Jack and the Big Society*', and '*The Mad Bankers Tea Party*'.

Two dominant stories of our time: '*It's Not Climate Change, You Just Need a New Air-conditioner – and they're on special*', and '*Your Country Needs You to Tighten Your Belts - but not ours*', are variants of stories that could be told in diverse ways. The same situations could be shown through different heroines and villains with alternative motivations; opposing plots and sub-plots with another twist. With creative storytelling techniques, they can all be exciting, convincing, emotionally appealing: what separates them is not the facts but the moral premise – the underlying values present in all stories, reflecting the vested interests of the storytellers. That is where we need to 'mind the gap': be aware of, and use, our 'narrative escape.'

Business corporations, too, hire consultants in story technique to help them create and disseminate their own narratives, not only for more effective advertising, but as a management tool in developing staff loyalty and embedding corporate values into the minds of their employees. It is an open market: story techniques are available to job-seekers, too, but they are advised to understand the company story and write themselves a character-part within its plot.

This is not about conspiracies. We don't need conspiracy theories: the potential to be mislead and manipulated is already built into our mental wiring – the downside of being so clever but not clever enough. It is a disturbing thought: to reflect on our fundamental need for stories and propensity to believe them and comply, amid the changing forms and distribution of power and influence. Identifying the predominant cohorts of myth-makers and truth-pedlars who have consciously enlisted storytelling as a tool of influence should give us pause: increasingly, behemoths have the stage. It makes us vulnerable.

Perhaps it is not only the persuasive force of power-brokers that creates our fragility; our predisposition to obey may be reinforced by our own weakness, as Russian film director, Aleksandr Sokurov observed during an interview about his "tetralogy of power" – films focusing on Hitler, Lenin, Emperor Hirohito and, latterly, Faust:

" ... [power] doesn't really exist. It only exists to the extent to which people are ready to submit to it ... Even during Stalin's terror. People had choices. They could betray, or not betray, for example. ... They wanted it. Because it's the most comfortable position for most people. We enjoy being forced. It takes responsibility off your shoulders. People are more afraid of responsibility than anything else."

There has rarely been a more urgent time for being aware of the 'narrative escape'; of the importance of fully understanding and questioning the narratives that surround us, and for holding fast to our own values and inner stories.

"It may be that we are puppets – puppets controlled by the strings of society. But at least we are puppets with perception, with awareness. And perhaps our awareness is the first step to our liberation." (Stanley Milgram)

Narratives are not limited to words: as enabling as language has been, it has its limitations. Some stories are so imperative that when words are not strong enough to overcome the prevailing noise, actions must carry the message. Mohamed Bouazizi, a vegetable vendor in Tunisia, resorted to burning himself to death; a narrative act that sparked a revolutionary movement in northern Africa. Repeated self-immolation by Tibetan monks has yet to penetrate the global chatter.

What we believe and do now is drafting the next chapter in our story – identifying the villains and heroes, the plot lines and twists, and ultimately the final denouement. We have the opportunity and the technology to write it for ourselves, have our own narratives heard. What will be the arc of our human story? Traditionally, all stories have a moral content – that has been their underlying force – the question is: whose values will predominate?

"If you got story, heart...then speak yourself, stand for it!" (Bill Neidjie).

Will we weave our own narrative, or was George Orwell wrong only on the timing: not 1984 but 2084?

~~~

Selected Sources, References and Further Reading

There is considerable overlap in the topics covered in some of these references, particularly where collaboration has been productive. I have listed them under topics for which I made most use of them in this study.

On the evolution of language:

- **Bickerton, Derek.** (2010) *Adam's Tongue: How Humans Made Language, How Language Made Humans.* Hill & Wang.

- **Corballis, Michael.** (2003) "From Hand to Mouth: the gestural origins of language", in *Language Evolution.* Editors, M. Christiansen & S. Kirby. Oxford University Press, p.201-218.

- **Chomsky, Noam.** (1972) *Language and Mind.* Harcourt Brace. [Universal grammar.]

- **Deacon, Terence William.** (1997) *The Symbolic Species.* W.W. Norton. [Quote: "Absence of evidence is not evidence of absence."]

- **Fitch, W. Teumseh.** (2010) *The Evolution of Language.* Cambridge University Press.

- **Jackendorff, Ray.** (2002) *Foundations of Language.* Oxford University Press

- **Harris, Marvin.** (1989) *Our Kind.* Harper and Row. [Anomalous size of H. erectus brain. Quote: *"equally efficient in storing…"*, and quote of Edward Sapir.]

- **Kenneally, Christine.** (2007) *The First Word: The search for the origins of language.* Viking.

- **Lieberman, Philip.** (2006) *Toward an Evolutionary Biology of Language.* Harvard University Press. [Reconstruction of anatomical parts for speech.]

- **Pinker, Stephen.** (1994) *The Language Instinct.* Penguin. [Mind modules for speech and thought.]

- **Pinker, Stephen, & Paul Bloom.** (1995) "Natural Language and Natural Selection" in *The Adapted Mind.* Editors, J. H. Barkow, L. Cosmides, J. Tooby. Oxford University Press.

On neuroscience and the mind:

- **Pinker, Stephen.** (1997) *How the Mind Works.* W. W. Norton. [Mind modules for concepts of space, time, matter and causation.]

- **Provine, Robert R.** (2001) *Laughter: A Scientific Investigation.* Penguin Books.

- **Ramachandran, V. S.** (2011) *The Tell-tale Brain.* Heineman. [The brain's synthesis of neural stimulation, chapter 3. Mirror neurons in the evolution of language, chapter 4.]

- **Ramachandran, V. S.** (2000) *Mirror Neurons and Imitation Learning as the Driving Force Behind "the great leap forward" in Human Evolution.* Edge lecture [Quote: *"..once you have a certain minimum.."*]

- **Rizzolatti, G., L. Fogassi, & V. Gallese.** (2001) "Neurophysiological mechanisms underlying the understanding and imitation of action." *Nature Reviews Neuroscience,* 2, 661-670.

On foraging societies and references to other cultures:

- **Edward B. Banning.** (2011) "So Fair a House: Göbekli Tepe and the Identification of Temples in the Pre-Pottery Neolithic", in *Current Anthropology,* 52(5) 619-660 [suggests Göbekli Tepe structures were houses not temples.]

- **Bell, Diane** (1983) *Daughters of the Dreaming.* MacPhee Gribble/George Allen & Unwin. [The *jukurrpa* rituals and 'women's business'.]

- **Carrington, John F.** (1949) *The Talking Drums of Africa.* Carey Kingsgate, quoted in James Gleick's, *The information.* [The Loleke 'talking' drums.]

- **Forde, Daryll,** editor. (1954) *African Worlds.* International African Institute/Oxford University Press. [Shilluk creation myth.]

- **Lee, Richard Borshay.** (1979) *The !Kung San: Men, Women, and Work in a Foraging Society.* Cambridge University press. [Social organisation of small foraging groups.]

- **Neidjie, Bill.** (1989) *Story About Feeling.* Edited by Keith Taylor, Magabala Books (Kimberley Aboriginal Law and Culture Centre). [Opening quote *"this story e coming..."* from "Laying Down" p.1. Closing quote *"if you got story.."* p.vi.]

- **Schmidt, Klaus,** for updates on excavations at Göbekli Tepe, see the website of the German Archaeological Institute: www.dainst.de

On psychology and the psychology of fiction:

- **Baron-Cohen, Simon.** (2011) (Professor of Developmental Psychopathology, University of Cambridge, and Director of Cambridge Autism Research Centre) "Evil is in reality a lack of empathy", article in *The Weekly Guardian* 8 April 2011 p.32.

- **Blackburne, Livia.** (2010) *From Words to Mouth.* 40K Books (e-book format). [Psychology of reading.]

- **Coyne, Sarah.** (2011) "Backbiting and bloodshed in books: short-term effects of reading physical and relational aggression in literature." In *British Journal of Social Psychology* 1 September 2011, published on-line. Reported on Miller-McCune journalist web-site.

- **Gabriel, Shira, & Ariana Young.** (2011) quote from, "Reading fiction 'improves empathy', study finds", by Alison Flood on *The Guardian* newspaper website, guardian.co.uk 7 September 2011. The original research is published in the journal *Psychological Science.*

- **Greene, M. C., & J. K. Donahue.** (2011) "Persistence of belief change in the face of deception: The effects of factual stories revealed to be false." *Media Psychology,* 14:3, 312-331.

- **Johnson, Dan.** (2012) *Personality and Individual Differences.* On-line pre-publication, reported by Keith Oatley on *Psychology Today* blog, 24 November 2011 at http://www.psychologytoday.com/blog/the-psychology-fiction

- **Keen, Suzanne.** (2010) *Empathy and the Novel.* Oxford University Press.

- **Milgram, Stanley**: quotes and experiment details from website maintained by Dr Thomas Blass – http://www.stanleymilgram.com [Experiments on obedience to authority.]

- **Oatley, Keith.** "Emotions and the story worlds of fiction", in *Narrative impact: Social and cognitive foundations,* p.39-69. Editors, M. C. Green, J. J. Strange, & T. C. Brock. (2002) Mahwah, NJ: Erlbaum.

- **Oatley, Keith.** (2011) Quotes from, "Reading fiction 'improves empathy', study finds", by Alison Flood on *The Guardian* newspaper website, guardian.co.uk 7 September 2011. [Dr Oatley has a PhD in fiction psychology and is himself a novelist.]

- **Stafford, Tom.** (2011) *The Narrative Escape.* 40K Books (e-book format) [Quote: *"That we make-up a reality at all,.."*]

- **Stern, Daniel.** (1985) *The Interpersonal World of the Infant.* Basic Books. [The range of sound and gesture communication between mothers and babies.]

Other references:

- **Darwin, Charles.** [Definition of mathematician.] *Chambers Dictionary of Quotations,* quoted by John D. Barrow in "Pie in the Sky: Counting, Thinking and Being" (1992)

- **Dawkins, Richard.** (2005) *The Ancestor's Tale: A Pilgrimage to the Dawn of Evolution.* Mariner Books. [The science of evolution, and in particular, a rebuttal of the idea of directional 'advancement'.]

- **McKee, Robert**. (1999) *Story*. Methuen.

- **Sokurov, Aleksandr.** (2011) Interviewed by Steve Rose and quoted in *The Weekly Guardian*, 9 December 2011 p.38 [Film director, quote *"(power) does not exist..."*]

About Trish Nicholson

Dr Trish Nicholson began a 30 year writing career as a columnist and feature writer, later drawing on her background as an anthropologist to travel and work in many countries, researching and writing on cultures, tourism, and travelogue. Living through some extraordinary situations, she developed a passion for storytelling. Her short stories have been placed in international competitions and published in anthologies. Inside Stories combines her experience with wit, honesty and compassion to inspire both writers and readers. She lives in New Zealand – Aotearoa – Land of the Long White Cloud.

Trish's titles for Collca:

- *From Apes to Apps: How Humans Evolved as Storytellers and why it Matters* (http://collca.com/fata)
- *Inside Stories for Writers and Readers* (http://collca.com/is)
- *Journey in Bhutan: Himalayan Trek in the Kingdom of the Thunder Dragon* (http://collca.com/jib)
- *Masks of the Moryons: Easter Week in Mogpog* (http://collca.com/motm)

Trish's website: www.trishnicholsonswordsinthetreehouse.com

Follow Trish on Twitter at www.twitter.com/TrishaNicholson.

About Collca

collca

Collca is an electronic publisher specialising in non-fiction bitesize ebooks for popular ereading devices such as Amazon's Kindle, Apple's iPad, Barnes & Noble's Nook and Kobo's eponymous ereader. We cover a wide range of subjects including biography, health, reference, sport and travel. Our titles are available from hundreds of popular ebook retailers all around the world.

We currently publish seven series of ebooks:

- *BiteSize Biography* (http://collca.com/biography)
- *BiteSize History* (http://collca.com/history)
- *BiteSize Introduction* (http://collca.com/intro)
- *BiteSize Science* (http://collca.com/science)
- *BiteSize Travel* (http://collca.com/travel)
- *In the Footsteps of....* (http://collca.com/itfo)
- *Lighter Shades of Grey Trilogy* (http://collca.com/lsgt).

In addition we publish a number of titles that do not fit into any of the series.

We also publish a number of apps for Apple's iPad, iPhone and iPod Touch devices. These are mainly history titles in the following series:

- *History In An Hour* (http://collca.com/hiah)
- *The Irish Story* (http://collca.com/tis).

We're always keen to find additional authors to help us expand our publishing programme. If you would like to know more about writing for us, please visit www.collca.com/writeforus.

To find out more about Collca including up-to-date details of all our titles, please visit our website at www.collca.com.

You can also follow us on Twitter at www.twitter.com/collca.

Subscribe to Collca's Newsletter

Have you enjoyed reading this book? If so, why not subscribe to Collca's FREE newsletter to learn all about our current, new and forthcoming ebooks and printed books.

The newsletter will be sent to you approximately twice a month.

To subscribe, please visit www.collca.com/newsletter

We look forward to welcoming you as a subscriber.

Lightning Source UK Ltd.
Milton Keynes UK
UKOW03f1903200813

215704UK00001B/1/P